Hey—

I'm not particularly scared of marriage. I'm not scared of much in this life. Having survived a near-death experience, and then spending the next ten years dodging more bullets, I find I can put things in perspective. Marriage isn't for me. Katharine isn't for me. I wish to hell she still thought I was dead, so that she could get on with her life. I'm not worth mourning.

Of course, she's not mourning me right now. She wants to kill me herself. How do I get into these messes?

Mac

Please address questions and book requests to: Harlequin Reader Service
U.S.: 3010 Walden Ave., P.O. Box 1325, Buffalo, NY 14269
Canadian: P.O. Box 609, Fort Erie, Ont. L2A 5X3

Reluctant Grooms

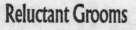

ANNE STUART

LAZARUS RISING

Harlequin Books

TORONTO • NEW YORK • LONDON
AMSTERDAM • PARIS • SYDNEY • HAMBURG
STOCKHOLM • ATHENS • TOKYO • MILAN
MADRID • WARSAW • BUDAPEST • AUCKLAND

HARLEQUIN BOOKS
225 Duncan Mill Road, Don Mills,
Ontario, Canada M3B 3K9

ISBN 0-373-30101-4

LAZARUS RISING

Copyright © 1991 by Anne Kristine Stuart Ohlrogge

Celebrity Wedding Certificates published by permission of
Donald Ray Pounders from *Celebrity Wedding Ceremonies*.

This edition published by arrangement with Harlequin Books S.A.

® and TM are trademarks of the publisher. Trademarks indicated with
® are registered in the United States Patent and Trademark Office, the
Canadian Trade Marks Office and in other countries.

Printed in U.S.A.

A Letter from the Author

Dear Reader,

It all started as a reaction to a miniseries on TV. You know, one of those tear-jerking ones where the first hero dies, the heroine mourns him for a good two hours of the four-hour program until she finally settles for the new hero, a very pale substitute for the original. I started thinking, what if you wasted ten years of your life desperately mourning someone who never really died? Wouldn't you be mad as hell?

It was fun taking Katharine's rage and transformation and making a love story out of it, and her returned-from-the-dead, bad-boy hero deserved all the trouble she gave him. I wrote *Lazarus Rising* just before I wrote a very odd book called *Night of the Phantom*, and my books have probably been getting progressively stranger. I hope you like one of my earlier forays into strange situations.

Anne Stuart

Chapter One

"I'd like to propose a toast," Henry Osmand, Sr., better known as Hank, said in his deep banker's voice, honed to perfection for soothing rattled investors. "To my son Henry and his Kay, who are planning to marry in early January. We all know she'll be a welcome addition to the Osmand clan."

An enthusiastic murmur rose up from the assembled Osmands and their friends, and Katharine Lafferty found herself swept into a series of hearty, scented embraces. She glanced over to see Henry's tall, upright figure being pounded with hearty backslaps, and she had to stifle a smile. Henry wasn't one for displays of affection, and that tight smile on his handsome face was a little strained at the edges. Serves him right, she thought, as elderly cousin Lucy swept her against her massive bosom. He was the one who'd told his gregarious father he could make the announcement at Thanksgiving dinner, with seventeen of his wealthiest relatives present. He was the one who'd pay the price.

"I couldn't be happier," Aunt Mildred said, taking over from cousin Lucy. Since her sister, Hank's wife, had died, she'd become the family matriarch, a role that suited her kindly, overbearing nature to a tee. "You and Henry are made for each other. We'd been so hoping he'd find a nice girl and settle down, and the moment you took a job at the bank we'd been keeping our fingers crossed."

Katharine murmured something vague and pleasant, secretly amused. At thirty years of age she scarcely considered herself a nice girl, but the aunts and cousins were right. She and Henry were a perfect match. The youngest senior vice president of Dexter Savings and Loan in Dexter, Washington, and son of its president, Henry was handsome, charming, sober and hardworking. Katharine wasn't one to flatter herself, but she knew she was passably attractive, and as sober and hardworking as Henry himself was. Together they'd be a model of industrious, compatible marriage and, in time, when they had the requisite 2.3 children, those children would also be bright, attractive overachievers.

There it was again, the sudden lancing in her stomach. Katharine carefully extracted herself from second cousin Ernest's grip and edged toward the kitchen, a smile glued to her face. Indeed, despite the pain in her stomach she felt like smiling. Thanksgiving had been noisy, frenetic, overwhelming, and she'd loved every minute of it. There were times when she was alone in the dark of night, unable to sleep, when she wondered whether she was in love with Henry or with his huge, boisterous family, even including his slightly overbearing father. It was a question she didn't dare examine too closely, especially with her stomach in an uproar.

For the first time in days the huge, old-fashioned kitchen in Henry's father's house was deserted. The dishwasher was humming, the serving platters stacked in the dish drainer, the food put away. Katharine grabbed her purse from the counter, pulled out the white plastic bottle and poured a generous amount of liquid antacid down her throat with a shudder. That was the damnable thing about an ulcer, she thought. She'd always hated liquid medicine, and now she had to live on it.

The door opened, and Henry's sister Melissa stormed in, her beautiful gray eyes, identical to Henry's, bright with unshed tears. She took one look at Katharine, seemed ready to head straight back out the swinging kitchen door, and then thought better of it. She sank down at the table, put her head in her arms and started to sob.

For a moment Katharine didn't move, the taste of antacid thick and heavy in her mouth. She didn't like scenes, didn't like raw emotions, and the last thing she wanted was Melissa sobbing all over her gray silk dress. She wondered whether she could run for it, skirt the table and make it back into the noisy front room without seeming too crass.

"I'm so miserable!" Melissa wailed into her arms, a clearly unnecessary statement. Once more Katharine considered whether she could ignore her cue, and then decided she'd have to listen. After all, Melissa was going to be her sister-in-law, and a bridesmaid to boot. When you got involved in a large family you had to accept certain responsibilities.

She moved to the refrigerator, poured herself a glass of milk and joined Melissa at the table. "What's wrong?" she asked dutifully. "Not that you have to talk about it...." she added quickly, hoping Melissa would dismiss her.

"I have to talk about it," Melissa howled, lifting her face. Katharine stared at her in fascination. Melissa had all the Osmand good looks, and even with a tear-streaked face she looked beautiful. Her eyes looked fuller, and her skin was pale and damp.

When Katharine cried her nose turned red, her cheeks were blotchy, her eyes were puffy and her nose ran incessantly. She looked horrible when she cried, and she had already spent too much of her thirty years looking at her tear-streaked face.

"Don't cry," she said automatically to Melissa. "Tell me what the problem is, and maybe we can do something about it."

"You wouldn't understand," she snuffled, reminding Katharine that she was only nineteen years old.

Katharine had the sense not to smile. "Maybe not. Try me."

"It's Nick!"

Katharine's razor-sharp memory immediately dredged up the sulky, handsome image of Melissa's current boyfriend. "I noticed he wasn't here," she said. "Have you two broken up?"

"He thinks we should date other people," Melissa sobbed. "He says we're getting too serious. But I don't want to see other people!"

"When did this happen?" Katharine kept her voice sympathetic and soothing. Personally she thought Nick Van Kemp was a spoiled, shallow creep, and that Melissa could do much better, but she was wise enough not to express that opinion.

"On Monday."

"Then why are you so unhappy now?" It was a reasonable enough question, but it set Melissa off again.

"I tried to keep it to myself," she said nobly, ignoring the fact that she'd spent most of the day heaving dramatic, heartfelt sighs and staring out the window into the rainy afternoon. "But the sight of you and Henry, so happy together, was simply more than I could bear."

"I'm sorry," Katharine said helplessly.

"Oh, it's not your fault. You and Henry are perfect for each other. Both so cool and unemotional. You'll have a wonderful life together, while I face a world of misery!"

"You'll get over it," Katharine said, hoping she didn't sound too heartless. "These things take time, but sooner or later they pass."

Melissa stared at her with all the disbelieving superiority of youth. "How would you know? I don't think you could even begin to understand what I'm going through. You with your safe life and your safe little future. What do you know about broken hearts and shattered lives?"

Katharine rose from the table, leaving her glass of milk untouched. She knew her face was pale, stiff, and she knew Melissa was too self-absorbed to notice. "You'd be surprised," she said mildly. And without another word she walked back into the noisy living room, a cool, friendly smile plastered to her face.

"THINGS WENT WELL, don't you think?" Henry murmured as he walked her up the sidewalk to her small, tidy little house. "I think the family is very fond of you."

"I'm very fond of them," she said, fumbling with her key. A light drizzle was falling, her stomach was burning and she was suddenly very tired.

"They're looking forward to a January wedding. It should be perfect, don't you think? Aunt Mildred's already making plans."

Katharine managed a faint smile. "I'll be glad of her help. Christmas is hectic enough, without a wedding thrown in on top of things."

Henry frowned. "You didn't tell me you objected to a January wedding."

"I don't object, Henry. I'm just saying things will be hectic."

"Not with you around. Everything is always calm, serene and ordered when you're involved," he said with the air of one bestowing a great compliment. "Besides, how crazy can Christmas be for you? You don't have any family to shop for. Which reminds me—will anyone be coming to the wedding from Ohio?"

Katharine shook her head. "No one," she said calmly. "There wasn't much family to begin with, and they're all dead." Her voice caught a bit on that word, secretly horrifying her, but Henry didn't notice.

"Well, that just means we'll be able to invite more people in town," he said easily. "It should be good for business."

"Very wise," Katharine said.

"You'll take care of the newspaper announcement, won't you, darling? I'm up to my ears in work."

"Of course. Do you want to come in?"

Henry looked up at her house, frowning slightly. "Not tonight, I think. It's been a long day, and you're looking a little pale. Is your ulcer acting up?"

"A bit," she agreed, wondering why she felt so relieved.

"Too much gravy and pecan pie," Henry announced.

Katharine hadn't touched the gravy and pecan pie. "You're probably right," she said. "I'll see you at work." She was a tall woman, and she didn't have to reach up to brush her lips against his.

For a moment his lips softened against hers, and she felt his arms go around her. "Maybe we should go away together," he murmured. "After all, we're basing this marriage on mutual respect, shared interests and sexual compatibility. We haven't even gotten to testing the last part yet."

"If we have the other two, the sexual part will work out," Katharine said with her usual serenity, and Henry nodded.

"Of course, darling. We've just been working too hard. We'll have to take a vacation, learn more about each other...."

"There's always our honeymoon," she suggested with the trace of a smile.

Henry smiled back. "That would be original. Waiting until after we're married. There's something about it that appeals to me. Yes, why don't we do that? After all, it's only a few weeks away."

"Unless animal passion overwhelms us first," Katharine said.

Henry just stared at her blankly.

"A joke, Henry," she explained patiently.

"Sometimes I don't understand your sense of humor, Kay," he said. "And thank heavens we're too civilized to be prey to animal passions. Look at the mess Melissa is making of her life."

"Hurrah for civilization," Katharine murmured.

"You're in a very strange mood tonight, Kay. Maybe I ought to come in and we can discuss this."

"I'm just tired. I'll see you in the morning, Henry."

"In the morning, dear." And he moved briskly down the sidewalk, his tall, slender body upright in the faint drizzle.

Katharine turned on all the lights in her house, a wasteful act that Henry would have soundly chastised. She took a shower, poured herself a shot glass of Maalox and sank down on her beige sofa, ignoring the bare walls and neutral colors. Her stomach was roiling, despite the medication, and her long fingers were trembling slightly. Melissa's words kept echoing in her head. "What would you know about a broken heart?"

She could feel it coming. Her old friend, her old enemy. That mindless, uncontrollable despair that swept over her at odd times. It had been more than a year since she'd last had a bout, and she'd hoped, since she met Henry, that those dreadful times were finally over for good. But she knew what she'd find if she walked to the small, rectangular mirror. Puffy eyes, blotchy face, running nose. She'd see mindless, uncontrollable grief, the kind that comes from a heart not only broken, but smashed beyond recognition. And she knew that after ten long years she still hadn't finished grieving.

IT WAS ANOTHER THANKSGIVING, in another lifetime, another universe. She was twenty years old, and ready for the first foolish action of her entire well-planned, studious, dutiful life. Crammed into Marcy Welton's Trans Am with Marcy and four other members of their tiny, exclusive sorority she so desperately wanted to join, she stared across the snowy street to Guido's All-Night Laundromat and tried to ignore the nervous fluttering in her stomach, the nervous fluttering that would turn to a full-fledged ulcer by the time she was twenty-eight.

"There it is," Marcy said in her rich, cultured voice. "Think you can do it?"

Katharine just stared for a moment. It was after eleven o'clock on the Friday after Thanksgiving, and the brightly lit laundromat looked deserted. "Couldn't I do something else?" she asked in a very small voice. "Ellie had to run across campus in her underwear. I could do that."

"There are plenty of lesser sororities you could join if this seems too much for you to handle," Marcy said in a silky voice.

Katharine hated Marcy with an intense passion, and she wasn't too fond of the other members of Alpha Alpha Alpha who were with them in the car, there to witness her ignominy. But her mother wanted her to join, insisting that Tri Alpha was the best sorority on the small suburban campus in eastern Ohio, and that any other would simply be a failure, one of many, on her only daughter's part.

"I can handle it," she said between her teeth. "I just have to get this guy to go out with me, not sleep with him, right?"

"Right," Marcy said. "Of course, a stud like Billy Ray might not know the difference, but a Tri Alpha has to know how to deal with these situations. Are you ready?"

Katharine bit her lip and nodded. "Ready."

She was halfway across the deserted street when Marcy's voice followed her. "Remember," she cooed, "we'll be watching."

The bright, fluorescent-lit room filled with washing machines was blessedly deserted. In the distance she could detect the noise of a radio, the murmur of voices, the smell of cigarette smoke, but for now no one was in sight.

She took the washing machine closest to the door, opening the lid and dumping her pillowcaseful of laundry inside. Marcy Welton was the fiend incarnate, to come up with this particular test of worthiness, she thought, shoving quarters in the slot with a vengeance. She glared down at the machine as it churned into action. It was probably the first time the washing machine had been used in weeks. Everyone in the small city of Calhoun, Ohio knew that Guido's was simply a front for the gambling syndicate in that section of the state. It wasn't open all night for people to do their laundry; it was open for bettors and their ilk.

Billy Ray could usually be found propping up the Coke machine in the laundromat. Ostensibly he managed the laundromat, making change for the little old ladies and selling soap, but no one had any illusions about his real job. Particularly when his duties took him on campus to some of the wilder fraternities whenever there was a big game in the offing.

Billy Ray thought he was God's gift to the females of Calhoun, Ohio. Tall, well muscled, with wavy blond hair, big white teeth and baby-blue eyes, he was the best-looking male any of the giggling members of Tri Alpha had ever seen, and it had taken someone with Marcy's devious brain to match him up with a closet nun like Katharine.

She hadn't needed to tell them her sexual experience was nil. She'd been on campus a year and a half, and during that time she'd politely but firmly rejected all the advances made to her by the various students. She had no time to waste on social amenities as she pursued a particularly demanding course of studies. Sarah Jane had drilled into her the need to succeed, the need not to be sidetracked by a handsome face or a broad pair of shoulders. A lifetime of poverty, of being raised by a demanding, overprotective single mother like Sarah Jane, had taught Katharine that there was little time for relaxation. She had to get ahead, she had to make her mother proud of her.

Unfortunately, for the first time her mother's requirements included Alpha Alpha Alpha. And Marcy Welton had decided that Katharine's initiation fee was a date with Billy Ray, the bad boy of West Calhoun.

She stood by the washing machine, uncertain what to do next. The Trans Am was still across the street, and she could feel their eyes boring into her back. The voices in the office grew closer, and she felt the butterflies in her stomach begin to dip and soar. A moment later two men stepped out of the office, stopping short when they saw her.

Billy Ray was bigger than she remembered, taller and broader than the man beside him. But for some reason the other man drew her gaze. He was older than Billy, probably in his mid-twenties, with brown hair, dark blue eyes and a tough, cynical face that was nowhere near as pretty as Billy's and infinitely more devastating. He glanced at her, then dismissed her, turning to his companion.

Billy Ray was staring at her and positively drooling. She knew why. She'd taken her ordinary good looks and dressed them up. Her long straight blond hair had been tousled and curled, her shirt unbuttoned halfway down exposing a lacy bra stuffed with tissues, her skirt was halfway up her thighs and her makeup had a very clear message. Billy Ray received that message, his tongue hanging out as he stripped her with his avid eyes.

"You going to make that delivery, Billy?" his companion demanded in a voice slightly roughened by cigarettes and an East Coast accent she couldn't quite place.

Billy shook his head, not tearing his gaze away from Katharine's. She felt like a frightened rabbit, mesmerized by the big bad wolf, but she wasn't quite sure what to do about it, so she simply stood there at the washing machine and tried to look self-assured. She'd spent most of her life pretending to be self-assured, and by now it was almost second nature.

"You make it," Billy said. "I'll take care of things around here."

"I'm sure you will," his companion drawled. Katharine could feel his piercing eyes run over her, then bounce back to Billy. "Watch your step, Billy."

"When I need a nursemaid I'll hire one."

"I'll put the ad in the papers for you," the man said, unmoved. And without another word he walked past them, out into the chilly November night, leaving Katharine alone with her worst nightmare.

Billy kind of sidled up to her. "Well, hello there," he said. "What brings a pretty little college girl like you down to this part of town?"

She hadn't meant to look like a college girl that night. But then she realized her laundry bag had Calhoun University emblazoned across it, and her class ring still sat loosely on one slender finger. "Laundry," she said in a shaky voice.

"Sure." He leaned against the washer next to hers, and he smelled of some cheap cologne. He wasn't as handsome up close—his eyes were a little too small and mean looking. "What happened to all the laundry rooms on campus?"

"Some problem with the plumbing," she said breathlessly.

"Sure," Billy said again. smugly. "Listen, sweet cakes . . . what's your name?"

"K-K-Katharine."

"Katharine. I like that. I'll call you Kathy. Listen, Kathy, you picked one of the slowest washers in the place. It's gonna take at least half an hour to wash your undies. Why don't you come on into the office and have a brew? I'd like to take you out, but we gotta wait until Danny gets back from his rounds."

"Who's Danny?" she asked, stalling for time.

"Some guy from Boston who thinks he's my boss. But he ain't. Not for long," Billy said with an affable grin that looked frankly terrifying. Katharine had the sudden forlorn thought that this wasn't a bad boy she'd been sent to flirt with. This was a dangerous, perhaps even evil man. And all her usual tricks for defending herself from unwanted college boys were going to do her little good tonight.

"I . . . I think I'd better get home," she said nervously, starting to sidle away from him.

"You just put your laundry in," he said, grabbing her arm with one meaty hand. He used a little too much strength, enough to thoroughly intimidate her, and Katharine knew she'd have bruises the next day. "Come on, Kathy, don't be frightened. Come on and have a beer. It'll relax you."

He wasn't giving her any choice. He didn't even seem to be aware of her reluctance as he dragged her back toward the office. "Please," she said, trying to break his grip. "I really don't want to."

He ignored her, dragging her into the office and slamming the door shut behind them before releasing her. "Don't give me that, chickie baby. You didn't come here to do any laundry. You came to check out the local action, and I'm more than ready to oblige. I've learned that college girls love to slum, and I'm more than willing to provide them with a little rough and ready."

"You don't understand..." she said desperately, skirting the edge of the desk and coming up against another closed door.

"Sure I do, babe. Trust me, I can show you a real good time." And he lunged for her.

The doorknob behind her gave, and she fell into another room, a small, dark room completely at odds with the seedy setup out front. For a moment she didn't move, transfixed by the television screens, the massive computer setup, the banks of telephones.

And then Billy was on her with a roar. "Nosy bitch!" he snarled, grabbing her and slamming her up against the wall. "I guess I'm going to have to give you something better to think about." And his wet, slobbery mouth covered hers as she felt the front of her shirt rip open.

I'm going to be raped, she thought distantly, shoving at him. *I'm going to be raped, and there's not a thing I can do about it, and it's all my own stupid fault.*

A moment later he'd tumbled her to the floor, not the hard, stained linoleum of the laundromat, but a thick carpet beneath her back. She tried to scratch his eyes, but he jerked out of the way in time, responding with a numbing slap across the face. She could feel the tears of fright and anger running down her face, but she didn't say a word, didn't beg, didn't plead, but fought with all her strength, knowing it was useless, knowing the rough hand between her knees was going to move upward, knowing she was going to be brutally violated....

She was vaguely aware of the door opening, shedding a small pool of light around them. She kept fighting, struggling, hitting at the oblivious Billy while he pinned her down, when suddenly a rough voice caught his attention.

"How many times do I have to tell you not to use this room for your...courting?"

Billy lifted his head, still keeping Katharine's smaller frame clamped beneath him, and swore. "Get the hell out of here, Danny."

"Oh, I'd be happy to. But I don't think the lady's willing."

"It's none of your damned business."

"That's where you're wrong." And suddenly Katharine felt Billy's huge weight plucked from her, and she watched with amazement as the smaller man simply threw him against the padded wall of the room.

Billy bounced, then slid to the carpet, stunned. The other man walked over to her and held out a hand, his expression bland and unreadable. "Want to get up?" he inquired politely, his own eyes sweeping over her disarranged clothing. "Or were you enjoying yourself?"

Katharine ignored his outstretched hand and staggered to her feet, wiping the tears from her face with a shaking hand. He didn't move, didn't make any effort to touch her, but she wasn't fooled. What she hadn't noticed before was that this man was just as dangerous, in his own way, as Billy Ray was. And far more attractive.

"I'm going home," she stammered, and started out the door, past Billy's unmoving figure.

He barely gave him a glance as he followed her. "I'll drive you."

"There's no need," she said, practically running across the linoleum. "I'll be fine."

He caught up with her by the door as she was struggling into her coat. His hands weren't as hurtful as Billy's had been, but just as inexorable. "I'll drive you home," he said flatly. "There are a few things we need to get clear."

She looked at him, frightened brown eyes staring into implacable blue ones. "Like what?"

"Like what you're going to say about what you saw in that room. Like who was sitting in that Trans Am watching the place? Are you with the cops?" He let his eyes run down her front. "Are you wearing a wire?"

She followed his gaze, realizing with horror that her blouse had been torn open and her bra ripped, exposing far too much skin to his dispassionate gaze and the chilly night air.

"It doesn't look like it, does it?" she snapped, finally goaded beyond endurance.

"Looks can be deceiving. Come along, little girl. The Trans Am has deserted you, and I don't advise walking. Billy Ray is going to come to in a short while and he'll be out for blood. He can't blame me—he works for me. So he's going to have to blame you."

"I don't want to go," she said stubbornly, but she was being patiently led to a dark red sports car parked in the shadows outside the building.

"Tough. You got yourself into this mess," he said, shoving her into the front seat and buckling the seat belt around her, "and you're going to have to do some fancy explaining to get yourself out of it."

Chapter Two

Despite the blast of warmth from the car heater, Katharine felt chilled. Even with her coat pulled tightly around her she kept shivering, and her surreptitious glance at the man driving the car with an economy of movement was scarcely warming. He had a hard face for someone so young, Katharine thought. Handsome, in his own way, as Billy Ray. And possibly far more of a threat.

"Are you going to kill me?" Her voice was flat, conversational, and she congratulated herself.

He cast a glance in her direction. "Why would I do that?"

"To keep me from telling the police about what I saw in the back room."

To her surprise he grinned. "Honey, the police already know exactly what I have in that back room."

"Then why haven't they closed you down?"

"Clearly you don't understand the free enterprise system."

"Clearly I don't. You want to explain it to me?" she questioned tartly, surprised at her own daring.

"I want you to explain to me what you were doing in my place tonight, flirting with Billy Ray. And no, I'm not going to kill you. If I were, I would have let Billy finish what he started."

She shivered again. "I forgot to thank you."

"So you did. Where are we going?"

"I beg your pardon?"

"Where do you live?" he asked patiently.

"None of your business."

He reached over and pulled her purse from her lap. She tried to stop him, hitting at his hand, but he simply hit her back, hard, so that she subsided into the corner of the seat and wondered if she dared jump out at the next light.

"Katharine Marie Lafferty—" he squinted at the student ID card in the dim light as he kept driving "—111 West Canal Street. You don't live on campus?" He took a left turn, heading toward Canal Street, and Katharine's panic increased.

"Please, I don't want to go home," she said desperately.

"Why not?"

"My mother... my mother would worry," she said, biting her lip. That wasn't the half of it. Her mother would kill her, kill her with that cold, bitter condemnation, the biting disappointment at Katharine's eternal failure to measure up.

"Well, I sure as hell am not going to take you home to my place," he snapped.

"I wouldn't go!" she shot back, outraged that he might have thought she was suggesting any such thing. Though given her behavior with Billy Ray that night, he had every right to make such an assumption, she thought with a trace of unwanted fairness.

"Okay, we're agreed on that. Where do you want to go?"

"The Alpha Alpha Alpha building on campus," she said in a low voice. "It's to the left of the science building, on Bank Street...."

"So that's it." His voice was low and smug as he dropped her wallet back in her lap.

"That's what?"

"This is some sort of stupid sorority prank, isn't it? I bet when we get back to the campus I'll find the Trans Am parked outside the building, won't I?"

"No," she lied, hating how stupid and childish the whole thing sounded.

"No?" he echoed. "Honey, it's that or you're working for the police, and I wouldn't take kindly to that possibility. The time's come for some answers, and if you don't offer them of your own free will you're not going to like how I go about getting them."

She didn't doubt him for a moment. At least he'd turned the car again, away from her mother's ranch-style house on Canal Street and back toward campus. "You're right," she said in a sulky voice.

"About the police?"

"About the sorority. It's pledge week, and Tri Alpha is the best sorority on campus. The one my mother wants me to join." She pushed her thick hair away from her face. "We all have tasks we have to complete before we'll be pledged. Everyone knows that Guido's is a front for..." Her voice faltered.

"Go on," he said affably.

"For a gambling operation," she said, glaring. "And people had seen Billy Ray around. I was supposed to get him to go out on a date. It seemed easy enough—I didn't have to do anything more than that."

"A date," he said with a snort. "I doubt Billy Ray's ever gone on a date in his life. His idea of flirtation is to ask a girl which way she wants it. Surely your sorority buddies knew they were sending you into the lion's den."

"Of course they didn't..." she said, her voice trailing off in sudden uncertainty. "That is...er..."

"Any particular reason why they'd want to throw you to the wolves?" he asked with sudden perception.

Ice princess, Katharine thought with sudden pain, remembering the mocking name she'd heard whispered. They'd set her up, deliberately, without the slightest concern for her safety. "I can't imagine," she said out loud.

They drove on in silence for a while, an edgy sort of silence that Katharine had no intention of breaking. She'd never been so acutely aware of another human being in her entire life. He was expensively dressed, in gray flannel slacks and a tweed jacket, which seemed better suited to a young executive than the college students she was used to. Except that was exactly what he was—a young executive, albeit with a criminal organization. He had nice hands, she thought, concentrating on them as they expertly handled the steering wheel. Not big, hamlike things like Billy Ray, but long fingered, deft looking without a trace of delicacy. Good hands, she thought, shivering again and pulling her coat closer around her.

"So what are you going to do about it?"

His voice startled her. It was a deep voice, a little raspy, with an urban edge to it that wasn't unpleasant. "Do about what?"

"Don't be obtuse. You're smarter than your actions suggest, Katharine. What are you going to do about tonight?" He pulled up outside the huge Victorian building that housed Alpha Alpha Alpha, right behind the telltale Trans Am. The building was ablaze with lights, and Katharine knew they'd be waiting for her, waiting for a report.

She unfastened her seat belt and turned to face him, suddenly, crazily loath to leave the uneasy cocoon of his car, his presence. "You say the police already know about your back room, so it wouldn't do me any good to tell anybody, if that's what you're worried about."

"Oddly enough, that's the least of my worries. I can take care of myself. I'm worried about what you're going to say to those bitches inside. Are you going to tell them the truth?"

"Why wouldn't I?" she asked curiously.

"It would give them a hell of a lot of satisfaction. You got exactly what they expected."

"So I did. What do you suggest?"

"It's not my place to make suggestions. I'm just your knight in shining armor."

She snorted. "Not quite. Anyway, I'm asking. What would you do if you were in my place?"

"That's not very likely."

"Stop quibbling."

"I'd lie," he said flatly. "I'd swagger in there, a sexy grin on my face, and tell them mission accomplished. It's the one thing calculated to drive them crazy."

"You're good at this," she said with unwilling admiration.

"Hey, revenge is my specialty," he drawled. "Of course, it's up to you...."

"It's perfect," she said, leaning across the seat with obvious concern to stare at her reflection in the rearview mirror. Her eyes were huge in her pale face, her mouth faintly tremulous. "The problem is, I look a little too worried for someone who just had a sublime sexual encounter," she said with a shaky laugh.

"We can fix that." She had no idea what he intended. In one moment she was staring at her reflection, in another she was in his arms, his mouth on hers, his hands holding her head still for his kiss.

It was devastating. Just as unbreakable as Billy Ray's, but far more expert. He held her still as his mouth discovered hers, his tongue pushing past her faint protest, his lips a damp seal on hers. She thought distantly that she should fight him, but she didn't want to. In the heat and darkness of the idling car she wanted this. Wanted his mouth on hers, kissing her with a completeness that defied anyone who'd ever kissed her before. Wanted the hands that slid beneath her coat, ripping the few remaining buttons from her blouse and cupping her breasts through the torn bra. Wanted more, wanted what she'd been denying ever since she reached puberty and boys started demanding. She wanted him.

He moved his mouth away from hers and she whimpered, a low sound of protest, as he trailed kisses down the side of her neck. She felt the tiny nip of his teeth against her sensitive skin, and she jumped, startled, almost impossibly aroused, as his mouth closed again over hers. And she kissed him back, her arms sliding around his neck.

He finally pulled away, but she was too shattered, benumbed to move. She lay back against the seat, staring up at him with a dazed expression. "Next time don't stuff Kleenex in your bra," he said with a hint of laughter.

That made her sit bolt upright, her sensual lassitude shattered. "Next time..." she sputtered.

"Go in there and wipe those smug smiles off their faces," he suggested, leaning back.

She opened the door with shaky hands and slid out. "Thank you," she stammered, pulling her coat tightly around her.

"Anytime, Katharine. Just sashay in there and act like you enjoyed it."

A sudden, absurd elation filled her as she looked back into his tough, handsome face. "As a matter of fact, I did." And she shut the door behind his burst of surprised laughter.

KATHARINE FOUND HERSELF wishing he could have seen their expressions when she did just what he suggested. She never knew she'd be able to manage such a hip-swinging walk, but the knowledge of Marcy's disappointment was a powerful incentive. Indeed, her expression had been absolutely priceless as Katharine casually let her coat drop open, exposing her ripped blouse and the prominent love bite on her neck.

She'd said one thing to the avid females staring at her, not what she wanted to say, but something far more effective. "Piece of cake," she'd murmured with a salacious grin, tossing her hair back over her shoulder. And without another word she'd headed up the wide front stairs to the room they'd allotted her on a provisional basis. The room she knew now she wasn't going to accept, no matter how much her mother railed at her.

There was a mirror over the dresser, and she paused in the act of undressing, marveling at how different she looked during the tumultuous events of that evening. Before she'd left in the Trans Am she'd checked out her appearance carefully, from the artfully tousled hair, so different from her usually straight mane, to the heavily made-up eyes, the provocative clothing.

She'd seen her reflection in the laundromat window when she'd been ushered out of the place—torn clothes, tear-streaked face, shaky demeanor. She'd seen the traces of it when she'd looked in the rearview mirror of the Aston Martin, before he'd kissed her.

That kiss had been stunningly effective. She no longer looked like an assault victim. With her bee-stung lips, the love bite on her neck, the torn blouse and dazed, smiling eyes, she looked like someone who'd been well and fully loved. Pulling the wadded tissues out of her bra, she found herself smiling. What would she look like if he hadn't stopped?

She had every intention of finding out. During the past few years she'd wondered whether something might be wrong with her, whether there might be a crucial hormone missing, or something of that ilk. No one who'd propositioned her, from the gorgeous football star to the randy, undeniably sexy English professor, and all the men and boys in between, had ever tempted her in the slightest. It was both a relief and a frightening discovery to realize she just hadn't met the right man.

The problem was, the right man was a professional criminal who probably viewed her as amusing. And on top of that, she didn't happen to know his name. Billy Ray had muttered something, but she hadn't been in any condition to pay attention to details like that.

It didn't matter. Whoever her mysterious savior was, she had suddenly become obsessed by him. And knew enough about men to know that he was interested. She was young enough, naive enough to believe in happy endings and love ever after, if you just worked hard enough for it. And she was prepared to work very hard indeed.

DANIEL T. MCCANDLESS, Danny to friend and foe alike, had had real doubts about the girl from the moment he set eyes on her. Guido's Laundromat came equipped with the latest in surveillance technology—he and Billy Ray had had plenty of time to watch her as she fiddled with the big washer and glanced around nervously.

A college kid, he'd dismissed her. Pretty, with those big chocolate-brown eyes and thick hair, and the kind of body he was partial to. Long, endless legs and a generous swell of breast that he wasn't quite sure he believed. But he liked women, not girls, and he liked them with a little more mileage on them. Miss Coed looked as innocent as a newborn babe, despite her heavy makeup and artfully tousled hair.

Innocent young women did not turn up at Guido's Laundromat, no matter what the hour. Neither did college girls. Whatever she wanted, it wasn't to wash that small load of brightly colored clothes.

She'd barely noticed him when they'd stepped out of the office. Those wonderful eyes of hers had been riveted on Billy Ray, a fact that had caused him only a moment's irritation. Even Danny knew that Billy was gorgeous, just the sort of pretty boy to appeal to an adolescent female. He'd headed out into the night, squashing down his slight misgivings.

And then he'd seen the car parked outside, engine running, windows steamed up, and his squashed-down instincts had come fully into play. He'd gone back to warn Billy Ray that this whole thing might be a setup, and found Miss Coed in the midst of being raped.

By the time he dragged her out into the chilly night and shoved her into his car she was shivering. By the time he got the truth out of her he was more amused than irritated. Besides, it had given him a chance to slam Billy Ray against a wall, and anything that gave him an excuse to hit Billy couldn't be all bad.

He'd been a fool to kiss her, but then, he'd been in a curiously playful mood that night. The start of the holiday season always got him to thinking about his family, and that tended to make him riled up, hostile, ready for anything. Anything tonight came in the form of Miss Katharine Marie Lafferty, with the sweetest, most untutored mouth he'd ever tasted.

Either the men of Ohio didn't know how to kiss, or Katharine was almost unnaturally innocent. Billy Ray would have eaten her alive, almost had, as a matter of fact. He didn't like to think what would have happened if he'd ignored his misgivings. He wasn't the squeamish sort, but he had an aversion to seeing helpless creatures tormented.

He'd stepped in, like a knight in slightly tarnished armor, and had the satisfaction of flattening Billy in the bargain. He had the strong sense he was going to have to repeat that action at least once more before Billy learned his lesson. He didn't trust Billy, but then he didn't really trust anyone. Billy was ambitious in his own shortsighted way, and he resented like hell the fact that Danny had been brought in over him. There was nothing he'd like better than to see Danny meet with an unfortunate accident.

If he had the sense, the nerve he knew he was going to need if he continued in this line of work, then he ought to see that Billy met with an accident first. It didn't make sense to let a lighted stick of dynamite sit in your back pocket, and getting rid of Billy would only increase his prestige to their mutual employers. There was no sentimentality in the mob—they recognized cunning, nerve and ruthlessness. Danny had more than his share of those qualities, but he couldn't quite bring himself to cold-blooded murder.

Chances are that time would have to come. He'd spent the past five years working his way up from numbers runner in the slums of south Boston to a fairly successful manager, and he'd been able to stay secure in the gambling rackets. He didn't like prostitution, white-collar crime bored him and he despised drugs. He'd seen too many lives wasted, too many people he cared about dead or ruined, to want to profit from that insidious white powder. So far his bosses had respected his squeamishness, but those days were limited the higher he climbed in the organization. He wasn't the kind of man to settle for limited success—he had brains and ambition and doing something halfway wasn't worth doing at all.

But for now he was content to spend his time in Calhoun, Ohio, keeping tabs on a minor pimple like Billy Ray, keeping the money flowing smoothly. He'd been sent to the Midwest to learn the local angle of the business, and so far things had gone well. People tended to pay on time, the women were warm and friendly and not too demanding, and the weather was an improvement over Boston.

Hell, he sort of liked the business. He understood gamblers, even the addicts. They had a restless, reckless streak he knew far too well. He considered he was providing a service. If some people couldn't handle it, couldn't control their gambling, that was their problem. They didn't close liquor stores because some people were drunks, did they?

He pulled his aging, carefully maintained Aston Martin up outside the laundromat. He could see Billy's hulking form in the window and he sighed, switching off the car and flexing his hands. He was in the mood to punch someone. While he was trying to forget it, the smell, the feel, the taste of Katharine Marie Lafferty was lingering in the back of his consciousness, burning in his gut. He'd seldom been around good girls in his life, but he found this particular one undeniably appetizing. He hadn't taken her, much as he wanted to, and that noble forbearance on his part was taking the shape of intense frustration. The best way to work off that frustration was to slam his fist into Billy's jaw.

Billy was sprawled at the table in the laundry room, a can of beer in his hand, a sulky expression on his face. Danny stood inside the door, waiting, but Billy made no move other than to nod in his direction.

"That's it?" Danny asked, closing the door behind him. "You aren't going to try to break my neck?"

"Hell, no," Billy said morosely. "She probably would have been more trouble than she was worth." He glanced up at him, a sly expression in his faintly bulbous eyes. "Was she?"

"Billy, I was only gone twenty minutes," Danny protested.

"So? That's more than enough time."

"For you, maybe. I like to make things last." He strolled over to the washer and lifted the lid. Her clothes were still inside, a damp circle of bright colors wrapped around the agitator. "You might as well go home," he murmured, shutting it again. "You don't look too well."

"I got a headache, thanks to you. And to that lying college girl." He made the phrase sound like a dire insult. "I've got some unfinished business with her that I'm going to attend to...."

"The hell you are," Danny growled.

Suddenly Billy grinned. "I thought you didn't have enough time to have her."

"I didn't. But I'm staking my claim." It was an instinctive, quixotic lie, created to protect the last remaining innocent on this earth from a brute like Billy. "Touch her and I'll break your arm. And that's for starters."

"You and who else?" Billy taunted him.

"Think I can't do it?"

"I think this town isn't big enough for the two of us."

"You been watching too many John Wayne movies, Billy. This town, this setup is plenty big for both of us. As long as you remember who's boss."

"And what if I don't like taking orders from you?"

"Take it up with Guido." He knew damned well a sneaky little bully like Billy would do no such thing. It was too straightforward for him. He'd do his best to take Danny out the first chance he got, from the back, like the coward and bully that he was. Their uneasy truce had shattered, all because of a stupid schoolgirl prank.

"I may do that. In the meantime, I'm outta here."

Danny watched him go, his tense shoulders not relaxing until he heard Billy's souped-up Mustang peel away from the laundromat. Reopening the washer, he took the small load of laundry and tossed it in one of the huge dryers, shoved in a quarter and watched the brightly colored clothes whirl. His claiming of Katharine had been nothing more than an invention to keep Billy away from her. It wasn't until he was alone in the laundromat, the thump and swirl of the dryer hypnotizing him, that he realized he'd meant every word he'd said. He wanted her. And smart or not, he had every intention of having her. It was time little miss schoolgirl learned how the other half lived.

Chapter Three

It hadn't taken more than the cool, gray light of day to make Katharine see reason. She couldn't throw away a lifetime of hard work and ambition on a whim. Even if the shadowy rescuer of last night was the first man she'd ever actually been overwhelmingly attracted to, it was probably nothing more than a fluke. When—no, if—she saw him again he'd probably seem far less romantic. Last night her reactions had been fuzzed by relief and gratitude. In the daylight she'd see him as the two-bit hood he really was, running a second-rate gambling operation out of a cheesy laundromat in the poor section of Calhoun.

Of course, he might be running a first-rate gambling operation, with the cheesy laundromat simply a cover. Certainly the brief glimpse of technology she'd had was impressive. Either way it didn't matter. Whether he was an upscale crook or a small-time operator, he wasn't the sort of man for Sarah Jane Lafferty's only daughter.

Besides, if she finally found one man almost irresistibly attractive, chances were she'd find others. She was just pickier than most, Sarah Jane's daughter after all. It was no wonder she had a hard time relaxing around men. Her own father had taken off before she was even three, leaving an embittered Sarah Jane to raise, no, to push into precocious adulthood, their only child. All her life Katharine had done her best to please her exacting mother, to make her proud of her. If at times it seemed like a doomed effort, she could no more stop trying than she could stop breathing.

Sarah Jane had managed to belittle and dismiss any boy brave enough to seek Katharine out, and it hadn't taken much for her to view them with her mother's eyes. Boys were a waste of time, her mother had told her early on. Men were an annoying necessity, as long as you didn't lose your heart to them.

Katharine had always assumed she didn't have a heart to lose. Her life was neatly planned, by her mother as much as herself. After she graduated from high school as class valedictorian, she entered Calhoun University, planning to join the best sorority, speed through four years of college in three, and go on for graduate studies to a prestigious Ivy League college, of necessity on full scholarship. Her mother wanted her to major in business, but for once Katharine had followed her own heart. She took the requisite business courses, but she took an equal number of art courses. Deep in her heart of hearts she wanted to paint, did paint in the drafty old classroom of the fine arts building, strange, colorful pictures that had her old professor both censorious and impressed.

That was the one part of her life she kept apart from her mother's rigid control. And now, for the first time in her life, she was going to tell her mother no. She was going to tell her she had no intention of joining Alpha Alpha Alpha and its slimy, back-stabbing coterie of small-minded witches. Even if it had meant freedom from the tiny back bedroom in the shabby ranch house she shared with her mother, she couldn't do it. Better to survive another year or so of her mother's watchfulness than cater to someone like Marcy Welton.

And if she had found someone like her anonymous rescuer to finally awaken her slumbering passions, then she'd be able to find someone else, someone more suitable. Someone who fit her mother's notions of what was proper, what was admired, what would complement her daughter and reflect suitably on Sarah Jane.

In the meantime, she had to stop thinking about him. She had enough problems as it was, worrying about how she was going to deal with her mother, without wasting her time thinking about a romance with a dangerous stranger.

She was scurrying along the sidewalk between classes, her head down as she contemplated how in heaven's name she was going to tell her mother her decision about Tri Alpha. One thing that would be sure to appeal to Sarah Jane was the financial aspect. One reason they'd chosen Calhoun University was the simple fact that Katharine could live at home, saving a great deal of money. If she'd pledged to Tri Alpha she would have taken up residence in that tiny room she'd been allotted last night, out from under Sarah Jane's vigilance. And the cost could have been prohibitive.

No, she'd point out to Sarah Jane that it was simply too expensive to join Tri Alpha, despite the social good it might do her in the future. Maybe next year.

She was so caught up in worrying about her mother's probable reaction to this strategy that she didn't notice the car that drove up beside her, slowing down to keep pace with her preoccupied stride. Didn't notice until a familiar, deep voice called her name, distracting her from her troubles and presenting her with a new one.

"Hey, Katharine," the voice said.

It was the red sports car. How she could have been oblivious to a red Aston Martin was beyond Katharine's comprehension, but oblivious she'd been. The man inside was a different matter. He'd put the car in neutral and was leaning across the seat, looking at her through the open window. And damn him, he was even better looking in daylight.

"I don't think I'd better talk to you," she said, concentrating on the books she clutched tightly in her arms. "Last night was an aberration, a mistake...."

"I bet," he murmured. "Do you want to go for a ride?"

"Listen, Mr...." She stopped, telling herself she shouldn't be tempted. "I don't even know your name."

"Danny. Daniel T. McCandless. Let's drive out to Pelham Park."

"I don't think this is a good idea," she said somewhat desperately. "I really appreciate your coming to my rescue last night, but I think I should stay where I belong."

He grinned. "You won't learn anything that way."

"I won't learn anything if I cut classes," she said, clutching her books even tighter. She wanted to get into that car. But to do so would betray twenty years of values drilled into her, to do so would be to betray her mother's determined plans for her.

"You'd be surprised," he said, unruffled. "Besides, I've got something for you."

She eyed him warily. Just to complicate matters, Marcy Welton's Trans Am was driving down the road in the opposite direction, full of Tri Alphas, and slowly enough so they could get a clear view of the ice princess. "Billy Ray's head on a platter?" she asked dryly.

"That might be arranged. No, something a little more... personal." He held up a teal-and-black lace bra, slinging it around his finger. "You left this behind. Among other things. I particularly liked the lavender teddy...."

She got into the car. When she tried to snatch the bra from his hand he pulled it out of reach, tucking it in his jacket pocket before pulling away from the curb with a surprising squeal of tires. She hadn't thought he'd noticed the Trans Am cruising slowly by, but Daniel T. McCandless wasn't someone to miss much. He flashed a mocking smile toward the avid watchers, his long fingers drumming on the leather-covered steering wheel, and Katharine thought he probably would have liked to salute them a bit more crudely.

"You should have seen their faces last night," she said, breaking the silence. "I thought their eyes were going to bug out of their heads." She giggled at the memory. "This morning was even better."

"What happened this morning? Did you fill them in on fictional details?"

"No. I figured their own imaginations would do a better job than mine would. It was when I told them they could take their sorority and... stuff it that they really freaked. I thought Marcy Welton was going to faint. No one's ever told her to go suck an orange before.''

"Why did you?" he asked. "I thought this was what you wanted, entrance into the holy of holies. Why throw it all away on a matter of foolish principle?"

"Don't you have principles?"

"I can't afford 'em," he said flatly, glancing over at her out of those dark blue eyes. "So why'd you throw it all away?"

"I didn't want to turn around and find myself trying to do to some poor girl what they tried to do to me, for no other reason than malice. It's always easier to give in to your worst instincts instead of your best, and I didn't want to live with people like that. Where are my clothes?"

"In the back. When we get to the park we can put the seats down and get them."

She looked at him, startled. His words were completely casual, he drove easily, his hands loose and efficient on the steering wheel, and his expression was relaxed. Maybe he didn't mean what she thought he meant.

Then again, maybe he did. She almost protested, then thought better of it, leaning back against the leather seat. For whatever reason, she'd made her decision once she'd gotten in the car with him. She hadn't given in over any desperate need to retrieve her clothes—she'd already figured they were a lost cause.

No, she got into his car because she couldn't resist him. She was drawn to him as thoroughly as a moth was drawn to a flame. And she was in just as much danger. She wouldn't get away with her wings singed. She was going to burn up.

"So where were you heading?" he asked.

"Do you really care?"

"Not particularly," he admitted. "But you've got an odd expression on your face, and I figured if I came up with some small talk you might forget about jumping out of a moving car."

"I'm not going to jump," she said calmly. "Thank you for bringing my clothes. I didn't think it would be a very good idea if I went back to the laundromat to get them."

"I'm glad to see you're capable of showing some sense after all. Billy Ray wasn't too happy with you last night, and what he lacks in brains he makes up for in his ability to hold grudges."

She looked up at him, startled. "He wouldn't do anything, would he?"

"Fortunately for you he doesn't even know your name, much less where you live. I also threatened him with a slow death by torture if he so much as laid a finger on you. But that doesn't mean you're entirely safe."

"It doesn't?"

"He could hang around campus until he ran into you. And he doesn't give a damn how many threats I toss his way—he'd like an excuse to try to bring me down. I'm in a competitive business, and Billy's not only a subordinate, he's a rival." He glanced over at her. "No, if I were you I'd be real careful."

"You're just trying to scare me."

"Why should I do that?"

To put it into words sounded both idiotic and conceited, and yet she couldn't let it drop. If he didn't recant his warning, she'd end up a nervous wreck. "Because if I'm frightened I'll be vulnerable, and if I'm vulnerable you could . . . you could . . ."

"Have my wicked way with you?" Danny supplied with a faint grin. "I don't think I have to scare you into it."

"You don't?"

He shook his head, slowly, and she could feel an odd, tingling sort of warmth spreading upward, over her breasts, and downward, between her legs. "Just be careful of Billy Ray, all right? I've warned him, but that could just make matters worse."

"What did you tell him?"

"That I wanted you for myself." This time he didn't look at her to gauge her reaction. His gaze was concentrated on the road ahead of them as he maneuvered the twists and turns into Pelham Park, the most notorious make-out spot in Calhoun.

The parking lot that looked out over the rolling landscape was deserted. For one thing it was too cold for casual sex, and it was still broad daylight. Danny slid the car to a stop, put it in neutral and turned to her.

"Why'd you tell him that?" she asked, her voice faintly husky.

"I always tell the truth," he said. "Even when I lie." And he pulled her across the front seat, and into his arms. The steering wheel was digging into her back, but she scarcely noticed, too mesmerized by the warm, hard body beneath her to think about anything else. He hadn't kissed her yet, he merely looked at her, slowly, his gaze hot and searching, as if he were memorizing her face.

She looked back, clear-eyed, frightened and yet determined, and the longer she looked the more certain she was. This wasn't a man she was going to get over. This wasn't someone she could simply ignore as inconvenient to her future plans. This was the man she'd been waiting for, all her life, and now that she'd found him things were never going to go back into their safe, comfortable little order.

His hands were beneath her loose-fitting parka, sliding up under her sweater, hard, rough-textured hands on the soft skin of her back. She didn't move, utterly still as his hands unfastened the back clasp of her bra with the deftness born of too much practice, and her eyes looked into his as his hands moved around the front, up under the loosened bra to cover her breasts.

"No padding today," he murmured, his voice slightly raspy as his thumbs danced across her hardened nipples. "You don't need it. You're perfect." And he brought his mouth to hers, very gently, his lips just grazing hers.

The quiet moan in the idling car was hers. The arms sliding around his neck were hers. The mouth that pressed against his, the tongue that reached out, searching, were hers.

"Easy, easy, now," he said softly against her lips. "We have plenty of time. This is just a little taste." He nipped at her mouth, gently, teasingly, and Katharine shivered in his arms, pushing her small breasts against his clever hands, pushing her mouth against his in an untutored need to have him deepen the kiss.

And then he gave in to her mute pleading, slanting his mouth across her lips and kissing her full force, with a passion that skirted the edge of brutality. She whimpered in fright for a moment and then kissed him back, pressing closer, closer still, wanting to be absorbed into his very flesh, wanting to sink into him, to be lost in this mesmerizing kaleidoscope of heat and dampness and pleasure and passion.

His hands left her breasts, tangled in her hair and pulled her head away from his. He was breathing deeply, his eyes faintly glazed, and she knew he was just as aroused, just as astonished as she was. She tried to move closer, but he held her away. "None of that, love," he admonished her. "It makes no sense to do it in the cramped front seat of a sports car when I've got a nice big bed at home. We'll go there. I just wanted to make sure I was reading you right."

She looked at him, still caught up with the idea of his nice big bed at home. "Reading me right?" she echoed uncertainly.

"I wanted to be sure that was lust, not just gratitude in those beautiful brown eyes of yours."

"Lust?" she said, nibbling the side of his neck above the black turtleneck he wore. "That's such an ugly word."

"What would you call it? You're about to go to bed with a man whose name you didn't even know. You're so turned on you feel like you're about to explode in my arms. If that's not lust, what is it?"

"Love," she said simply, astonished that he didn't understand. "I'm in love with you."

"Good God!" he choked, looking horrified. "You don't even know me."

"Don't you believe in love at first sight?" She continued kissing him, ignoring the sudden tension in the muscles of his neck.

"Honey, I don't believe in any form of love at all. I believe in having a good time, period."

She wasn't discouraged. "You'll find out," she murmured, coming back to his lips and pressing hers against them.

He pushed her away. "Stop it!" he snapped.

"Stop kissing you?"

A faint, last trace of amusement shadowed his blue eyes. "No, you can kiss me all you want. Anywhere you want. Just stop talking about love like a romantic kid. You don't have to love someone to go to bed with them, Katharine. It's much better if you don't try to fool yourself into believing that. You can't spend your life thinking you're in love every time you want to go to bed with a man."

"I won't," she said, kissing his throat. "Once is enough."

"Katharine..." he said, exasperated.

"Let's go back to your apartment," she murmured beneath his ear. "I want to see your nice big bed."

"That's not all you'll see," he muttered. "Listen, Katharine, you have to promise me you won't try to convince yourself you're in love with me or we're not going anywhere."

"I promise," she said promptly.

His expression was doubtful. "As easy as that?"

"I don't need to convince myself. I already know."

"Cut it out." He picked her up and set her back on the passenger seat. "How many times have you told yourself you were in love with someone?"

"Never."

"You mean you went to bed with the other men in your life out of pure lust, and it's only me who gets saddled with your first case of true love?" he drawled.

"No. I mean that I waited until I fell in love before I decided to go to bed with someone." She was getting tired of this argument, and without his arms around her, his hard body beneath her, the shivering, heated passion was fading into a case of minor irritation.

"You mean..." Horrified comprehension finally dawned. "You mean you've never gone to bed with anyone?"

"Not until now," she said brightly.

"Uh-uh," he said, slamming the car into reverse and knocking her against the leather-covered dashboard. "Not now either."

"What do you mean?"

"I mean that I'm not going to be the recipient of your first childish passion. I don't want anyone in love with me, looking for happy ever after and marriage and babies. I've told you once, I'm looking for a good time, not a commitment. I don't want you to love me, I don't even want you to think you love me, and delicious as your body is, I don't want it with all that emotional baggage."

She sank back, clinging to the leather seat with clenched fingers, pain and disbelief washing over her as he skidded back out of the park, a determined expression on his face. "You're turning down love?" she asked, not quite believing it. "How could you? Love is the most precious thing in the world...."

"Love is a pile of crap, a bunch of lies fed to women to keep them docile and housebound, a bunch of lies fed to men to keep their nose to the grindstone forty hours a week, fifty years of their lives. Love is a joke, and I'm not having any of it."

"Where are you taking me?"

"Back to where I found you. Maybe you can walk in late to your class."

"I want to go to your apartment," she said, her voice breaking with sudden tears.

He pulled to a stop, too fast, and once again she went hurtling toward the windshield. His arm shot out to stop her, and for a moment she clung to him.

He shook himself free, grabbed the clothes from the back and piled them in her arms. "It's been an education," he said, his voice remote. "But next time stay on your own side of the tracks."

She still didn't move, even when he leaned across her, his arms brushing her breasts, and opened the passenger door. "Don't you want me?" she asked.

For a moment she thought he'd soften, that he'd close the passenger door and take her away. But then his expression closed up. "Honey," he drawled, his voice sharp and cruel, "I should have known from those amateur kisses that you were a virgin. Frankly I prefer a woman who knows what she's doing to a clumsy novice. Come and see me when you've had a little more experience in learning how to please a man."

"Why you egotistical, sexist moron," she said, fury wiping out even the shame that had been her first reaction. "You slimy, contemptible, worthless piece of..."

He shoved her, not too gently, out of the car. And then, as an afterthought, he took the teal-and-black lace bra out of his pocket and tossed it in the road in front of her. "See you," he said, and pulled away from the curb without a backward glance.

The campus was almost deserted at that hour, everyone still deeply immured in their classrooms. At least no one had witnessed her ignominy. She squatted down and picked up the bra, now covered with muddy snow, and tucked it into her own pocket. Staring after the rapidly disappearing sports car, she fought against the crushing sense of inadequacy that threatened to overwhelm her. All her life she'd only wanted to please her mother, to love her mother. And she'd never been good enough, smart enough, hardworking enough for Sarah Jane's exacting standards, and that love had always been thrown back in her face.

Now it was happening all over again. She'd been judged and found wanting, and her foolish declaration of love had once more been thrown back in her teeth. She wasn't experienced enough for him, she wasn't cool and calculating enough to take and provide pleasure without involving her heart.

All she had to do was go on to her classes, work twice as hard and tell herself she hated Danny McCandless. After all, he was nothing but trouble, and not the sort of man any decent girl would want to have anything to do with.

But she couldn't do that. It made no sense, but she meant what she'd said. For some reason she loved him, and all the hard work and stern self-reproaches weren't going to talk her out of it. That left her with only two choices.

Number one, she could spend her life mourning a lost love and end up old and bitter and alone like her mother.

Or number two, and far more appealing, she could refuse to take no for an answer. Go after him, win him over despite his denial of the very existence of love, and maybe there could be a happy ending after all.

And if that didn't work, she thought, shoving the rest of the clean laundry in her pockets, there was always revenge.

IT HAD BEEN A CLOSE ESCAPE, Danny thought as he drove fast, too fast, back to the grittier sections of Calhoun, Ohio. He'd almost made one of the biggest mistakes, and it all came with thinking with his zipper instead of his brain. Hell, he was as bad as Billy Ray. He'd looked at Katharine Marie Lafferty and wanted her. Almost enough not to realize the mess he'd be getting into.

Fortunately, she was too damned innocent to realize the daunting effect her little confession would have on a man like him. She seemed astonished that he wouldn't want her love, wouldn't welcome it gratefully.

He cursed under his breath, remembering that hurt expression on her face. Remembering the sweet, untutored taste of her mouth, the feel of her small, perfect breasts beneath his hands.

There was no room in his life for virgins, for love, for Katharine Lafferty. And if she were only a little bit older, a little bit wiser, she'd know there was no room in her well-ordered life for a no-good like him.

Now if only he could convince himself of that notion, once and for all, he'd have a much easier time of it. But he had the depressing suspicion it was going to take more than common sense to make him forget her.

Chapter Four

"So who was he?" Janelle demanded, sinking her plump body down across from Katharine in the cafeteria and digging into her hot fudge sundae.

Katharine kept her eyes glued to her calculus text. Janelle was her best friend and confidante, as far removed from the witches of Tri Alpha as a female could be, and yet for once Katharine didn't feel like baring her soul. She was still too confused, uncertain about what she wanted, to share those feelings with even her most trusted friend. "Who was who?" she murmured, turning the page without seeing it.

"This is a small campus, Katharine, and you're my best friend. Word travels fast. You didn't really go out with Billy Ray, did you?"

She raised her eyes to meet Janelle's worried gaze over the melting hot fudge sundae. "What if I did?"

"You should have talked to me. Joining Tri Alpha isn't worth it, and I would have told you so. You're just so blindly obedient where your mother's concerned...."

"Eat your sundae, Janelle."

"I can't. I'm worried about you."

"Don't be. I didn't go out with Billy Ray. I got rescued by a knight in tarnished armor. I turned Tri Alpha down, my mother's not speaking to me and I don't care. How's that for changes?" Her voice was faintly defiant.

Janelle immediately scooped a huge spoonful of ice cream into her mouth. "Wonderful. So tell me about this knight."

"There's nothing to tell. He brought me back to the sorority like a perfect gentleman."

"And picked you up the day before yesterday in an Aston Martin when you were on your way to calculus. This has got to be serious. I've never known you to cut a class."

"I never have before." She closed the book. "Did your spies tell you he dropped me back on the campus less than half an hour later and drove away from me like a bat out of hell?"

"I don't have spies," Janelle said, aggrieved. "I don't gossip. People talk to me, but I don't tell them anything, you know that."

Katharine sighed. "I know. I'm sorry. I'm just a little ... upset."

"Marcy Welton said he was the best-looking man she'd ever seen in her life. She said he made Billy Ray look like a nerd. So how come I've never seen this stud?"

"He's Billy Ray's boss."

Janelle let the ice cream drip from her spoon as her mouth dropped open. "You mean he's a gangster?" she gasped.

"For want of a better word, I suppose so," Katharine said uneasily. "He's in charge of whatever's going on at the laundromat."

"We all know what's going on at the laundromat, Katharine, even a naïf like you knows," Janelle said, putting her spoon into the rapidly melting mess and shoving the dish away. "So he and Billy fought over you and the boss won."

"What makes you say that?"

"Billy Ray was seen with a very impressive black eye and a chip on his shoulder the size of Cleveland."

A chill ran down Katharine's backbone. "Seen where?"

"On campus, a couple of hours ago. Why?"

"What was he doing here?"

"Who knows? Professor Carlyle has a gambling problem, and I imagine there's a lot of action on the upcoming football games. Billy's been around here often enough—

how do you think Marcy came up with her nasty little idea? You don't think she hangs out in places like Guido's Laundromat?''

"I have no idea what she does, and I could care less." There was no need to panic, Katharine told herself. Billy had been on campus before, she'd even seen him herself a time or two before she went off on her idiotic quest. Chances were she'd run into him again, sooner or later.

Danny had been exaggerating any possible danger. Billy wouldn't dare touch her, hurt her. He probably wanted to forget all about what happened as much as she did, and if he ran across her he'd probably ignore her.

"So are you going to tell me what happened, or are you just going to sit there with a faraway look on your face? Marcy Welton's spreading it around that you did it with Billy Ray, but I told her she was lying through her teeth. So what about this gangster in shining armor? Are you going out with him?''

"I told you he dumped me back on campus yesterday and drove away as fast as he could. If it was up to him he'd never see me again."

"Is it up to him?"

Katharine considered it. "What do you think?"

Janelle shook her head. "I think you can be very dangerous when you have that expression on your face. Why did he dump you?"

"He told me he didn't like virgins."

Janelle's mouth was a round O. "You're kidding."

"Nope."

"And what are you planning to do about it?" she demanded.

"I don't really have any choice in the matter, do I?" Katharine countered.

Janelle let out a premature sigh of relief. "I'm glad you're being reasonable. The best thing you can do is forget about him."

"It is. But that's not what I'm going to do," Katharine said, her voice ruthless.

"Oh, God," Janelle moaned. "I don't think I want to hear this."

"Then don't ask."

"I can't help myself. What are you going to do?"

"It's very simple. I'm just going to have to go out and get some experience."

SHE WAITED UNTIL Sarah Jane left the house that evening. It had been easy enough to avoid her mother's intense scrutiny. Sarah Jane was so offended by Katharine's refusal to join Tri Alpha that she was maintaining a frosty, disapproving silence. That silence made the usual searching questions as to Katharine's day and plans impossible, and Katharine spent the afternoon and evening in her room, trying to concentrate on calculus.

It was a losing battle. The moment she heard her mother back out of the driveway she slammed her textbook closed, ripping off her clothes as she ran for the shower.

Tonight's transformation was a little easier than the one she'd managed three nights ago, when she'd made her abortive visit to Guido's Laundromat. By the time Janelle showed up outside the little ranch house she was finished, stepping out into the nippy autumn evening with her mother's cloth coat wrapped around her in lieu of her parka.

Janelle let out a low whistle as Katharine slid into the front seat. "You look gorgeous," she said.

Katharine glanced at her reflection in the mirror, remembering all too vividly looking into Danny's rearview mirror and what had followed. "The makeup's not too much, is it?"

"Maybe just a little. But you look fabulous. I really don't think this is a good idea, Katharine. Why don't we go back on campus and find someone safe? Vahsen's Tavern isn't the sort of place nice women go."

"Do I look like a nice woman?"

"No. And that's the problem. People are going to think you're a . . . a . . ."

"That's the point. Danny made it clear he wasn't interested in an inexperienced little schoolgirl. I have to prove to him that I'm not what he thinks I am."

"But Katharine, you are!" Janelle insisted, driving slowly through the evening streets of Calhoun. "I don't understand why you're doing this."

Katharine leaned back against the vinyl seat. "I don't know why, either," she said in a quiet voice. "But I couldn't just slink away, give up. This was the only thing I could think of. Vahsen's Tavern is the biggest dive in East Calhoun. Danny must hang out there. If he sees me there he'll think twice about protecting my innocence."

"Is that what he's trying to do?"

Katharine squirmed. "That's what I'm taking a chance on. He told me he wasn't interested in inexperienced girls, but I'm guessing it was only his way of trying to protect me."

"He saved you once from Billy Ray and now you're convinced he's a noble prince?" Janelle said with her customary shrewdness.

"I'm taking a chance on that, yes."

"And if you're wrong?"

"If I'm wrong, I'll survive, sadder but wiser. I can't really explain what I feel about him, Janelle. I just know I'm drawn to him, in ways I don't even begin to understand."

"It's called infatuation," Janelle drawled.

"I wish it were that simple. Wish me luck?"

"It depends what constitutes luck. I hope to God you get out of there safely. That'll have to do. Are you sure you don't want me to wait for you?"

Katharine shook her head. "We both know this section of town is too dangerous. Besides, I don't know how long I'll have to wait. It's eight-thirty now—he might not show up till later."

"He might not show up at all."

"That's a possibility. Don't worry, I've lived in this town all my life."

"Not in East Calhoun, you haven't. How are you planning on getting back home?"

"Danny will drive me."

"And if he doesn't?"

"Then someone else will."

"Katharine..."

But she was already sliding out of the car, before the sudden wave of panic could turn into a debilitating swell. "I'll call you tomorrow," she promised, squaring her shoulders and turning to face the seedy-looking tavern. And it took all her hard-earned self-control to keep from running after Janelle as she drove away, leaving her in the center of the worst section of town.

The bar was noisy, smoky and ill lit when she stepped inside. She swallowed an instinctive cough, glanced casually around her, and kept her face impassive as she realized that in a crowd of twenty or thirty customers there were only two other women, both of whom looked as if they plied the world's oldest profession.

She heard the wolf whistle as she crossed the floor on the high-heeled shoes she'd chosen to show off her undeniably nice legs. It was too crowded, and she was too nervous, to see whether Danny was there yet. Certainly everyone in the place was watching her. If he was there, he'd see her soon enough.

Only one bar stool was unoccupied. She climbed onto it, fighting the impulse to keep her mother's coat wrapped safely around her, and she wondered whether she could surreptitiously button another of the buttons. She'd forgone the tissues tonight, but her meager cleavage still felt far too obvious. She looked down at the bar in front of her, the greasy rings left by somebody else's drink, the pretzel crumbs and peanuts strewn across the surface.

"What'll you have?" the bartender growled.

"White wine?"

"You got an ID?" he demanded. He was big and evil looking, with a cast in one eye and a stubbled chin.

"Since when have you been so fussy about IDs, Frank?" a smooth voice interrupted them. Too smooth for Danny's deep, rough tones, Katharine thought with a sudden prickling of doubt, turning to face the man who'd come up behind her.

He was a tall, lean man, ageless, and impeccably dressed. Too impeccably dressed, from the tasteful diamond on his right hand to the shiny leather shoes that Katharine instinctively knew were custom-made. He snapped the fingers on his diamond-adorned hand, and the white wine appeared in a smudged glass.

"Allow me to introduce myself. I'm Leon Spengler. You must be new to Calhoun."

Katharine cast a glance around her. She was no longer the center of attention in the seedy bar. Once Leon approached her everyone else went back to their own business.

She looked back at him. He must be a powerful figure in this run-down section of town, yet for the life of her she couldn't imagine why. His clothes were so fancy they were almost effeminate, and his whole manner was smooth and unthreatening. "I've lived in Calhoun all my life," she said ingenuously. "I've just never spent much time in this part of town."

Leon smiled. "Slumming can be very illuminating."

"Oh, I didn't think I was slumming..." she protested quickly.

"Then why are you here?"

She considered telling him the truth. Leon looked like the sort of man who knew everything and everyone—if anyone could lead her to Danny, he could.

But there was a difference between could and would. And for some reason she didn't quite trust him. "I was looking for work," she said, the lie instinctive. "I'm a student, and I need some extra cash."

Leon positively grinned. "You came to the right man, lady. I can help you make all the pocket money you could ever need."

"Get away from her, Leon." Danny's rough voice broke through.

Leon turned to look into Danny's chilly blue eyes. "I saw her first, man."

"No, you didn't," Katharine said softly, slipping off the bar stool. Danny was positively vibrating with rage. If she'd ever had any doubts about her ability to affect him, those doubts were effectively laid to rest.

"Horning in on my business, Danny?" Leon said coolly. "This is the best-looking prospect I've seen in a long time. What do you want her for? I thought you were above such things."

She could see the struggle Danny was going through; she could almost read his mind. On the one hand, he wanted to walk away, deny that she meant anything to him. On the other hand, he didn't want to leave her with Leon, though she couldn't imagine why. If anyone seemed harmless in this evil-looking bar, Leon did. "Just keep your slimy hands off her, Leon. She's not that sort of girl."

"Everyone is that sort of girl if they have enough motivation," Leon said smoothly. "What's your problem, Danny? Just what does she mean to you?"

Danny glanced down at her, and Katharine held her breath, waiting. Waiting for a declaration of undying love, even if they both knew it was a lie. She'd put everything on the line, and now the future lay in his hands. All he had to do was say something.

"What does she mean to me?" he paraphrased. Then he shrugged. "Not a damned thing, Leon. You can have her." And he turned and walked away, through the crowded bar and out the door.

She must have made some sort of sound, some quiet gasp of distress. Moments later she found herself sitting in a booth that had been instantly vacated, her glass of white wine in front of her, Leon looking at her out of sad, dark eyes.

"You put your money on the wrong dude, lady," he said. "Danny's not the type to help you out. He's got a limited chance for success in his chosen profession. He's got too many scruples getting in his way."

"What do you mean?" she asked numbly, staring at the wineglass in front of her.

"Word on the street has it that he's good. Too damned good. But he's not going to get very far if he isn't willing to dirty his hands in some of his employers' sidelines. And Danny strikes me as an ambitious man."

"I don't know what you're talking about," she said, taking a sip of her lukewarm wine.

"You trying to tell me you don't know what he does for a living?"

"I know."

"Then you should realize that he's not the man to turn to if you're needing some money. Leon can take care of that. I have the connections, the network set up, and all you have to do is get paid for what you give away for free." He shook his head with comical sadness. "Women are so lucky."

Katharine forced herself to close her gaping mouth. "You're a pimp," she said in hushed, horrified tones.

"What did you think I was, honey, a social worker? I can guarantee you all the work you want, anytime you want, any way you want, and all I'll take is my usual fifty percent. You could work one night a week and have enough for a new car. You could . . ."

"I'm not interested," she said, pushing back from the table and knocking over her wine.

Leon grabbed her wrist and forced her down again. While the same pleasant smile was on his face, the pain he was inflicting on her wrist was agonizing. "People don't say no to Leon," he informed her. "You think Danny can help you? He won't touch the drug or prostitution trade with a ten-foot pole. That's the problem with these inner-city white boys—they think they can dabble in the business and not get their hands dirty."

"Please let me go," she begged in a hushed voice.

"Honey, are those tears in those beautiful brown eyes?" Leon chuckled. "I can up your price if you know how to cry on cue."

"I don't want to do this. I don't want to have anything to do with you."

"I can change your mind," he said simply.

"Okay, Leon, let her go."

She hadn't realized Danny had returned, she'd been so petrified with terror. Immediately her wrist was released, and she cradled it in her other hand, fighting to keep the tears from spilling down her face.

"Change your mind, man?" Leon questioned. "If you're thinking of running her yourself, I wouldn't advise it. She's going to need some persuading, and I've got experience in doing just that."

"She's not looking for work, Leon." Danny was controlling his fury with an effort. "She's a stupid college student who doesn't know what she wants, and she's getting out of here right now." His hand on her arm as he hauled her up wasn't any more gentle than Leon's iron grip, but it was far more welcome.

"You think about it, girl," Leon murmured, leaning back and watching the two of them out of hooded eyes. "Danny can't do anything for you, but I can. You get tired of him, you come back and ask for Leon."

She wanted to run out of the bar. Every eye in the place was watching her through the haze of cigarette smoke, and she knew from the tension in Danny's hand gripping her that he wanted nothing more than to haul her out of there as fast as he could. But he forced her to take her time, his face dark and unreadable.

The Aston Martin was parked outside, the motor running. He shoved her into the front seat and slammed the door after her, moving around to the driver's side with economy of motion. After one look at his expression she slid down in the leather seat, buckling her safety belt and holding on for dear life as he took off at a speed better suited to the Indy 500 than a city street.

The night was dark, the glaring lights from East Calhoun receding in the distance as Danny drove, his jaw set, his eyes staring straight ahead. They were past the city limits, driving into the night, when he finally spoke.

"What the hell did you think you were doing?"

She flinched at the controlled savagery in his voice. "Looking for you," she said, cursing the fact that her voice wavered.

"Dressed like that?"

"I . . . I wanted to show you that I wasn't just an innocent schoolgirl." It sounded impossibly lame right now, when less than twenty-four hours ago it had seemed like such a good idea.

"Nothing could have proved more how innocent you are," he snapped. "You're just lucky you ran into Leon."

"Lucky?" she shrieked. "He was a white slaver."

"He's a businessman who knows what he's doing. And what he was doing tonight was scaring you."

"You mean he didn't think I'd be a good prostitute?"

"Don't sound so aggrieved. You weren't planning on entering that profession, were you?"

"Of course not!"

"Leon needs his girls committed. If they don't scare easily then he works out an arrangement. He would have let you go sooner if I hadn't made an ass of myself." He reached for a cigarette and lit it, the flame flaring brightly in the darkened car.

"Why did you?"

"I guess I've gotten in the habit of rescuing you from your own stupidity. You sure this wasn't one more task you had to accomplish to join your sorority?"

"I told you, I told Tri Alpha to go . . . suck eggs," she finished.

His laugh was mirthless. "You aren't going to survive too well in East Calhoun unless you learn how to curse. I guess I'm going to have to teach you."

She held her breath, watching him in the darkness. There was no softness in his expression, no warmth. "What else are you going to teach me?"

He glanced over at her. "Maybe I'll teach you to think twice before jumping into trouble. Or maybe I'll teach you not to judge things at face value." He looked straight ahead, taking a deep drag on his cigarette. "Most likely I'll teach you to be sorry you were ever born." And he turned off the highway, onto a side road.

Chapter Five

The roadside tavern was dimly lit, and a light snow had begun to fall around Calhoun, Ohio. Danny pulled the Aston Martin up between a battered red pickup and an old Chevy, switched off the engine and turned to her. "We need to talk," he said.

"We can talk in the car."

He shook his head. "You need a cup of coffee," he said flatly, "and I sure as hell need a drink. Besides, I think the less time I'm alone with you the safer we'll both be."

Some of the misery was beginning to abate, and fresh stirrings of hope made her lift her head. "Don't you trust yourself?" she taunted softly.

"Hell, no. And even worse, I don't trust you. Move your butt, Katharine. It's cold out here."

At first she couldn't see much difference between the Redwood Café and the sleazy dive she'd just been rescued from. It was equally smoke filled, equally noisy, equally redolent of beer and onions. "This isn't much of an improvement over Vahsen's Tavern," she murmured, glancing around her as she slid into a booth.

He shook his head in disgust. "It just goes to show why you shouldn't be allowed out without a keeper. Vahsen's Tavern is a dive. Half the dope deals in Calhoun go down there, not to mention Leon plying his trade. Even the police think twice about setting foot in there, and you waltz in, innocent as a baby, and expect to get out in one piece."

She was glad the place was dark. She could feel the heat in her flushed cheeks, and only hoped Danny wouldn't notice her embarrassment. "So?" she said bravely. "What makes this place any different?"

"This place is just what it seems, a roadside café where people come to eat, drink and dance. And maybe, just maybe, place a few harmless bets if someone's around to take them. That's a far cry from drugs and prostitution."

"That's what Leon said," she murmured.

"What do you mean?"

"He said you were too squeamish for anything but gambling, but that sooner or later you were going to have to come down off your high horse and dirty your hands. Is that true?"

"Is what true? That I keep away from certain aspects of the business? That doesn't make me any less guilty, you know. I work for a very large organization, a nationwide family with international connections. Just because I personally don't get involved with drugs doesn't mean I'm guiltless. The income I generate goes into the same pot, gets spread around with all the other money. I may not have brought cocaine money into the coffers, but cocaine money helped pay for my car and my nice suit." He voice was very bitter, so harsh that Katharine ached for him.

"It is a nice suit," she said in a quiet voice. "Nice car, too."

Danny grimaced. "I can always take you back to Leon. With his expertise you can have a car of your own. Maybe not an Aston Martin, but a little Fiat would be nice."

"Don't."

"Then grow up, Katharine. It's a big, nasty world out there, and you've been in school too long. Keep away from East Calhoun, from Vahsen's Tavern and people like Leon. And most importantly, keep away from me." His voice was savage, but Katharine was growing ever more sure of herself.

"Should I walk back home?" Her voice held a trace of laughter. "Or are you going to buy me that cup of coffee while you lecture me? If you are, I'd rather have a glass of white wine. Maybe this place has a better vintage."

"You'll have coffee," he snapped. "And be glad I don't make you hitchhike."

"That'd be the day. You're so busy acting like my mother that I don't expect you'll let me go to the bathroom without you."

"If this were Vahsen's I wouldn't," he agreed, giving the order to the bored-looking waitress. "Listen, Katharine, this is for your own good."

"Why do people always say that when they're trying to get their own way?" Katharine demanded of the ceiling. "That's one of my mother's favorite phrases."

"That's the second time in less than sixty seconds that you've compared me to your mother. Stop it."

"Then stop acting like my mother."

"Stop acting like a schoolgirl."

"I am a schoolgirl, damn it. It's not my fault." They were glaring at each other across the table, and for the first time she noticed a tiny, crescent-shaped scar by the corner of his mouth. She wanted to kiss that scar, run the tip of her tongue over it. She wanted to taste the whiskey he'd just taken a gulp of, she wanted . . .

"Don't look at me like that," he said in a harsh undertone. "This is hard enough for me, without you looking like you want to . . ."

"I just want to kiss you."

"Well, don't. Katharine, I'm no good for you. I'm in a dirty little business, and Leon's right, it's just going to get dirtier. I don't know why you're so attracted to me, but for your sake you ought to go back to your classes and your college boys and forget you ever met me."

"I can't. I love you, remember?"

"We've met three times, each for no more than half an hour. What's that got to do with love?"

She shrugged, stirring sugar and cream into the coffee she had no intention of drinking. "I've been practical all my life. I've done what my mother wanted, I've worked hard and done very well. For the first time I'm feeling something that doesn't make sense, and I don't feel like analyzing it or trying to talk myself out of it. I love you, period.''

"Period," he echoed glumly, draining half of his dark glass of whiskey. "What happened to your father?"

It was such a non sequitur that for a moment she simply blinked at him. "My father?"

"Did he die, divorce your mother, run off?"

"Ran off, and I don't think there was any divorce. Sarah Jane tells people she's a widow, but I don't think anyone believes her. We've never heard anything since he took off, and I don't expect we will."

"How old were you?"

"Three. I don't even remember him. I remember the fights, of course. The screaming, the dishes breaking, the noise and darkness. But I don't remember him."

"What about your mother's boyfriends? Hasn't she wanted to get married again?"

She didn't like this conversation. Reaching over, she snapped his almost empty glass of whiskey and drained it. It took all her self-control not to choke on it. "How can you drink that stuff?" she gasped.

"You drive me to it. You didn't answer my question."

"My mother doesn't have boyfriends, or relationships. There's always been just the two of us. Why?"

"I'm trying to figure out why you've picked on me. I must be some sort of father figure. I can't be the first man who's ever kissed you, even though you kiss like it. So you must be looking for some older man...."

She couldn't let this go on for a moment longer. "Older man," she exploded. "Just how much older than me do you think you are? You can't be more than twenty-five, and I'm twenty."

"I'm twenty-four," he said flatly. "And I'm centuries older than you'll ever be in your entire life."

"Why do you say that?"

The second drink he'd signaled for arrived, and he took a sip, delaying. "Because I grew up on the mean streets of south Boston. I've seen things you'll only read about in books, that is, if you like those sort of books, which I doubt. You probably read romances. I've seen more violence, more crimes committed than most people can even imagine. By the time I was twelve years old I'd been running numbers for three years, and I was considered one of the best in the business. By the time I was fifteen I was running my own shop, and by the time I was eighteen I had charge of half the numbers operation in Roxbury.''

"What in the world are you doing in the middle of Ohio?'' Her coffee was cold and bitter, but she drank it anyway, for something to do.

He leaned back, watching her out of narrowed eyes. "Let's just call me a visiting professor. I told you, my organization is nationwide. They thought their operation in Ohio needed some beefing up, and they decided I was the man to do it.''

"And are you?''

He shrugged. "Billy Ray's a vain, cocksure fool. Someone has to keep him in line. I'm like the Lone Ranger. I come to town, fix things up and then take off into the sunset.'' There was no missing the mockery in his voice. "So there's no room in my life for sweet little girls and falling in love.''

"I've got the message.''

"Do you? I wish I could believe that. You're as stubborn as a blind mule.''

She let a slight smile play around her lips. "Let's just say you've managed to convince me.''

He drained the second glass of whiskey, setting it down on the Formica-topped table with a snap. "I don't want you coming around me, Katharine. I don't want you showing up at bars in the combat zone, at the laundromat or anywhere else I happen to hang out. I don't want you batting those beautiful brown eyes at me and looking hurt, I don't want you tempting me. This is for your own good as well as mine.'' He rose, tossing money down beside his empty glass.

For a moment she didn't move. "Are you going to drive me home?"

"Yes, I'm going to drive you home!" he said with barely repressed violence. "And I don't want arguments, or conversation along the way. I'll drop you off at your mother's house and then I don't ever want to see you again. Understood?"

She had no choice. "Understood," she said quietly, sliding out from the booth.

She was as good as her word. She didn't say a thing during the too-fast drive back into town. He drove with a controlled savagery, every line in his body radiating anger and frustration. It should have been some salve for her bruised ego. He wouldn't be so angry if he didn't want her.

But he didn't want her enough to risk his fast track to the top of organized crime. He didn't want her enough to risk anything, despite the fact that she was more than willing to throw her safe future away for him. He simply didn't want her enough.

The ranch house was dark, and Sarah Jane's car was still gone from the driveway. For the first time she spoke. "How did you remember where I lived?" Her voice sounded hoarse, strained, as he put the engine in neutral, not turning it off.

"I'm good with numbers," he drawled. "Goodbye, Katharine. Have a good life."

For a moment she didn't move. *How can I have a good life,* she wanted to demand, *if I don't have you?* But she didn't say the words out loud. He didn't want to hear them, and she'd be wasting her breath.

She reached for the door handle, then thought better of it. Turning back, she reached for him. He tried to duck, but he wasn't fast enough. Sliding her hand behind his neck, she kissed him, pressing her mouth against his closed lips in a desperate farewell.

His resolve lasted seconds. And then he hauled her into his arms, his mouth opened against hers, and he was kissing her back with a thoroughness that stole her breath, her life, her sanity. Yanking open her coat, his hands slid up inside her sweater to cup her breasts. She could feel the steering wheel against her back, the gearshift under her knees, and nothing mattered but his hands on her breasts, his tongue thrusting into her mouth in a fierce demand.

She had the sense to make the first move. When he tore his mouth away from her, gasping for breath, she scrambled out of his arms, back across the seat, and opened the door into the cool night air.

She thought of a hundred different things to say, and rejected all of them. Instead she simply ran up the front walkway to the ranch house, resisting the almost overwhelming need to turn and look at him one last time.

She was inside the door, leaning against it, when she heard him rev up the engine and drive away. She shut her eyes, breathing deeply, her whole body tingling. She could only hope he was hurting as much as she was. Every inch of her skin felt hot, prickly. Her mouth was damp, bruised, her breasts swollen, her entire being on fire with need. Damn him and his crazy resolve.

"I WISH I COULD GET OVER the feeling that someone's watching me," Katharine said, keeping her eyes lowered to the hot fudge sundae topped with whipped cream, marshmallow, nuts and cherries.

It was four days later, and she was with Janelle once more in the almost empty Student Union Center. Dusk was closing in around them, an eerie, pre-Christmas dusk, and the wind was whipping through the bare trees outside the windows.

"Maybe it's Danny," Janelle suggested, having heard more than her share of Katharine's frustrations. "Maybe he's having second thoughts."

Katharine shook her head. "He wouldn't do that. Besides, it's probably all in my imagination. I haven't seen anyone. I just get this uneasy feeling between my shoulder blades."

"It's probably caused by sexual frustration," Janelle, the budding psychologist, announced sagely, digging into her own sundae.

"I don't think so. If anything, it's causing me to eat like a pig. I don't think my mouth has been empty for the last three days, except when I've been asleep. I've probably gained five pounds."

"That goes to prove how unfair life is," Janelle said. "If you get miserable and gain five pounds you simply look more...more luscious. If I get miserable and eat I look like the Pillsbury doughboy. No, don't say that I don't. I won't believe it, so don't waste your breath. If it's not sexual frustration, then why do you have these paranoid delusions?"

"Who says they're delusions, paranoid or otherwise?" Katharine pushed her empty dish away from her and wondered what else she could eat. Her stomach was burning a hole inside her, and still she kept eating, anything from bland food when it got too bad to spicy Mexican food when the burning let up for a while.

"You really think you're being watched? That's crazy!"

"You aren't going to get very far as a therapist if you tell people they're crazy."

Janelle grinned. "I intend to start a new style. You've heard of est and scream therapy? Well, I intend to pioneer truth therapy. I'm just gonna call 'em like I see 'em, and let the chips fall where they may."

"Great," she said sourly. "Remind me not to go to you for counseling."

"You don't have the sense to go to anyone for counseling. You're just going to eat yourself into a tent and still look gorgeous doing it, and then some handsome prince will come along and haul you away."

"I don't want a handsome prince," Katharine wailed. "I want Danny."

"So you've told me, and him, a dozen times. The fact remains that he doesn't seem to want you," Janelle said ruthlessly. "I think maybe you'd better see whether this feeling of being watched is all a neurotic fantasy on your part, or whether someone is really following you."

"And what if someone is?"

"Isn't that obvious? Let him catch you. What you need, Katharine, is a distraction. And someone's attracted to you enough to chase you around the campus. Maybe he's the answer to your prayers."

"No, thank you," she said with dignity, deciding against a double order of french fries and a cheeseburger. Her jeans were getting a little tight, and heaven knew there wasn't enough money in the family coffers for new clothes. "The very idea gives me the creeps. I'm facing a life of celibacy, Janelle. I'm not interested in taking up with a Peeping Tom."

"Suit yourself. Are you ready for a ride home, or do you want to drive me crazy and eat more?"

"No more food. I'll go over to the fine arts building and do some work. I'm feeling too restless right now—I need to paint."

"You mean you need to splash gaudy colors onto a canvas and call it art."

"I mean I need to spend some time alone doing what I want to do," she said calmly. "Professor Lindstrom gave me a key to the studio—I can work for a while and not be bothered, and then I'll walk home. I could do with the exercise."

"You're planning on walking home in the dark when you think someone's been following you? Aren't you asking for trouble?"

"Maybe," she said thoughtfully. "When it comes right down to it, who else would follow me but Danny? Maybe he's having second thoughts. If he sees me walking home he'll probably make me get in the car so he can lecture me."

"And..."

She grinned. "And then I improvise."

"You're a hopeless romantic. It'll probably be Jack the Ripper and they'll find your mutilated body in a gully."

"Gruesome, aren't you? Jack the Ripper's been dead almost a hundred years. Besides, the one sport I'm good at is track. I can outrun any pervert."

"I don't like it. It was bad enough leaving you in that awful dive last Monday. If you really think someone's watching you, you're out of your mind to walk home alone."

"No one's watching me. Or if anyone is, it has to be Danny. I promise you, Janelle, I'll be safe. I don't have a death wish. I just don't think I'm quite ready to face Sarah Jane tonight."

"You'll have to face her sooner or later."

"She's going to a two-day conference in Akron this weekend. She's leaving with a co-worker tonight, and she won't be back until Monday. If I can put off going home for a little while longer, I'll be free and clear."

"Katharine..."

"I'll be fine, Janelle. I know what I'm doing."

Two hours later she wasn't so sure of that. The time spent in the deserted art building had been frustrating and unproductive. Instead of the bright colors cheering her up, she'd simply wasted canvas by daubing everything with browns and blacks. She'd given up finally, knowing she was only working herself into a state of depression so deep that nothing would pull her out of it short of nachos, and her stomach hurt too much for the customary solace of Mexican food.

The night was dark and moonless when she left the building. The campus was deserted—Christmas break had started early and most of the students had scattered. It was a cold, windy night, with a promise of snow in the air, and if people were busy doing their holiday shopping they were doing it far from the residential streets Katharine strode through.

At least that peculiar feeling between her shoulder blades had left her. If someone had been watching her as she walked around campus, that person had wisely gone in out of the cold. It was probably some lovesick student who was already back in the bosom of his family. The idea of someone stalking her, watching her, was absurd.

Sarah Jane was long gone by the time she reached home. Katharine had taken her time, dawdling along the way, trying to come up with some new plan to assault Danny's defenses, but for once her inventive mind failed her. For the moment, on that cold, dreary December night, it seemed as if the situation was completely hopeless. She'd done everything she could, thrown herself at him, given him her best arguments, and still he'd managed to push her away. If she had any sense at all she'd give up, concentrate on any of the fellow students who'd been more than interested. Young men with a much more promising future than that of a second-rate hood.

She was so caught up in her misery that she failed to notice that the front door was unlocked. She used her key out of habit, then had to turn it twice, when she first locked herself out. By the time she stepped inside, some of the abstraction was beginning to fade, and the first uneasy tendrils of fear came slithering down her backbone.

She half expected some monster to jump out of the dark at her as she reached for the light switch, which had always been too far away from the front door. Why hadn't she listened to Janelle? Why had she gone wandering off on her own, tempting fate? Something was in the house with her, something evil, something that wasn't going to let her turn on the light and banish the dangerous shadows.

She felt along the wall, her nervous fingers coming in contact with the switch. A second later she flicked it on, flooding the room with light, flooding her body with relief.

Until her eyes focused on the man sitting in her mother's delicate armchair, his large body sprawled against the chintz flowers, a beer in one hand, a gun in the other.

"I've been waiting for you, sweet cakes," said Billy Ray with an evil grin. And rising from the chair, he started toward her.

Chapter Six

She almost made it back to the front door. He caught her just as she reached the handle, slamming her back against the door. "Not so fast, Katharine. That's your name, isn't it? I've been watching you for days, waiting for the right chance, and now I've got it. That old lady won't be back for quite a while. Long enough for me to get what you promised last week and then backed out on."

"Please," Katharine moaned, hating her fear. "Please don't kill me."

He merely laughed, putting the gun in her ribs. "You behave yourself like a good little girl and I won't hurt you. Much."

Through her blinding panic she was aware of one thing. Instead of dragging her to one of the bedrooms, he'd opened the front door and was pushing her outside. If he was taking her away, she might have a fighting chance. She could jump out of his car, she could start screaming when they reached a stoplight.

The neighborhood was deserted as he half dragged, half pushed her down the sidewalk. The Mustang was parked across the street, and in her love-blind absorption she'd never noticed it. He shoved her in, followed her and took off into the night with squealing tires.

She scrambled over to the passenger seat, huddling against the door, her hand edging surreptitiously toward the door handle. He didn't seem to notice, and for the moment it wouldn't have mattered if he did. The speedometer needle was creeping up toward sixty—to jump out would have meant certain death.

He knew the back streets of Calhoun too well, snaking through them without ever coming against a Stop sign or a traffic light. In the reflected light from the street lamps Billy looked almost eerily beautiful, with his sulky, well-shaped mouth, blond curls and limpid blue eyes.

"Where are you taking me?" she asked finally.

"Why, to the scene of the crime, of course," he said cheerfully, turning a corner with a total disregard for the oncoming traffic. His eyes glittered in the darkness, and there was an excitability about him that wiped out any lingering hope. He was on something, some kind of drug, to make him that reckless. "You know, Danny should never have warned me away from you. I got better things to do than waste my time chasing after women. Enough of them chase after me to keep me busy. But once he told me to keep away from you, I knew what I had to do. He's eaten up inside over you—I know the signs well enough. And taking care of you will be the icing on the cake. He'll go nuts." Billy chuckled.

"You're making a big mistake."

"I don't think so."

"He doesn't give a damn about me. He's told me in no uncertain terms that he doesn't want to have anything to do with me."

Billy's smug grin faded slightly. "You're lying."

"I wish I were. If he told you to keep away from me, it was only to get at you, not to protect me. You're not very bright, are you?" As a last-minute comment it didn't rank high on her list of wise remarks, but she was too frightened and too rattled to think before she spoke.

He slammed on the brakes, and she hurtled toward the dashboard, catching herself as she was about to go headfirst through the windshield. "Don't call me stupid," he said in a low, dangerous voice.

"He doesn't care about me." Like a fool she pushed on. Her only chance lay in making him so mad at Danny that he forgot about her. He was already driving again, faster than ever, and her one chance at leaping out of the car was gone. "He just wants to bug you. And you're falling for it, kidnapping me, endangering yourself, like he wants you to. He'll be able to get rid of you now, and all because you made a stupid mistake."

"I said don't call me stupid!" he roared. "I'm going to take you back to the laundromat and I'm going to do you right in front of Danny, and then I'm going to put a bullet between his eyes while you watch. What do you think of that?"

"I think you're crazy."

"I don't like that much better than being called stupid," he snarled. "We'll see who's crazy and who's stupid when the night's over. We'll see who's still alive."

"You said you weren't going to kill me."

"Hey, a guy can change his mind," Billy announced with sudden affability. "It depends on how nice you are to me tonight."

She was going to scream. She told herself she was going to start screaming, and nothing would stop her, not his threats, not his gun, not anything. It took every ounce of her fast-disappearing control to squash down the hysteria. She couldn't afford to get hysterical now. Her life depended on it. Danny's life depended on it.

"What makes you think Danny's going to let you do this?" she said, proud of how deceptively calm she sounded.

"He's not going to have any chance. I already took care of him. Right now he's sitting in the computer room behind the laundromat, tied up and gagged. He won't be moving until I bring you back. I'm not as stupid as you think." There was an aggrieved note in his voice, and Katharine wondered whether she ought to change her tack. Flatter him. If Danny was already captured, then he wouldn't be able to rescue her as he had so conveniently a week ago. She was the one who was going to have to do the rescuing.

Maybe fate, or God, would be on her side. Maybe half the population of East Calhoun would be doing their laundry. He couldn't very well drag her past a crowd of witnesses with a gun to her side, could he? Glancing over at his tense, excited expression, she realized he might be hopped up enough to do just that. But at least there would be a fighting chance that someone would either stop him or call the police.

She'd forgotten that Guido's Laundromat was nothing but a front for the gambling operation. No one did laundry there, no matter what time of day or night. Katharine had lost track of time, but it couldn't be much later than seven-thirty or eight o'clock when he pulled the Mustang up behind Danny's parked sports car. The laundromat windows were brightly lit, illuminating the rows of white machines inside. Illuminating the empty room.

"Come on, don't be shy," Billy said with a high-pitched giggle, clamping his hand on her wrist. "Your audience is waiting." He climbed out of the car, pulling her with him. She stumbled, banging her knees on the cement curb, but he paid no attention, hauling her after him.

The streets were deserted. If anyone happened to be watching from an upstairs window, she knew with a sudden depressing certainty that they wouldn't call the police, wouldn't even come forward when her body was found in some ditch. Why hadn't she listened? Why hadn't she remembered Danny's warning, why hadn't she paid attention to that feeling that someone was following her? Why had she been so blind and besotted with Danny that she was going to die because of it?

She tried to keep her movements clumsy, slow, but he paid no attention, shoving her up the short flight of steps to the front entrance, banging her against the doorjamb as he pushed her into the back room. She could see the locked door to the computer room ahead of her, and she knew Danny was back there, tied up and waiting. Once Billy got her inside there would be no hope for either of them.

She let her weak legs buckle beneath her, and she collapsed onto the cheap green carpet, knocking her head against the old metal desk. Billy swore at her and kicked her in the ribs. "Get up, damn you," he said.

She knew she should get to her feet. She knew he'd kick her again with his pointy-toed boots, but she couldn't do it. Her feigned collapse becoming all too real, she buried her face in her hands, awaiting the blow.

"I wouldn't do that if I were you," Danny drawled.

The gun flashed, and there was a belated, deafening sound, followed by the unmistakable smell of smoke. She screamed, even as she cursed herself for being a coward, and tried to crawl under the desk. Something thumped on the carpet beside her, and she lifted her head, half expecting to see Danny lying in a welter of blood.

Danny was lounging in the door of the computer room. He had a black eye, and he had a gun in his hand. Billy was slumped on the floor, holding his hand and cursing steadily.

Danny stepped over Katharine, barely giving her a glance, and kicked Billy's abandoned gun out of reach. "You had enough, Billy boy?" he demanded in a deceptively smooth voice. "Or would you like more? You and I both know that I could get rid of you with no questions asked, no nasty body showing up to cause embarrassing questions. I could—" he aimed the gun directly at Billy's groin "—give you just what you so richly deserve."

Billy squirmed away. The blood was running through his fingers, staining his jeans. "There's no need, man," he said hoarsely, his manic air vanished. "Be cool, be cool. We can work this out. I didn't hurt the lady. Just gave her a little scare. You know I wasn't planning on doing anything. Just shaking you up a bit. I wouldn't be fool enough to try to take you down."

"You're the biggest fool I know, Billy," Danny said gently. "Or close to it. Maybe I'm a bigger one, for not finishing you off."

"Hey, man, you're not a fool," Billy said, scrambling backward. "You know better than to ice me. That's not your style, is it?" A hint of an ill-timed sneer had crept into Billy's pain-filled voice.

"I could change my style." Danny's voice was thoughtful. "I want you out of here, Billy. I've already called Guido and given him the word, and they're sending someone new down. You find someone to take care of that wound with no questions asked and then you disappear. I don't ever want to see your face again. If I do, you might end up with a face as ugly as your rotten little soul."

"Don't you worry about my soul, Danny. Worry about your own."

Danny had turned away, but he paused, looking back. "Is that a threat, Billy?" he asked in a silken voice.

"No way, man. Just telling you you don't need to worry about me."

A tense silence filled the room. In the background Katharine could hear phones ringing, the muffled sound of a television set, but neither of the men moved. Finally Danny turned away, reaching strong hands beneath Katharine's elbows and hauling her to her feet. "I'd be in touch with Guido if I were you," he said to Billy as he ran his eyes over her face with remote, professional detachment. "He's going to have a few things to say to you."

Tucking his arm around her, he led her from the room, closing the door behind them with a quiet click. He released her for a moment, long enough to pick up Billy's discarded gun and drop it in one of the washing machines. Pulling some quarters from his pocket, he set the machine in motion, the hot water pouring in on top of Billy's lethal weapon.

She wasn't quite sure what happened next. Somehow he bundled her into his car, fastening the seat belt around her with gentle solicitude. That was her last clear memory. Somehow he got her into his apartment, got her to swallow a glass of strong, dark whiskey, and wrapped her in quilts and blankets. She fell asleep instantly, with his scent around her, and her last conscious thought was that she'd finally managed to get into his bed.

She woke up screaming. She was trapped, held down, and she was going to die unless she fought her way out of the cocoon of darkness that was threatening to smother her.

Light flooded the room, illuminating a barren room she didn't remember seeing before, one that looked disconcertingly like a prison. She blinked against the blinding glare, shocked into silence, the screams dying in her throat like bile as she slowly realized where she was.

Alone, in Danny's bed, the quilts and blankets wrapped around her, pinning her down. He was standing in the doorway, a wary expression on his face. His dark brown hair was rumpled, and he was wearing nothing but a hastily donned pair of jeans. He had the gun in his hand, the gun he'd used to shoot Billy. He must have been asleep in the other room, and come running when he heard her scream. He stepped into the room, setting the gun down on the dresser, and she realized his hand was shaking slightly.

"You okay?" he asked, his voice even deeper than usual from sleep.

She nodded, then shook her head. "I'm sorry I screamed. I must have had a bad dream."

"Billy's long gone, Katharine. There's no way he can get in here, even if he were fool enough to try. And it was no accident that I shot his right hand. He won't be able to hold a gun for weeks, maybe longer. You're safe."

Funny, she didn't feel safe in the middle of his empty bed, with him looking at her like that. She knew he was going to turn away, walk away from her, closing the door behind him, and she knew she couldn't bear to be alone for one more minute.

"What time is it?" she asked, not really caring, just trying to prolong his presence.

"What? Oh . . ." He glanced down at his bare wrist, and she followed his gaze, up his tanned, muscled arm to his bare chest. He stepping into the room, coming up beside the bed, and pointed to the clock on the nightstand. Four-thirty in the morning. It would start getting light in another couple of hours. If she could just make it through the darkness, maybe she'd be all right.

"You okay?" he asked again, his voice rough with concern.

She shivered, wrapped in the quilt, and thought of Billy. "I don't want to be alone," she said in a very small voice.

"Katharine . . ."

She was plucking at the quilt with nerveless fingers, and she kept her gaze lowered, afraid he'd see the unshed tears swimming in them, afraid he'd know what an absolute coward she was. "I mean, couldn't we talk? Or play poker, or chess, or something? I'm not trying to seduce you, Danny. I just don't want to be alone." A tear dropped on the quilt, splashing against her hand, and she hoped he wouldn't notice.

He squatted down beside the bed, and his large, strong hand covered hers with surprising gentleness. "I know you're not trying to seduce me," he said wryly. "After what you've been through that's got to be the last thing in the world you'd be interested in. The problem's not with you, schoolgirl. The problem's with me."

She looked up then, her face level with his, and met his rueful expression. "What do you mean?"

"It means that I've done my noble damnedest to keep away from you and all that temptation in your sweet mouth. It means that I can't sit on the bed with you and hold your hand and comfort you like an older brother. I've got limits, and I'm already past them."

Somewhere in the midst of that short speech things shifted. The fear and darkness that Billy had closed down over her shattered and broke, and hope began to spike through. His hand still covered hers, and she could feel the warmth in his skin, the strength in his fingers, and she shivered again, this time not in fear. She turned her hand under his, so that her palm rested against his and their fingers entwined.

"Danny," she said. "Billy didn't rape me. He didn't . . . touch me. He frightened me. And if you hadn't stopped him I'm sure he would have hurt me very badly. Maybe even killed me. But all he did was frighten me."

His face was set and still. He had the bluest eyes she'd ever seen, clear and steady, and yet she couldn't even begin to guess what he was thinking. "What are you telling me?" he said, not pulling away from her.

"That I'm not asking you to hold my hand," she said, terrified of her own daring. "I don't want you to comfort me like an older brother. I want you to make me forget all the things Billy said he was going to do to me. I want to think and feel nothing but you." And before she could chicken out completely she leaned forward and pressed her lips against his.

She took him off guard, and he jerked back, startled, so that she was half afraid he was going to run from her in disgust. But instead he reached out and caught her, steadying himself, and the hand in hers tightened as he put his other hand behind her head and took charge of the kiss, opening his mouth against hers.

This was different from his other kisses. He'd been diffident before, but there was no longer any trace of uncertainty. He'd made up his mind, and she knew that this time there was no going back for either of them. He was going to make love to her, completely, and after tonight she was never going to be the same.

She tilted her head against his powerful onslaught, willing herself not to panic as he kissed her with a force and passion that was overwhelming. Releasing her hand, he pushed her against the mattress, following her down, half beside her, half on top of her. His hands cradled her face as he kissed her, slower now, tasting her, nibbling at her, giving her a chance to respond.

Her hands came up and touched the smooth skin of his sides. He was hot, and sleek, and she ran her fingers up his back, caressing him with growing wonder and desire.

He rolled away for a moment, reaching for the thick quilt and pulling it away from her. She hadn't realized that somewhere along the way she'd undressed or, more likely, been undressed. She was wearing a baggy cotton T-shirt that had to be Danny's, and her bikini panties.

He was sitting on the side of the bed, looking down at her out of his hooded eyes, and his breath was coming rapidly. "Do you want the light on or off?" he asked harshly.

She shook her head helplessly. "I don't know."

"Change your mind?"

"Can I?"

He grew very still, and she could see the tension throbbing through him. "If you have to."

She sat up, sliding her arms around him. "You're not getting out of it that easy," she murmured. "I'm not backing down."

"Schoolgirl," he said roughly, "you're asking for heartache and trouble."

"Danny," she countered in a gentle voice, "I've already got it."

He didn't turn off the light. Instead he pulled the quilts and blankets off the bed entirely, dumping them on the floor, so that the double bed was covered only with a dark blue bottom sheet and half a dozen pillows. If she'd felt vulnerable before, it was nothing compared to what she was feeling now. And yet, despite his promise, she knew there was no changing her mind.

His hands covered her small breasts beneath the loose-fitting cotton knit. She could feel her nipples harden, despite the warmth of the room, and she could feel the knotting heat in her stomach move lower, between her legs. He leaned forward, and his mouth covered her breast where his hand had been. He sucked her deep into his mouth, through the clinging material. She whimpered, but he didn't mistake the sound for pain or protest. He moved his head to the other breast, and the damp material against her was an added arousal.

An arousal that rapidly became a frustration. She wanted his mouth on her skin, his tongue against her breast. She wanted his hands on her, his body covering her, she wanted everything almost as much as she was suddenly frightened of it.

There was no room for her fears. As if he could read her mind, he pulled the T-shirt over her head and sent it sailing onto the pile of quilts on the floor. Her breasts were too small, she knew it, and yet he was looking at her with a fierce desire in his darkening blue eyes, and she knew she pleased him. He slid his hand over her flat stomach, between her legs, and she could feel that she was damp against the lavender silk panties. He didn't seem to mind. He let his hand trail lightly, almost as an afterthought, as his mouth concentrated on her breasts.

"Does your mother know you wear such racy underwear, Katharine?" he murmured against her breast. "Does she know where you are right now?"

Katharine didn't bother to answer. Her breath was coming in strangled rasps, particularly since he'd moved his long fingers inside the leg of the panties, to touch that embarrassing dampness with clear appreciation. She arched against him with a strangled sound of pleasure, and she could feel the tension shake through him.

He ripped away the panties, as if he couldn't stand the frustration any longer, and he kissed her mouth again, with a fierce hunger that flamed her own.

"Touch me," he murmured against her mouth. "You can't expect me to do all the work."

In fact, she had. She slid her hands up his strong arms to his shoulders, reveling in the smooth, sleek hide of him, still unsure of herself. "I don't know what you want," she whispered.

He lifted his head to look down at her, and there was a trace of amusement beneath the burning glow of desire. "I was thinking of something a little lower than my shoulders," he suggested, taking her hand and bringing it to the zipper of his jeans.

She jerked back nervously, shocked by the feel of him, the size and shape of him beneath the tight jeans, but he dragged her hand back, holding it there for a moment. "What were you expecting, schoolgirl?" he taunted softly.

But she was beyond reacting to his gibes, mesmerized by the feel of him beneath the heavy denim and frustrating zipper. She ran her hand over him, and he arched against her, moaning deeply. She started working on the zipper, but the pressure against it was making it impossible for her clumsy fingers.

He covered her shaking hand with his own. "Slow down," he murmured. "If we're going to do this right we have to take our time."

"I don't want to take my time," she said, squirming. "I want to get it over with."

"Get it over with?" he echoed, not moving for a moment. "I thought you wanted this?"

"I do, I do. But I certainly don't expect to enjoy it the first time. It's going to hurt."

For a moment she was afraid he was going to leave the bed, walk away from her and her big mouth. She was so nervous she wasn't thinking before she spoke, a chronic weakness of hers.

And then an absolutely devilish grin lit his face. "It may hurt," he agreed. "But if you're not expecting to enjoy it, then you picked the wrong man to go to bed with. I expect you to enjoy yourself as much as I will." And he rolled back on top of her, covering her body with his, covering her mouth with his, as his jeans-covered legs entwined with her bare ones, and that was her last coherent statement.

He kissed her senseless, into a liquid pool of helpless need and wanting. He kissed her mindless, taking conscious thought and effort and sending them spinning into the wind. He kissed her soulless, until nothing existed but the hard body covering hers, the heat of his wanting pressing between her spread legs, his hands supporting most of his weight as he loomed above her.

He stripped off his jeans, tossing them over the end of the bed. She shut her eyes, too nervous to look at him, but he made no move to touch her again, waiting until she grew brave enough or curious enough to look at him.

"That's better," he murmured, leaning forward until he pressed against her, hard and heavy against her vulnerability.

If there was pain she was scarcely aware of it. With his hands beneath her hips she reached for him, feeling the steady invasion with a transfixed kind of wonder. It seemed to her as if she'd waited all her life for this, for this man, and when he finally rested deep inside her she wrapped herself around him, arms and legs and heart and soul, clinging to him, astonished at the power of it all.

She hadn't realized there was more to it. As he began to move, thrusting into her with a sinuous force that was just short of devastating, she knew that she hadn't even begun. There was something, just out of reach, as she lay beneath him on that sagging bed, something impossibly wonderful and immeasurably frightening. She fought it. She wasn't ready for it—too much had happened and she couldn't bear it. . . .

"Don't fight it," he whispered in her ear, his voice no more than a thread of sound. "You've come this far—don't stop now."

"I'm frightened," she whimpered, feeling the tremors ripple over her body as she arched to meet him.

"I know," he said. "I know." But there was no mercy in him, no pity. He wouldn't let her retreat.

He rolled over on his back, pulling her on top of him, and she was too overwhelmed to do more than follow his lead, letting his strong hands settle on her narrow hips and teach her the motions. The sensations were even more intense, and she tried to pull away, but he was having none of it. He rolled again, pulling her with him, and they went off the bed, onto the thick pile of comforters on the floor.

She could feel it coming, and all her panic couldn't stop it. Before she realized what was happening her body exploded, destroyed by something she couldn't even understand. She felt him go rigid in her arms, joining her, and she clung to his sweat-slick body in desperation, the only familiar thing in a world gone crazy.

When she came down to earth she was crying, punching him in the shoulder in helpless confusion. "Hey, don't beat on me," he said weakly, holding her tightly in his arms.

She didn't know why she was crying. She didn't know why she was hitting him. So she just cried harder, burying her face against his hard shoulder and sobbing.

For some reason he didn't seem to mind her irrational behavior. He simply moved off her, tucked her against his side and pulled one of the comforters from underneath them to cover their bodies, not bothering to climb back up on the rumpled bed.

"I told you this was a bad idea," he said in a resigned voice, stroking her hair.

"Why?" she demanded on a broken sob, loving the feel of his hand on her hair, loving the feel of his body wrapped around hers, loving but frightened of the tremors of reaction that were still shimmering through her body.

"Because as long as I kept my distance I was safe. Now it's too late."

"Too late for what?" The tears were fading into no more than an occasional watery hiccup.

"Too late for me," Danny said morosely. "I'm in love with you."

And at that, Katharine started sobbing all over again.

Chapter Seven

Danny fed her warm Coke, saltines and canned peaches for breakfast, all the while watching her out of his brooding blue eyes. Blue wasn't the right color for brooding eyes, Katharine thought as she nibbled on the slightly stale crackers, but Danny managed a creditable job. He looked as if he'd just made the worst mistake of his life, and he also looked as if it was all he could do to keep his hands off her. Such disparate reactions were both confusing and gratifying, but they certainly didn't help her sort through her own reactions.

The silence finally got to her. "Lovely day, isn't it?" she said inanely, reaching for another saltine.

Danny glanced out the kitchen window to the sleety gray day. "Lovely," he said morosely.

"Have you lived here long?" she persevered.

"Six months."

"Where did you live before that?"

"Boston."

"Can you manage more than one-word answers?"

"No," he said flatly.

"Look, I'm not used to this sort of thing," she said, exasperation and tears simmering beneath the surface. "I don't know how to behave the morning after. Maybe I was supposed to pull on my clothes and sneak out before dawn. Maybe I'm supposed to sit here in absolute silence until you decide to talk to me. Maybe I'm supposed to..."

"Absolute silence sounds pretty good to me right now," Danny drawled, tipping back in the metal-and-plastic kitchen chair.

"I think going home sounds even better," she said, pushing away from the table.

His hand shot out and caught her wrist, yanking her back down again. "I wouldn't advise it."

"Why not?"

"For one thing, there's no guarantee that Billy's well and truly gone. I knew what I was doing when I shot him, and that hand should be useless for a long time. It still doesn't hurt to be too careful."

"And?"

"And what?"

"You said 'for one thing.' That suggests there's another reason why I shouldn't leave."

"Because then I'd have to follow you and bring you back here."

"Why?"

"Don't ask stupid questions."

"Why?" she repeated stubbornly.

"I told you, I'm in love with you," he said between clenched teeth.

"Oh, yeah? Well if this is true love I think I might prefer indifference," she snapped back. He was still holding her wrist in an iron grip, and while he didn't hurt her, she knew perfectly well there was no escaping until he was willing to release her. "Let go of me, Danny."

He considered it for a moment. "What are you planning to do?"

"Take a shower."

He released her. "All right. After that we have to talk."

She knew she wasn't going to like his subject of conversation. She also knew that there was no way she was going to avoid it, short of crawling out the bathroom window. "All right," she said evenly. "We'll talk."

The shower stall was small and rust stained, but the water came out full blast and deliciously hot. She left the door to the bathroom open with a deliberateness worthy of a Mata Hari. It took him exactly three minutes to join her in that cramped metal stall.

"Damn you," he muttered against her ear as the water poured down on both of them. His hands molded her wet body against his, the warm, silken texture of his skin unbelievably arousing. "You know I should never have touched you." He cupped her rear, pulling her up against him, and she flung her arms around his neck, burying her face against his shoulder.

"Why not?" she whispered, breathing in the smell of the water against his heated skin, wanting to drown in it, as his hand reached between her legs.

"It was the worst thing I could have done for both of us. I'm no good for you, Katharine. Any future I've got is with the kind of people you shouldn't even know exist. And you're no good for me. You make me think things are possible, things I've given up long ago. I'm a bad boy, Katharine, and you're a good girl. We don't belong together."

She slid her hand down between their bodies until she reached him. He was strong and hard in her hand, powerful, and it took all her control not to panic. Carefully she circled him, tugging gently, and he responded with a savage groan, pushing against her. "Then why did you follow me in here?" Her own voice was faintly breathless. He was so much taller, so much broader than she was that most of the shower was washing over him, leaving her damp and sheltered against him. He was still stroking her, almost absently, with a hypnotic deftness that made her knees weak, made her heart race, made her pulses pound.

"Because I want you," he groaned. "I want you more than I've ever wanted anyone in my entire life, and it doesn't seem to matter how dangerous, how wrong it is. I need you, Katharine. Now." He lifted her up against the metal wall, wrapping her legs around his waist as he sank into her. She expected pain, but instead there was a shuddering kind of wonder that rippled through her. She clung to him, burying her face against his chest, as his big hands held her against the wet metal. Slowly he withdrew, the strength in his arms, in his body astonishing, and then he plunged back in again, filling her with his heat and power. She bit her lip, afraid she was going to cry out with the wonder of it, and once more he withdrew, only to fill her again, and again, and again, until she was sobbing against his shoulder, this time not afraid, this time wanting what she knew he could give her.

The tin shower vibrated beneath the force of his thrusts, the water rained down around them, and suddenly it all turned to blackness as her body exploded into nothingness, shattering beneath his overpowering strength. He was with her this time, her name a muffled groan as he pushed her back against the flimsy metal stall.

She was barely aware of him releasing her, letting her slide down his body. Her legs wouldn't support her, so he scooped her up, turning off the water with one encumbered hand as he levered her out of the bathroom, just narrowly missing banging her head against the doorjamb. He set her wet body down on the bed with infinite care, pulling a quilt around her as she began to shiver with sudden chill, wrapping himself around her with the strength born of despair.

"There's no future with me, Katharine," he said in a low voice as his lips pressed against her damp hair. "You know that."

"I have no future without you."

"You're young, you'll get over me. . . ."

"The hell I will. Women in my family love just once. My grandfather died in World War II, and my grandmother mourned him for thirty-five years. Even my mother hasn't gotten over my father leaving, and heaven knows she's had plenty of other chances. We fall in love once and it's there to stay, whether it makes sense or not, whether there's a happy ending or nothing but heartache. I'm in love with you, Danny. It doesn't make sense, I shouldn't want to be, but there's nothing I can do about it. I'm yours. And if you don't take me I'll follow you around like a lost puppy, embarrassing you wherever you go."

He laughed without humor. "I could stop you."

"Then I'd go work for Leon."

She felt the sudden rigidity in his body. "Don't even joke about that. I've never killed a man, and I sure as hell don't want to start with Leon. But I would, if he ever put one finger on you."

"Then stop talking about sending me away. I'm here to stay. No matter what you say, no matter what anyone says. So you might as well stop arguing." She mustered up her fiercest expression, glaring up at him.

His grim expression momentarily lightened, and he dropped a kiss on her still-damp nose. "We'll argue about it later," he said. "For now I have better things to do."

Her eyes widened in amazement. "You do? I mean, so soon after . . . ?"

"Mmm-hmm," he murmured in agreement, pulling the quilt away from her. "Unless you have any objections?" His hand trailed down her flat stomach with impressive deftness.

"None at all," she said in a strangled gasp, arching her back beneath his practiced touch. "None at all. . . ."

THE TIME WENT BY too quickly. They had less than two days before someone would start demanding to know where they were. Sarah Jane would be returning home sometime Monday evening, and Danny, without explaining further, simply said he had to check in by Monday. Katharine was wise enough not to ask. If it hadn't been for Danny, she would have stayed in that stark, undecorated little apartment for as long as he'd let her. If Sarah Jane came home to an empty house she'd have no idea where to look, and right then and there Katharine didn't care how panicked her mother might be. All that mattered to her was Danny, being with him every single moment she could. It was as if she had the sense that it would all be torn away from her, too soon, and she needed to store away every touch, every glance, every teasing word against the long, lean times ahead.

She wouldn't have thought she could turn so wanton. In the past, that word had always seemed so negative. Now, with Danny's eyes on her, Danny's hands on her, his mouth trailing kisses she still blushed to think about, she felt deliciously, wickedly, gloriously wanton. The schoolgirl he'd mocked had disappeared almost completely, replaced by a woman who melted at a glance, a touch, a word.

But the most astonishing thing was Danny. Through some miracle he seemed as entranced with her as she was with him. When they weren't actually making love he was holding her, talking to her, teasing her or arguing with her. But some part, mind or body or soul, was always connected to her during those short days in his apartment. And to her amazement, she soon learned there was nothing she couldn't say, nothing she couldn't do, around him.

"You said you never killed a man," she said in the dark hours of Monday morning, curled up in his arms in the hazy afterglow of loving. "Could you? I mean, if you really had to, do you think you could?"

She could tell by the sudden stiffening in his chest that he didn't like that question, didn't like thinking about it. She also knew by now that he'd answer her honestly.

"I think I could. I've seen people die. It's amazing how fast it can happen. One minute they're alive, arguing over something in a back alley, and then moments later they're dead, a young life wiped out in a flash of temper."

"Would you kill if someone ordered you to? One of your bosses?"

"I don't want to talk about this," he said, sitting up.

"Could you?"

He stared at her bleakly. "If I had to. I told you there's no future for us. You want to spend what short time we have together married to a potential killer?"

For a moment she didn't move. "Why would we have a short time together?" she asked first, getting the lesser issue out of the way.

"Because people in my profession have a short life span. Live fast, love hard, die young as the song says. Sooner or later someone, like Billy Ray, or someone I haven't even met yet, will decide I'm in his way and that it's easier to get rid of me than go around me. And there you'll be, a widow in your mid-twenties, probably with babies to raise on your own."

"That's the second time you've mentioned marriage. Is this a proposal?"

"You don't want to throw your life away on me, Katharine." There was clear desperation in his voice. "You need to finish school, make something of yourself, not end up with a second-rate hoodlum from the back streets of Boston."

"Is this a proposal?" she repeated calmly.

"Yes, damn it."

"Then I accept. I don't want a career. I want to throw my life away on you, Danny McCandless. I want your babies, I want your name, and if it all ends in five years then those five years will be worth fifty with anybody else. How many times do I have to tell you that I love you? The longer I'm with you, the more I love you. By the end of five years I'll probably love you so much that it'll last me for the rest of my life."

He stared at her, his blue eyes dark and unreadable in the early dawn. "I'll quit," he said abruptly. "I'll call Guido and have him pass the word. I'll quit right now, and we'll find a way..."

"Then I won't marry you."

His eyes narrowed. "Explain."

"You can't give it up for me. You've been in the business for too long, come too far, to give it up on a whim. Granted, it's a dirty, dangerous business. But you've got to leave it for your own reasons, not for mine. Leave it when you're ready, Danny. For now, I want you as you are. Not who you think you should be."

A wry grin tugged at the corner of his luscious mouth. "How old did you say you were?"

"Almost twenty."

He shook his head. "You can't be. No one gets that smart in only twenty years." He leaned forward and kissed her, hard and joyfully, on her lips. "You got any idea what the marriage laws are like in this state?"

"The question's never come up before," she murmured, feeling suddenly shy.

"I'll find out. If we have to wait too long we'll fly to Nevada. You can get married twenty-four hours a day there, and believe me, I've got tons of connections. We could get the honeymoon suite in any hotel we want."

"I don't need a honeymoon suite. I need you. Just you." She slid her hands behind his neck and gently tugged him closer. He went willingly, that devilish grin dancing around his mouth.

"I'll check on Vegas later," he murmured, following her back down onto the bed.

IT WAS A BREATHLESSLY beautiful day in the second week of December. The air was very cold and crisp, and the bright blue sky was cloudless. She kissed him goodbye as he left for the laundromat, a long, lingering farewell that almost had him coming back into the tiny apartment and slamming the door behind him.

Instead she pushed him away with a playful shake of her head. "None of that. You have to do...whatever it is you do, and I have to go home and pack some clothes. Do you think it's warm in Nevada this time of year?"

"I don't think anyone ever notices the weather when they're there." He pressed a last kiss on her nose. "Just bring the basics. Once we're married and in our room I don't think you're going to be wearing anything."

"I'll be back in a couple of hours at the most," she said, feeling suddenly bereft at the thought of being without him, even for that long.

"It shouldn't take me much longer. Even if it does, I don't want you coming down there. Stay put. If I get held up I'll call you."

"But..."

"Don't come down to the laundromat, Katharine. I want to keep that part of my life away from you as much as possible." He caught her shoulders in his strong hands. "Promise me you'll stay put."

"I promise," she said rashly.

Four hours later that promise was burning a hole in her heart. It had taken her less than forty-five minutes to take a taxi back to her mother's still-deserted ranch house. Signs of Billy Ray's temporary occupation were still in evidence—the dead beer bottles, the toilet seat up, the cigarette butts ground into the coffee table. Katharine scooped up what she could, threw all her outrageous underwear and almost nothing else into a suitcase and tried to write her mother a note.

Words failed her. "Wish me luck—I'm getting married" was too breezy. "So long, sucker" was too harsh. "Thanks for everything" was a lie, and "I'll miss you" was an even greater untruth. She gave up, deciding she could always telephone from Las Vegas. In the meantime, all she wanted to do was think about Danny.

He'd been gone two hours and five minutes when she began to panic. By two and a half hours she was convinced he'd been in a car accident, by three she was sobbing around the apartment, by three and a half she'd become numb with misery. He hadn't made her promise not to call the laundromat, but there was no number listed for Guido's Laundromat, despite the raft of telephones she'd seen.

When he'd been gone three hours and forty-five minutes her stomach finally rebelled, and she threw up. When he had been gone four hours she couldn't stand it anymore and, grabbing her parka, she headed out into the chilly afternoon to do exactly what she'd promised not to do.

He lived in a seedy area of East Calhoun, just on the edge of the red-light district, but not by far. Taxis didn't come down in that area if they could help it, and she realized belatedly she should have called before she left the place. By that time she didn't want to go back—she had the overwhelming need to get to the laundromat and make sure he was all right. It didn't matter if he was furious with her for breaking her promise. She could stand a little rage, as long as she knew he was safe.

She was being a fool, she told herself as she hurried down the broken sidewalks, arms wrapped around her body in a vain attempt at keeping warm. Ever since her father disappeared out of her life without warning, she'd always been afraid of being abandoned. When she was growing up she used to panic when her mother was inexplicably late. She couldn't rid herself of the feeling that what mattered most to her was going to be ripped away without warning.

Which was absurd, she told herself, moving as fast as she could, just short of a run. Nothing was going to happen to Danny, nothing was going to happen to her. He'd be there, impatient and held up over some trifle, and probably quite angry that she hadn't waited meekly at home for his phone call. But she wasn't the sort to wait at home meekly. Not when panic was chewing up her insides.

She turned the corner, in her abstraction coming smack up against a road barricade. She stared at it numbly for a moment, wondering why in the world a busy downtown street would be blocked off. And then she looked up, toward the far corner to Guido's Laundromat. The flashing red lights from three police cars split the approaching dusk with a Christmassy light, echoed by the seedy street decorations.

She was unable to move. Someone brushed past her, and she whirled around, catching the arm of a distressed-looking matron. "What happened?" she demanded hoarsely.

The woman yanked her arm free. "What do you think happened in a neighborhood like this, honey? Couple of men got shot over at the laundromat."

"Who?"

The woman shrugged. "I don't live here, honey. Looked like a couple of white boys." And she scurried on her way.

Katharine heard a sobbing scream. She knew it came from her own throat, tearing at her insides, but she was too busy running, racing down the blocked-off street toward the haphazardly parked police cars.

There were two ambulances. One was just beginning to pull away, slowly, with no lights or sirens, but the other waited. A crowd of white-coated men surrounded someone on a stretcher, and she flung herself at them, sobbing.

Someone grabbed her arms, pulling her back. "Lady, let the paramedics do their job."

She could see Danny's dark brown hair, she could see blood on his pale, pale face. She struggled, but it did her no good. The burly blue arms holding her gave her a hard shake, whirling her around to face a lined, moon face set with weary, cynical black eyes. "Listen, lady, there's only a slim chance that he's going to make it. And he sure isn't if you go flinging yourself on top of him. He's got six bullets in him, and Billy Ray knew where to hit. So you just calm down and give them a chance to try to save him."

"Billy Ray..."

"He's dead." The man nodded toward the departing ambulance. "McCandless is going to be right behind him if we aren't lucky. Who the hell are you?"

Nothing was making any sense. She murmured her name to the man, still trying to pull away, but he held her fast. "I'm Lieutenant Siegal," he said, determined to get her attention. "Lefty to my friends. How do you happen to know McCandless?"

"We're getting married," she said brokenly, trying to look over her shoulder.

"Married, eh? You're gonna have to put that off for a while, by the looks of it. He's going to have a long recuperation. Best thing, anyway. You're too young to rush into marriage, especially with a bad 'un like McCandless."

"He's not bad," she said fiercely, yanking once more, but he held her fast. "He's kind and wonderful and..."

"He's a gangster lying in a street, pumped full of bullets by a rival. If he makes it this time who's to say he'll survive the next time? I'm speaking to you like a father, Kathy. I can call you Kathy, can't I? You use this time to think about what you're doing."

Suddenly the crowd of white-coated men stepped away, one of them turning to Siegal. "Sorry, Lefty. He's gone."

The man still didn't release her, but her view was no longer blocked. Danny was lying on a stretcher in the middle of the street. They'd stripped him of his clothes, and various tubes were still attached to his torn, bleeding body. But even she could see that his blood-soaked chest was no longer rising and falling.

"No," she screamed. "No, no, no!" Yanking herself out of Siegal's arms, she flung herself onto Danny's body.

Within seconds someone had plucked her off him, dragging her away with gentle insistent hands. Someone shoved her down on the cement steps of the laundromat, forcing her head between her knees so she wouldn't pass out.

She could feel darkness closing in, her skin a mass of prickles as she fought for breath. She opened her eyes and saw blood beneath her, blood on the cement steps, blood on her clothes. Someone stripped her parka off, but she didn't raise her head, didn't notice the December cold biting into her skin. Didn't notice the sharper bite of a needle as she slipped into an oblivion that she never wanted to rise from. Her last vision was Danny's body as they covered him with a sheet, covered his beautiful, dead face, shutting it away forever.

SARAH JANE PICKED HER UP at the hospital after they released her. Katharine didn't say a word, blessedly numb, and her mother didn't question her. Sarah Jane's mouth had been set in a thin, disapproving line, but apparently she'd been warned not to push someone already dangerously near the edge.

There was no funeral. By the time Katharine came out of her fog to ask what happened to his body, she was told it was cremated and the ashes shipped to his family in Boston. Everything was gone, wiped out as if he'd never existed.

Surprisingly enough, the only one able to help her at all was the tough, concerned Lieutenant Siegal. He kept showing up, checking on her to make sure she was slowly but surely surviving. She'd look at him out of dead eyes, manage the ghost of a smile at one of his terrible jokes and absently wonder whether he was coming to see her mother or her.

Katharine held on, just barely, until she found out that there was no chance of her being pregnant. And then the last of Danny died for her, leaving her dead inside. And all her mother's impatience, all Lefty Siegal's concern, all Janelle's worry couldn't reach her. She closed her heart off, neatly, thoroughly, and went on with her life.

Chapter Eight

Katharine woke up with a start as the gray, early-morning light began to filter through her tiny house. She sat up, grimacing at the sofa chosen more for its price and its neutral color than comfort, and wondered when she'd fallen asleep. She ought to be relieved. Usually these spells of mindless grief lasted days. At some time past dawn on the Friday after Thanksgiving she felt calm, drained and almost unnaturally serene. At least the periods of mourning were growing shorter.

She pulled herself to her feet, feeling decades older than her thirty years, and headed for the stairs. The house didn't contain many mirrors, but there was no avoiding her reflection in the bathroom, much as she wanted to.

Her face was deathly pale, her mouth crumpled with the memory of misery, her eyes red and swollen from hours of crying. "You've got to stop doing this to yourself," she said out loud. Her reflection simply stared back, witless and stubborn.

There was one advantage to all this, Katharine thought as she stepped into the white fiberglass tub and turned on the shower as hot as she could stand it. At least her ulcer wasn't bothering her. She never knew why, but after she had one of her spells her ulcer seemed to calm down for several days. Maybe all the poisons that ate into her stomach got washed away with her tears. Or maybe she was just too numb and dazed from the aftermath of an orgy of grieving.

The bank was closed for the long weekend, but that meant little to someone with her workaholic habits. The quiet, empty atmosphere would be perfect for catching up, even getting ahead, on several projects. And there'd be no one there to bother her with questions and demands. Hank was flying down to California to see an old friend and even Henry would be out of town working on his latest project. She could work awhile, then put her head down on her desk and cry for a while, then go back to work. And not a soul would know.

She grimaced at her reflection when she stepped out of the shower, at her pale face surrounded by her drenched hair. It was too long, but somehow she hadn't gotten around to cutting it in years, apart from an occasional trim. During the past ten years of college and graduate school, working her way up in the world of banking, she'd seldom paid much attention to clothes and hair styles. There were times she suspected she left her hair long because it had been long when Danny was alive, but that was only in her darkest moments. The rest of the time she figured she just didn't want to bother with a change.

By the time she was dressed in her usual weekend working outfit of khaki pants, tailored jacket and silk blouse, her still-damp hair braided and pinned behind her head, her stomach had begun to revolt, and she headed for the Maalox with a long-suffering sigh. Some day, if she were very good and worked very hard, the pain would be gone, all of it. The pain in her stomach, and the far more devastating pain of remembering Danny, ten years dead. In the meantime, she was going to have to figure out how to talk Henry into postponing the wedding.

It was a beautiful day in late November. The almost constant rains had vanished, if only for a moment, and the sun shone bright and clear on the neat, orderly streets of Dexter, Washington. She'd fallen in love with the small town the first time she'd seen it when she'd come for a job interview with the impressive Hank Osmand, Sr. It had looked like the town of her dreams, with perfect, nuclear families, a strong economy, stay-at-home mothers and faithful husbands. No drugs, no alcoholism, no abortion, nothing controversial or painful could mar the neat landscape.

After living there for almost a year, Katharine knew better. All those problems existed just as frequently as they existed in other towns. The people of Dexter were simply more adept at covering them up.

Until a few weeks ago, the local weekly newspaper, the *Dexter Argus*, had been part and parcel of that benign cover-up. But the arrival of a new managing editor had heralded changes, and the entire town was buzzing over the unpleasant addition of hard news and the paucity of social coverage.

Even Hank was strongly disapproving of old Mr. Price's choice of a new editor. "He had a tradition to uphold," Henry's father had fumed. "When he was ready to retire, why didn't he get someone like himself? Someone who understands this town, instead of an interloper like John MacDaniels?"

Katharine hadn't bothered to listen. While she appreciated the illusive peace and serenity, even thrived on them, there were moments when she found, to her shock, that she was bored by it all. The new editor was shaking things up, and as long as none of it hit too close to home, she was ready to be entertained.

The Dexter Savings and Loan was a bland, gray edifice in the center of town, dominating the place with its impressive, unremarkable architecture. She parked her Toyota in the empty parking lot and let herself in the back door, breathing in the faintly musty smell of security and money with a little sigh of relief. There was no pain here. No despair and passion. Just order. Safe, predictable order.

She should have known nothing was perfect. By early afternoon her back was aching, her eyes were stinging and her stomach was in full revolt. She was ready to push away from the computer and wallow in a good cry when she heard Henry's unmistakable footsteps in the hall outside her office. No one else walked like Henry. It was a firm, purpose-

ful stride, soft leather shoes on midquality carpet, and there
was never, ever a hint of hesitation. He didn't storm through
life like his powerful father; he didn't slink through it, either. He simply strode.

"I didn't expect to see you here today, Kay," he said, appearing in her office door. He never lounged, never leaned.
His well-shaped body was upright, as always, as if the sheer
force of his personality refused to allow him to slump.

She managed a game smile, pushing away a flyaway wisp
of blond hair from her face. "I didn't want to miss the
chance to catch up on some of my accounts."

Henry moved into the room. "I know you well enough to
know you don't have any catching up to do. You never let
anything slip behind. Such devotion is more than com-
mendable, it's the reason I urged Dad to hire you, and the
reason I fell in love with you."

"You fell in love with me because I'm a workaholic?" she
asked with just the hint of amusement in her voice.

As usual it was the wrong thing to say. Henry was a good
man, an honorable man, a loving man, but he wasn't a man
with a sense of humor. "You're not a workaholic, Kay. You
simply have your priorities clear. You have to work for what
you want, for the finer things in life. People don't just drop
them in your lap. You know that as well as I do, and you're
not afraid of going after what you want."

I'm afraid of everything, she thought with sudden clar-
ity, keeping her face still. *Everything but work.* "That's why
we're so well suited," she said gently. "I've been thinking,
Henry. About our wedding date..."

To her amazement he leaned across her desk and chucked
her lightly on the chin. "No rushing things now, Kay. God
knows, I'd love to simply elope, get it over with and get on
with our new life, but my father would have a conniption fit,
not to mention Aunt Mildred. She's already talked with Seth
Price at the *Argus* about invitations and announcements.
They're the best place locally to have these things printed up.
You could take a glance at what they've got when you drop
off the engagement announcement."

Her rational suggestions died on her lips in the face of his unusual enthusiasm. She knew perfectly well she couldn't refuse—Henry wasn't the sort to take objections seriously, and he knew just how to talk someone into doing something they didn't want to do. If he hadn't been an executive vice president of a bank he would have made a perfect used car salesman.

"All right," she said, not wasting her breath. "On Monday I'll go over there...."

"Kay, the invitations really can't wait. Seth says he'll put a rush on it, but it's still cutting things much too close. People should have at least a month's warning, and at this rate we'll be lucky if they get three weeks."

"We could always postpone the wedding." There, she'd said it, and the building hadn't collapsed around her.

Henry simply laughed. "I wouldn't ask that of you, darling. I know how eager you are, as eager as I am. No, it's a bit irregular, but we'll manage it. But you'll need to head down to the *Argus* now. Just tell the new editor you want to see the sampler books, if Seth isn't around."

"Henry, it's a holiday."

"Not for a weekly newspaper, particularly not at the start of the Christmas season with all their extra advertising to lay out. You've been cooped up here too long on such a nice day, anyway. Stretch your legs, pick out something tasteful for our wedding and then have an early night. You look exhausted."

She ignored the last remark, since there was little she could say. "I need to talk to you, Henry."

"And I need to talk to you, dearest. But not tonight. I have to meet with some banking people over in Bellingham, and you need your sleep. I'm not sure if I'll be back tomorrow—don't count on it. I'll call you when I get in."

"Henry..."

"It's after three, Kay. I expect the people at the *Argus* will be leaving early." There was the faintest hint of impatience in his voice. She could imagine him using that tone with their children. A child would shrink from that voice, shrivel at the disapproval. She'd have to work on ridding him of that trace of a domineering whine before she got pregnant.

"I was going to rewrite the announcement." She kept stalling.

"It's perfect the way it is. Humor me, Kay."

There was no withstanding Henry when he was determined to have his own way. With a sigh she pushed back from her desk, grabbed her purse and rose. She could feel Henry's eyes wander down her body, and she knew it wasn't with a trace of lust. "I wish you wouldn't wear pants when you're working," he said mildly enough. "You know I don't like them."

"This isn't a work day, Henry. This is my own time, and I'll wear what I please. Be satisfied that I'm not wearing jeans." She kept her voice patient and firm.

He shuddered. "I wouldn't let you wear them."

"You couldn't stop me," she said, a trace of asperity filtering through.

He looked startled. "You are in a strange mood today, darling. Not enough sleep can make anyone testy, I suppose. Fortunately I only need five hours a night. Once we're married I can help you make do on less."

Katharine, who cherished a good nine hours whenever she could get it, smiled tightly. "Maybe I can help you get a little more sleep," she said in a dulcet tone. "It might make you less dictatorial."

It didn't even faze him as he slipped her raincoat around her shoulders. "Maybe once we're married I'll have better reasons to stay in bed," he said, and dropped a kiss on her lips.

That kiss soothed her, calmed her enough to carry her halfway across town to the old three-story town house that housed the *Dexter Argus.* In her entire life there'd been no one to kiss her, touch her, soothe her as Henry did, all without expecting something from her in return. In actuality, the time she'd spent with Danny had been too brief, too full, to allow for something as simple as affection. And after the devastation of losing him, affection seemed far preferable to bone-shaking passion.

It was over, or close to it, she thought, glancing at her reflection in the rearview mirror as she reached the older section of town where the *Argus* offices were located. For the first time in ten years she was finally ready to let go of Danny for good. She didn't know why, but deep inside something told her that her mourning was finished. Life was ready to move on, after ten empty years. She was close to being free.

She parked with her usual haphazardness. That was one of Henry's few complaints about her, along with her occasional foray into tailored slacks. She drove with deliberate recklessness, too fast for conditions, parking badly. Her Toyota was a disgrace—scraped fenders, dented doors, scratched surfaces and the outside mirrors torn off. She knew she could do better, but she refused to try. It was her one form of rebellion, her one try at tempting fate. Her one rule was to watch out for other drivers. If she was alone on the road, no matter what the conditions, then there were no limits.

She'd have to stop that. If she'd finally decided to say goodbye to Danny, goodbye to lost love and lost dreams, then she'd have to stop surreptitiously trying to join him. She'd learn to parallel park, to slow down when the roads got icy. And maybe, for a wedding present, she'd buy Henry a pair of blue jeans.

She was smiling to herself as she ran up the front steps of the *Argus* building. The place was busy for the day after Thanksgiving, with a handful of people clustered around the computer screens that the far-thinking Seth Price had installed several years before.

"Hi, Kay," Liz Allen greeted her. They went to the same exercise class together, they moaned about their thighs together. "What are you doing here?"

She waved the neatly typed sheet of paper. "Engagement announcement," she said, ignoring the burning leap of her stomach.

"Congratulations!" Liz flung her arms around her. "I knew Henry wasn't as much of a stick-in-the-mud as he seemed. You'll make a great couple."

Her stomach knotted further. She smiled at Liz. "You'll get one of the first invitations. Speaking of which, I gather there are sample books here?"

"In Mac's office." She gestured toward a glassed-in enclosure. "He's fiddling with the pasteup of the next edition—you might as well give him the announcement if you want it in right away."

"There's no hurry."

"Sure there is. All men are cowards. Once it's in print Henry won't dare back out," Liz said, popping a sugar-coated doughnut in her mouth.

"Henry's not going to back out," Katharine said. "And neither am I. Where's your boss?"

"You haven't met him yet? Mac's a great guy—you'll like him. Don't pay attention if he's a little gruff—I think he thinks he needs to be that way to control all of us. And he's probably right. If only the man weren't so sinfully gorgeous I could get a lot more work done."

"Sinfully gorgeous, is he? I never did trust your taste in men. He probably looks like Pee-Wee Herman," Katharine teased.

"He's better looking than Henry, and that's saying a lot," Liz said. "You just got yourself engaged to a hunk, but Mac's got him beat by a mile. Go on ahead and rap on the door. He won't bite your head off. He's likely to bite mine if I don't get this finished."

"See you at the exercise class."

Liz groaned. "Don't I know it. Damned doughnuts."

Katharine had always liked the noise and smell of a newspaper office. The chaos, something she'd wiped out of her own life, called to her like an insidious siren song. A call she rejected strenuously.

Liz's sinfully handsome boss was bent over his desk, so her first glance was of a thick head of dark brown hair. She rapped on the doorjamb, but he didn't bother to look up.

"Yeah?"

She'd gotten used to people reminding her of Danny. If she hadn't spent the night thinking about him, she probably wouldn't even have noticed the similarity in their voices.

She walked into the room and dropped the engagement announcement on the desk in front of him, but he still didn't bother to look up. There was a cup of cold, congealed coffee on the desk, an overflowing ashtray, and she hated the thought of her neatly typed announcement being subjected to such rude treatment.

She wasn't any fonder of the rude treatment her own presence was meriting. She cleared her throat, but he still ignored her. "I'd like to see the sample books of wedding invitations," she said firmly.

He waved toward a littered table behind him, still not raising his head. "Over there somewhere. Help yourself."

Katharine ground her teeth. No wonder Liz had warned her. Gruff was too kind a word for the man. Rude, to the point of arrogance. And she hadn't even had the chance to be suitably mollified by his sinfully gorgeous face.

She was used to standing up to overbearing men. She was expecting a lifetime of it with Henry, and she made a habit of charming other recalcitrant males. "I'd prefer it if you help me," she said pleasantly enough, not moving.

He lifted his head then, his blue eyes meeting hers, and they held nothing but impatience. "All right then. I can give you five minutes."

Katharine didn't move. Sinfully gorgeous didn't begin to do him justice. He had clear, brooding blue eyes, the color of the sky over Montana. His hair was thick and brown, his chin strong and his mouth wide and sexy, even thinned into its current expression of impatience.

He also happened to look almost exactly like Danny McCandless. From a distance she heard his voice, the voice that was like Danny's, saying, "Lady, are you all right?"

Moments later she found herself shoved into a chair, someone's hand on her neck, ruthlessly holding her head down between her knees as the dizziness began to disintegrate. And she found herself remembering another time when she'd fainted, another time some man had forced her to sit like this. But it hadn't been Danny's voice she'd heard in her ears. Danny was dead.

She tried to sit up, but the man holding her there was strong and ruthless, and clearly she wasn't going to be allowed to straighten up until he decided she was ready. She had to see his face again. To face the ghost, and know it was a trick of lighting, an aberration brought on by a night of tears and grief. She couldn't have walked into this office and stared into Danny's face.

"Please," she said, her face muffled against her khaki pants. "Let me up. I'm all right now."

He hesitated, then released her. She sat up slowly, half afraid to look at him again. Afraid she had imagined the resemblance. Afraid she hadn't.

"Are you all right?" he demanded again, irritation and a trace of human concern in that damnably familiar voice.

"You..." Her voice came out strangled, unintelligible, and she had to clear her throat before she could speak again. "You remind me of someone I once knew," she said, staring at him. Once the initial shock was over she could see that he wasn't quite the same. His nose was different. Danny's had been straight; this man's had been broken at some point. And he was older, with lines bracketing that stern-looking mouth and fanning out from those midnight-blue eyes. Danny's color.

"Yeah, well, people have said that before," he drawled. "I've got a common face."

"I wouldn't say that," Katharine murmured, feeling marginally stronger. It was all just a horrible, twisted coincidence. First last night, with all the unwelcome memories. And now this, confronted by Danny's bad-tempered ghost. "I'm sorry I made such a fool of myself. I'm Kay Lafferty." She started to rise but he shoved her back in the chair.

"Don't take chances. I don't want to have to scoop you off the floor again," he said ungraciously. "I'm Mac

MacDaniels, but I figure you know that. Can I get you a cup of coffee? A shot of something? You look like you had a shock."

"Coffee would be nice," she said dazedly, not because she wanted any but because she couldn't tear her eyes away from his face, and she needed the excuse to stare some more.

He went to the open door of the office and called out a terse order to Liz. He moved with a sinuous kind of grace, one that reminded her of Danny. She supposed it must be the result of last night's crying orgy.

"I don't suppose you're in any mood to look at wedding invitations?" There was just the edge of humor in his voice, and she found herself smiling, really smiling back, as the foolishness of what she'd just done hit home.

"Maybe I'll take a rain check," she said, trying not to stare.

"Your fiancé won't mind?"

Guilt flooded her for a moment, and then she realized he meant delaying the invitations, not the strange, compelling thoughts she was having for a total stranger. "No, Henry won't mind," she said, turning with gratitude as Liz brought her a cup of lukewarm black coffee.

"Are you all right, Kay?" she asked, her eyes snapping with curiosity and solicitousness.

"I'll call you when she needs your help, Liz," Mac drawled. "In the meantime we can dispense with your presence."

Liz managed to stalk away, pausing long enough to give Katharine a conspiratorial wink. Katharine tried to stare at the floor, then lifted her gaze in unwilling fascination to meet his rueful expression.

"He must be some man to have that kind of effect on you," he said.

She didn't pretend to misunderstand him. "He was. He's dead now."

"I'm sorry."

She shook her head, trying to clear the cobwebs from her brain. "So am I. It's amazing how alike you are. Like his older brother or something. You didn't have any half brothers, did you?"

He shook his head. "I'm an only child. Son of Flora and Elroy MacDaniels of Maple Center, Vermont. And trust me, my parents would never have played around. Neither of them had the imagination."

She managed a dutiful smile, knowing he was trying to charm her, to put her at her ease, knowing she should be charmed. "I never thought two people could look so much alike," she murmured, taking a sip of her coffee and deciding death would be preferable. She set it down carefully. "Of course you have a different nose. And he had a scar..." Her voice faded.

The man calling himself John T. MacDaniels had a crescent-shaped scar by the side of his mouth. She remembered kissing that scar, tracing it with her finger, she remembered him telling her how he got it. She looked up then, into his suddenly wary eyes, and knew without question she was looking into the eyes of the man for whom she'd destroyed her life by mourning.

She felt faint again, but she wouldn't let that happen. Her roiling stomach intensified, and part of her considered throwing up in his untidy office. She wouldn't let that happen, either. For a moment she simply sat there, frozen. And then she ran.

She knocked Liz against a desk as she tore out of the first-floor office. She fell on the cement steps, skinning her knees and tearing her trousers, but a second later she was up and running again. She heard the satisfying crunch, the grinding, tearing sound of metal as she pulled her car out into the street, ignoring the oncoming traffic. And then she was gone into the gathering shadows of the night, as fast as her car could speed.

Chapter Nine

Mac MacDaniels watched the little blue car speed away into the night. Then he turned, shutting the door behind him and facing the shocked expressions of the people in the newsroom. Liz had managed to right herself, confusion and doubt on her broad, pretty face.

"Are you all right?" he barked, a little more roughly than he would have liked.

She nodded.

"How many maniacs do you number among your acquaintance? Is that lady the only one?"

"She's the sanest person I know," Liz said stoutly. He always liked the fact that she stood up to him, even while he tried to intimidate her, but right now he was more irritated than impressed.

"Who the hell was she?"

"Kay Lafferty. She works at the bank, and she's engaged to..."

"That's right, she brought her engagement announcement. You might want to pass on a word of advice, Liz. Tell her if she doesn't pull her personal life together I'd be willing to take bets that there won't be any wedding." He slammed the door behind him, shutting out their hushed comments. He was in a foul mood, and he didn't care who knew it.

He sat down in Seth Price's old chair, lit a cigarette and picked up her neatly typed announcement. There it was in

black and white, Kay Lafferty and her dull-sounding fiancé. Graduated from college in Illinois, master's degree
from Stanford University. A safe, normal-sounding life. No
mention of parents, but then, Osmand had enough family
in Dexter to make up for the lack. No, whoever and whatever Miss Kay Lafferty was, her wedding announcement left
him just as confused.

He glanced into the newsroom. It was past five, and people were grabbing their coats, heading for the door. They
had enough sense not to beard the lion in his den and bid
him good-night. He would have bitten their heads off.

He waited until they all left, Liz Allen being the last reluctant departee. Reaching for the phone, he began punching buttons. Lots and lots of buttons. And when a neutral
voice answered, with nothing more than a number, he simply said, "Get me Lefty Siegal."

A LIGHT SNOW BEGAN TO FALL sometime after midnight.
The thick white flakes tumbled down on the small, pictur-
esque little town, making it a fairyland of white. Making the
roads a living hell, Mac thought gloomily as he drove his
lovingly restored MGB through the empty streets of Dexter. He should be at home, asleep. Instead he was out driving.

It had become a habit with him, years ago, when no place
felt like home and no one could be trusted. Whenever he had
to think something through, he'd take off in his vehicle of
the moment. Sometimes it had been a broken-down old
beater, one that barely started, sometimes an anonymous
sedan, sometimes, when things were a little more to his lik-
ing, he'd have an old British sports car. Lefty had often
pointed out to him that this was a fatal weakness. Anyone
out to track him down would have a good starting point in
their search. The places that restored and maintained an-
tique British sports cars were few and far between, and if
someone wanted him they could find him by simply making a few phone calls.

So far no one had wanted him, he thought, easing up on the gas pedal slightly. Each little job had ended neatly, all loose ends tied up in a nice little bundle. Quite often he'd be dead. That had been Lefty's idea. It had worked so well when he'd first met him that they'd decided to make a habit of it. At the advanced age of thirty-four he'd died at least half a dozen times. And only once for real.

He frowned at the approaching headlights, flicking his own brights down for the briefest period of time. He didn't like thinking about the past. In his line of work that sort of thing didn't do him anything but harm. Each period in his life, each job, had ended, and there was no going back. No mourning lost chances, lost moments. It was always on to the next one, with no regrets.

But he had no choice in the matter. Lefty had professed to be just as confused as Mac was about the strange woman who'd recognized him, but he'd promised to put the computers to work on it first thing in the morning. Mac hadn't liked waiting that long, but he'd learned after working with Lefty for close to ten years that there was no pushing the man if he didn't want to be pushed.

So he was left on his own, trying to remember where the hell he'd seen Kay Lafferty before.

Her strong reaction made one thing very clear. He must have gone to bed with her at some point in the past ten years. But for the life of him, he couldn't remember where or when, or even which name he might have used.

It wasn't that he slept with that many women. For one thing, in his chosen profession sleeping around was a little too dangerous. When you made love you tended to let your guard down, at least a little. It was damned hard to carry on an affair and still keep your secrets.

Not to mention the fact that sleeping around, particularly with the sort of people he tended to deal with, had other, medical dangers as well.

But if he had to sit back and recall every woman he'd bedded since he first lost his virginity to Mary Margaret Mackin in the choir loft at St. Anselm's in south Boston, he'd be at the loss he was right now. Somewhere, sometime he'd had Kay Lafferty. He just couldn't remember when.

Thinking back to his initial impression of her, before she took a nosedive onto his office floor, he decided she really wasn't his type. He'd tended toward tiny, dark-haired women, with the occasional platinum-blond amazon thrown in for good measure. Ms. Lafferty's hair, what he remembered of it, was a drab sort of color between brown and blond. Her eyes had been shadowed and unremarkable, her body, in those colorless clothes, had looked decently rounded but nothing to get excited about. She'd been irritated at being kept waiting, and in that brief moment she'd struck him as someone who knew how to get her own way.

That was before her pale color turned paper white, her eyes went glassy with shock and her unremarkable body slumped to the floor. He'd caught her in his arms, but her faint, flowery scent brought no tender memories, the weight of her in his arms rang no warning bells.

Maybe he hadn't slept with her. Maybe he'd done her wrong, during one of his past incarnations. There were certainly enough people he'd destroyed during the past ten years, enough women left to mourn a shattered life or a lost loved one, thanks primarily to him. Maybe he'd last looked at her over the barrel of a gun.

He doubted it, though. There was something almost disturbingly normal about her. She didn't hang out with the scum of the earth, the dealers, the hit men, the blue-collar, white-collar, pink-collar criminals.

All the same, no matter who or what she was, he was going to have to shut her up. This was supposed to be his last job for Lefty. He'd earned his retirement, earned it with blood, sweat and tears. Mostly blood. And he wasn't going to let anything, or anybody, screw up his plans.

Lefty had ordered him to sit tight, not to say or do anything until he got back in touch with the information who Kay Lafferty was, but Lefty knew Mac well enough to realize he'd do exactly what he wanted to do. What he had to do. And what Mac had to do was go and shut her up, now, tonight, before she could make any phone calls that might jeopardize what he was doing. He couldn't afford to wait until morning, wondering what was behind that unremarkable facade. And he damned well didn't want to.

The tiny house on Cedar Street was trim and well taken care of. He'd driven by there half a dozen times during the past few hours, each time certain he'd find cars parked outside, lights blazing, while Ms. Lafferty shot off her mouth. In the beginning the lights had been blazing all right, but no cars had been parked near the place expect her blue Toyota.

The last time around the downstairs lights had been turned off, along with the outside spotlights. There was one light still shining from an upstairs window, neatly broadcasting which was her bedroom, but apart from that the house was still and quiet.

He parked about a quarter of a mile away, near a gully, and hoped the rapidly falling snow would discourage curious passersby. He checked the gun in the holster at the small of his back, considered whether he ought to get his silencer and then dismissed the idea. He'd never liked the added weight—it threw off his excellent aim by a dangerous fraction of an inch, and that infinitesimal amount could mean the difference between life and death. He wanted to be entirely in control of the situation tonight. There wasn't room for mistakes.

The houses surrounding hers were dark and silent by the time he reached her property. Everyone tucked up safely for the night, with no snoopy witnesses to inconvenience him. The lock on her back door was a joke, and she wasn't one of the few people in the town of Dexter who felt they needed a security system. A point toward her innocence, he thought. If she had anything to hide, her house would be as impenetrable as a fortress.

He glanced at the house as he moved through, silent despite the numbing ache in his left shoulder that hit him whenever things got tense. The house looked like the places he'd been living in. Bland, anonymous, generic. According to his local sources, she'd been in town for more than a year. If she was who and what she said she was, why did her house have all the personality of a motel room?

He'd been smart enough to wear running shoes, knowing what he'd have to do. They were wet from the snow, and he considered taking them off, then dismissed the idea. He might need to make a quick exit, and he didn't want to run barefoot through a couple of inches of snow to his car. He could if he had to, had done far worse, but he much preferred a modicum of comfort in his advanced age.

He compromised by dumping his leather jacket on the colorless sofa before starting up the stairs. One of them creaked, loud enough to wake the dead, but there was no sound from the bedroom above, no voice calling out in worry.

He reached the top of the landing before he noticed that the beige carpeting beneath his damp sneakers was stained with dark blotches. He stooped down, touching the wet spot and bringing his fingers to his nose. Blood. He'd seen too much of it in a lifetime not to know the feel and the smell of it.

Straightening up, he reached for the gun behind his back and pulled it out before he took one step farther. He didn't know who or what he was going to find beyond that open door at the end of the corridor. But he'd learned long ago to expect the worst.

He moved to the doorway silently, then paused, listening, gun ready. A second later he sprang inside, gun aimed with both hands. Then he dropped it, resetting the firing mechanism and tucking it back into his belt.

The figure lying on the bed didn't move. Her hair was loose now, flowing over her, and he realized it wasn't quite as colorless as the rest of her. As a matter of fact, it was a rich, tawny blond, thick and surprisingly erotic. He would have thought he'd at least remember hair like that.

He moved forward, peering at her. Through the thick strands of hair he could see her sleeping face, a face that was hauntingly familiar and infuriatingly mysterious. Her eyes were red and swollen from weeping, and the dried salty streaks on her cheeks attested to the bout of misery.

He knew where the blood came from. Somehow or other she'd cut the hell out of her right hand. She had managed to tie a clumsy bandage around it, something that looked as if it had once been a towel, but the blood was still seeping from it, staining the white bedsheets. He wondered whether she'd slashed her wrists in some blind despair and then changed her mind, and then he dismissed the notion. It looked as if her hand had suffered the brunt of the trauma, not her wrist.

It wasn't bleeding enough to be an artery, but it certainly was a mess. As silently as he'd come, he moved back into the hallway, looking for the bathroom.

The answer to her bloodstained hand was over the sink. A smashed mirror, shards of silver glass littering the sink, attested to it. She must have put her fist into it, he thought, staring at the spiky shards of his own reflection in the pieces of mirror still clinging to the medicine cabinet.

He grabbed several clean white towels from the racks, ran them in the bathtub and then carried them back into the bedroom. She was still sleeping, wiped out by tears or pain or possibly something more dangerous, and he knew he was going to have to wake her up. To make certain she wasn't going to end up a suicide a few scant hours after she'd been seen running out of his office like a bat out of hell.

If she was dead, if she had killed herself, he was going to have to do some pretty fast thinking. Lefty wouldn't be able to wait till tomorrow—they'd have to get rid of her tonight.

She was wearing a white cotton nightdress, sleeveless despite the cold night, and the flounces were spotted with blood. He touched her arm, gently, not wanting to terrify her any more than he had to, but she simply sighed, a broken, tear-filled sigh, and shifted away from him.

He glanced around, looking for drugs, looking for a bottle, but there was no sign of either. If she'd taken anything she probably wouldn't have bothered cleaning up after herself.

She stirred, rolling over onto her back, her thick hair falling away from her face. He stood over her, staring down, trying to remember where he'd seen her before. Whether he'd watched her as she slept, whether he'd kissed her awake, whether she'd ever meant anything to him at all. A second later he found he was staring into her open eyes as she looked up at him in confusion.

He slammed his hand over her mouth, cutting off the scream just as it started to erupt. "Don't do that," he said, pushing her down on the bed. "It won't help matters if you make a scene. Just calm down and I'll let you go."

He didn't know whether to trust her or not. There was confusion in her dark brown eyes, and the beginning tendrils of a hatred so fierce it almost shocked him. Maybe he hadn't slept with her after all, he thought. She looked more as though he'd murdered her one true love.

"Are you going to be quiet?" he demanded fiercely. "Don't try nodding, you'll break your neck the way I'm holding you. Just blink your eyes twice if you can keep from screaming your fool head off."

She blinked, twice, glaring at him, and he knew he was going to have to trust her. He released her slowly, ready to pounce the moment she started to scream, but she simply lay back on the bed, staring up at him.

He realized then that he'd climbed up on the bed, straddling her. It was a suggestive position, and with her hair flowing all around her she suddenly looked very desirable. Except for that hatred in her eyes.

"Get off me," she said, her voice clear and low. Unslurred, so he knew she hadn't taken anything.

He did so, more for his sake than hers. For an instant he'd been immediately, shockingly aroused, and he couldn't afford to let that happen. It was only as he turned to retrieve the wet towels that he wondered about it. He didn't usually let sex interfere with what needed to be done. His intense reaction to her was inexplicable. Unless his body had been remembering what his brain refused to tell him.

"How'd you hurt your hand?" he asked, wondering what excuse she'd give him.

"I imagined your face in the bathroom mirror, and I put my fist in it," she said flatly. "Why are you here?"

"Give me your hand."

"Go to hell."

"Fight me and you'll just make it worse," he said, grabbing her elbow and yanking her toward him. "You've already made a complete mess of yourself."

"I don't need your help."

"It's me or the emergency room, and I'd prefer you didn't start answering anybody's questions. Except mine."

She just stared at him. "Your questions?" she repeated with a rusty laugh. "By all means, let's answer your questions. The hell with mine.... Don't do that!"

But he'd already unwrapped the bloodstained towel, letting out a low whistle between his teeth as he surveyed the damage. It wasn't as bad as he'd thought, but bad enough. There were several long gashes, ones that could do with some stitches, but as far as he could tell there was no nerve damage. Over the years he'd developed an unwanted expertise with rough-and-ready first aid, with sensing what had to have professional help and what could survive without it. This one was a moot case.

"I'll drive you to the hospital," he offered.

"No, thank you. I'll be fine. Everything still works, it just hurts like hell and bleeds like a pig. Thank you for your concern, and go to hell," she said sweetly.

He ignored her, wrapping the cold, wet towels around her hand. "I'll bandage it so the bleeding will stop for now," he said, ignoring her insults. "But tomorrow you'd better go have it checked. Tell them you got drunk and put your hand through a window."

"That'll do wonders for my reputation."

"Your reputation is so squeaky clean it can stand it," he said ruthlessly, moving away from her and prowling around the bedroom. It was a shot in the dark, but from the flush of color on her face it was clear it had hit its mark. "I don't suppose you have any bandages?"

"I don't make a habit of this."

"Who does? We'll have to use a pillowcase." He ignored her protest, finding the linen closet with unerring instinct and grabbing a pile of white pillowcases. "This place looks like a hospital," he said, sitting back down on the bed and unwrapping the wet towel. "Don't you believe in colors?"

"No."

Just like that. He glanced at her, startled by the dead tone in her voice, but she was giving nothing away. Much as he hated to do it, he was going to have to ask her. Flat out. And if she wouldn't tell him, he was going to have to force it from her.

She said nothing while he bandaged her hand with swift professionalism. The bed sagged beneath his weight, but her body didn't roll toward his. He could feel the tension thrumming through her entire body, almost vibrating the bed with it. As soon as he could he released her hand, dropping it down onto the bloodstained sheets and stepping away.

"You're good at that," she said. "Have you had a lot of practice bandaging women who want to kill you?"

"Do you want to kill me?"

"Why not? You're already dead."

Clue number one, he thought. But which death? Had he known her in Wichita, when he was part of that tainted-meat scam? He'd supposedly died in a plane crash there. Or up in Winnipeg, when he had been working undercover as a stockbroker and had ended up drowning? Which life, which lie, had she been involved in?

He turned away from her for a moment, and heard her uncontrollable gasp. He knew what had caused it—the gun in his waist holster. He whirled around, not trusting her, but she hadn't moved. She still lay on the bed, her face pale with shock, her eyes almost black with anger and fear.

He took the gun out of its holster and laid it on the table, within her reach. "I'm not going to hurt you, Kay," he said in what he hoped was a soothing voice. "Not unless I have to."

She blinked in momentary confusion. "Why are you here?" she asked, her voice a niggling memory that jolted down his backbone and pooled between his legs. "Why are you using that name? Does Seth Price know who you are?"

"It's none of your business," he said gently, knowing a quiet voice could be far more intimidating than any threat.

Kay Lafferty didn't appear to be intimidated. "What are you doing here in this house? That's my business, isn't it?" She managed to sit up, grimacing with pain as she levered herself up on her wrist. She looked like a ghost, sitting in that bed, her white night dress, the white sheets, the white, unadorned walls surrounding them. He must look like the devil himself, dressed in snow-drenched black, he thought. *Good guys wear white, bad guys wear black. I guess that fits the situation tonight pretty well.*

"I wanted to make sure you know how to keep your mouth shut," he said.

"Why should I? Why should I cover for your lies? Who are you out to hurt?"

"No one, if I can help it. No one who doesn't deserve exactly what he gets."

"And who gave you the right to decide that?"

"Listen, Kay, I didn't come here to argue with you, I just . . ."

"Why do you keep calling me that?" she asked, a sudden vulnerable note breaking through her anger.

"Calling you what?"

"Kay."

"It's your name, isn't it?" He bluffed it through. He should have known not to jump to conclusions. She looked so innocent, he simply assumed she'd been a bystander, not a major player in some past action. But now it seemed as if she'd been using another name, and that could only mean one thing.

"My name is Katharine Marie Lafferty," she said, her voice icy. "And that doesn't mean a damned thing to you, does it? Does it?" Her voice rose a bit.

He could see no way out of it, short of overpowering her again, and that was one thing he very definitely did not want to do. Her breasts were rising and falling agitatedly beneath the innocent white nightgown, and the room smelled faintly of flowers. It had been a long time since he'd had a woman, and even longer since he'd had this particular woman. And for some reason unbeknownst to him, he wanted her.

"No," he said, aiming for a faintly apologetic tone and knowing he simply sounded cold, "it doesn't. I don't remember ever seeing you before in my life."

Chapter Ten

Katharine sat in the bed unable to move, buffeted by emotions too overwhelming even to feel. She looked at the man calling himself Mac, the man she knew was Danny, and the sense of unreality increased. Only the pain in her lacerated hand kept her grounded.

"Do you have amnesia?" she asked, grasping for any excuse. "Have you forgotten your name, who you are?"

She could see him hesitate, as if he was considering the notion. She waited for what she knew would be a lie, even hoped for it, but instead he opted for the truth.

"No," he said. "I don't have amnesia. I remember what I need to remember."

It was a direct slap, one almost thoughtless in its cruelty, but she flinched anyway, not yet inured. "Go away," she said.

"Not until you tell me..."

"I don't need to tell you a thing. Go away, Danny." She was proud of how steady her voice sounded, when she wanted to scream and cry and rage at him, the way she'd screamed and cried and raged throughout her house, culminating in the moment she'd smashed her fist through the bathroom mirror.

"Danny?" he echoed.

"That's your real name, isn't it? Daniel McCandless?"

He didn't bother denying it. "I must have known you in Boston," he said, his eyes narrowing. They were the same eyes, Katharine thought in desperation. The same midnight blue, shadowed with wariness and doubt.

"You didn't know me in Boston," she said flatly. "Obviously it doesn't matter where you met me. The association was brief enough to leave no impression on whatever passes for your memory. Just go away and leave me alone."

"It's not that simple. I need to know where I knew you. What happened between us?"

She managed a sour little smile, an expression alien to her usual serenity. "That's your problem, then. I'm not about to enlighten you. I want you out of here. If you don't leave I'm going to start screaming."

"Then I'd simply have to stop you," he said in a deceptively gentle voice, and unwillingly her eyes shifted to the gun lying on her dresser. "The problem is, Kay, that I'm here under a different name. Now even the least curious female is going to wonder why I should pretend to be someone else, and when someone I knew under what I can only assume were vastly different circumstances is that female, then I figure I'm in for some trouble. So you're going to need to convince me that you aren't going to ask people difficult questions, or feel the need to talk about the new editor down at the paper to your co-workers or your fiancé."

Every time she heard his deep voice call her Kay instead of Katharine it was like a fresh knife wound to her heart. It shouldn't be. Her ten years of mourning were nothing but a sham, based on a love that was clearly one-sided and unworthy of existing in the first place. "And if I can't convince you that I'm not the slightest bit interested in who and what you are?"

"Then I'm going to have to do something about it." The words were spoken very gently, but there was no missing the soft menace behind them. This wasn't a small-town newspaper editor with no hidden agenda. Whatever had happened to him during the past ten years, whatever had turned him from Danny McCandless, small-time hood, to the deceptive yuppie in front of her, those events had been powerful.

He frightened her. More than the gun on the table, the bleak, emotionless expression in his eyes frightened her. She looked up at him and knew that even if his body had survived that horrible afternoon ten years ago, a part of his soul had died.

She also knew there were worse things than any harm he might care to inflict on her. And the worst thing she could possibly imagine would be to sit there and tell him the sordid details of her lovesick past.

She swung her legs over the side of the bed, pulling the bloodstained nightgown around her and wishing she'd worn something a little more voluminous. She hadn't been expecting visitors. During her evening rampage she'd still held out the vain hope that she'd been mistaken, that despite the evidence of her eyes, her heart, that John MacDaniels wasn't really Danny. She never would have thought that she'd wish him dead, but death was better than this consummate lie.

"You don't frighten me," she said, wishing she meant it as she moved across the beige-carpeted floor on unsteady feet. He made no move to come closer as she pulled her bathrobe from the closet door and wrapped it around her, but she wasn't fooled. One false move and he'd be on her as quickly as he had when she first woke up. And she couldn't bear to let that happen again.

"Glad to hear it," Mac drawled. "Then maybe you'll be willing to tell me where it was that we met."

"In Ohio. West Calhoun, as a matter of fact. I used to work for a man named Leon when I was a teenager, and I used to see you hanging around." What was the name of that bar, she thought desperately. She needed details if she was going to convince him of this improvised tale. "At Vahsen's Bar and Grille," she added, pleased with herself.

He went very still, only his blue eyes alive in his face. "Vahsen's Tavern," he corrected pleasantly. "Was I one of your customers?"

She wasn't sure which way to answer this, what would sound more reasonable. On the one hand, he probably never had to pay for it in his life. On the other hand, she had to come up with a reasonable explanation for her intense reaction to his reappearance. "Just once," she said. "Leon sent me over one night. You can see why I don't want this to get around. It was way in the past, when I was a screwed-up teenager. If the good people of Dexter, my fiancé in particular, knew that I used to turn tricks, my life would be over. At least in this town."

"Very good," he said, moving across the room with a sudden, stalking grace. "Give me something to blackmail you with, and I won't push too much, secure in the knowledge that if you talked, you'd ruin your own life. Clever of you. There's only one problem."

He was too close. In ten years she hadn't been near him, and as her mind screamed out in anguish her body wanted to drift closer, lean against him, let him wrap his arms around her and hold her. Nervously she licked her lips, staying where she was. "What's that?"

"You've never turned tricks in your life. If I didn't know better, I'd think you were an aging virgin."

"Aging!" she shrieked.

"If you're a thirty-year-old virgin you're positively ancient."

"An endangered species," she agreed, wary herself. "I'm exactly what I told you. I don't have anything to hide."

"Except your stint as one of Leon's hookers," he said pleasantly. "All right, let's sample your wares." And before she could guess his intent he'd put his hand behind her neck and yanked her to him, his mouth meeting hers with ruthless force.

For a moment she was too shocked to do anything but let him kiss her, too bemused by the unexpected, almost forgotten taste and feel of him. This wasn't a polite kiss, a wooing kiss, even a seductive kiss. This was an insult rape of a kiss, his tongue in her mouth, the hand on her neck holding her still as he kissed her with a devastating thoroughness.

Suddenly, almost too late, her brain returned. She shoved at him, ignoring the pain in her hand, and he fell back against the open closet door. She shuddered, trying desperately to regain her tenuous control. "Don't ever do that again," she said, her voice a mere thread of anguished sound.

For a moment he looked dazed, and then his eyes narrowed. "If you were ever a hooker you were a piss-poor one. Haven't you kissed anyone in ten years, Katharine?"

Too late, she thought. Too damned late. She wiped her bare arm across her mouth, wanting to spit. "Go away," she said tonelessly. "Your secrets are safe with me."

He didn't move. "Your hand's bleeding again."

She glanced down at his homemade bandage, at the blood seeping through. "I'll survive. I can survive anything." She managed a bitter smile. "Like you, I can survive just about anything."

"You were a college student," he said, slowly remembering. "We had an affair."

It didn't hurt, she told herself. It didn't hurt at all. "A weekend," she said tonelessly. "And then you died. Tell me, was that all part of the plan? Whose body did I see lying in a pool of blood outside of Guido's Laundromat?"

"You were there?"

"I was there. I flung myself weeping on your corpse. You were dead. Why couldn't you have stayed dead like you deserved?" The rawness of her pain was starting to seep through, like the blood through her bandage, and she took a shaky breath, trying to force it back.

The man in her bedroom had no emotions. He didn't even flinch. "Sorry to disoblige you. Medical technology had other plans at the time. I don't remember much of it, but I've been told they were able to revive me in the ambulance. I was in intensive care for almost a month, but I survived."

"And what about Billy Ray? You haven't forgotten him, too, have you? The man who tried to kill you? What's he doing, selling real estate in Arizona?"

"He's dead," Mac said flatly.

"Now why do I have a hard time believing that?" she said, her voice mocking.

"I should know. I'm the one who killed him."

That silenced her, if only for a moment. And then the rage broke through again. "Why didn't someone tell me you were alive? Why did a policeman come and hold my hand and mourn with me when he must have known all along that you weren't really dead?"

"I can't imagine why. Unless the cop had the hots for you himself. As far as the hospital knew, I had no relatives in the area. No one who needed to be informed."

"It wasn't in the papers."

"I wouldn't know about that. I wasn't in much shape to be reading anything for a long time."

In fact, neither was she. For all she knew, there might have been something in a later edition about the survivor of the East Calhoun shoot-out. The only people who knew it would matter to her, Janelle and her mother, might not have said anything. But she didn't believe that, at least not of Janelle.

"So what happened after your miraculous return from the dead?"

"I got out of the business. It finally dawned on me that organized crime had a limited future, and I was better off changing my way of life, changing my name, changing everything I possibly could. The authorities helped me, in return for some much-needed information, and I went back to school as John T. MacDaniels."

"Just like that?"

"Just like that."

"And you never thought that maybe you ought to at least let me know you weren't dead?"

"You were better off believing it. What the hell could I offer you at that point? It was better this way. We had the memory of a short, sweet affair, and that's all."

"Your memory was remarkably short-lived," she pointed out to him coldly.

He ran a hand through his thick brown hair, suddenly looking harassed and very human. "We need to be civilized about this, Katharine. For old time's sake if nothing more. There's nothing mysterious about me being here—I'm just a newspaperman on a job. But I'd rather not have to start explaining all the sordid details of my past. The last ten years or so are all that matter. Anything before that is ancient history. It doesn't have anything to do with who or what I am today."

She couldn't help it—she laughed. "You expect me to be reasonable about this?" she said. "I don't care what happened to you. I suppose I'm glad you're alive, but really, after ten years it hardly matters, does it? It's not as if I spent the last ten years mourning you."

"I didn't say that you did." The very gentleness in his voice was the finishing blow to her hard-won calm. It shattered, like a crystal figurine, dissolving into shards of sheer, uncontrollable rage.

She was beyond asking, beyond ordering. There was a bedside lamp near at hand, a beige ginger jar. She yanked the cord out of the wall and threw it at him with all her force. He ducked, cursing her, but she was too fast for him, leaping across the bed and scooping up his gun, pointing it at him with shaking hands.

"I've asked you to get out, and I've told you to get out," she said, her voice raw. "Now I'm warning you."

He didn't move. There was a wary, waiting air to his body, one that told her he hadn't spent the past ten years in school and newspaper offices, no matter what he tried to tell her. "You've never held a gun before in your life," he said.

"No," she agreed. "But I kind of like it. Get out of here, Mac." Her voice was mocking as she called him by his new name.

"The safety's on, Katharine. You couldn't shoot me if you tried."

"You want to find out how ingenious I can be with machinery?" she asked. The gun was trembling in her hands, and she clasped it more tightly, wanting to shoot him, wishing she only knew how.

He stayed where he was for a moment longer. And then he walked toward her, very calmly, and plucked the gun from her hands. "Don't point a gun unless you know how to use it," he said gently. "Someone might shoot back."

She backed away from him, up against the wall, utterly weary. "Go to hell," she said, but there was no heat in her voice, only exhaustion.

"Trust me, Katharine. I've already been."

A moment later she was alone in her white-and-beige bedroom, leaning against the wall, knowing her legs wouldn't support her a moment longer. She didn't hear the door close, didn't hear the sound of a car starting, but she knew as surely as she knew anything that she was finally alone with her shambles of a wasted life.

How could her safe, ordered life dissolve in such a short time? How could she want her unending grief back, instead of this shattering rage that threatened to shake her apart? She'd thrown everything away, her youth, her passion, her heart and soul, on a fantasy. A dream lover, a tragic passion that had never really existed. While she was moving through life in a numbed daze, burning emotional candles to his memory, he was off living, really living. While all she'd done was exist.

She really did want to kill him. She wanted her old safe cocoon back, the safe, fuzzy cloud that had kept her from the world, not this place that was raw and new and unbearably painful.

But there was no going back. That was the first lesson she needed to learn. She'd spent ten years trying to go back, and look where it had gotten her. From now on she was going to look ahead. What had he said, that nothing but the past ten years mattered to him? She could go him one better. As of—

she glanced at her digital alarm clock—as of one-thirty-seven on Saturday morning, she was going to live life to the fullest. She was going to make up for ten years of mourning. And she was going to do her damnedest to do so in the shortest amount of time. Starting with her straitlaced fiancé. And she was never going to even think about Danny McCandless/John MacDaniels again.

Except to wonder, if he was just a straightforward newspaperman as he insisted, why had he come to her house with a gun?

MAC PUNCHED THE NUMBERS of the telephone with savage fury, each jab an imagined stabbing at Lefty Siegal's eyes. When the sleep-fuddled voice finally answered, Mac's first words were delivered in nothing less than a snarl.

"Why the hell didn't you tell me who Katharine Lafferty was?" he demanded.

"Mac?" Lefty's voice was suddenly alert. "What're you talking about?"

"Don't give me that crap. She told me some kindly cop came and held her hand and mourned with her after my untimely death. I can only assume that was part of your tying up of loose ends."

There was a long pause at the other end of the line. "Would you have wanted me to handle it any differently, Mac? Should I have told her you were still alive?"

"Of course not. What I can't figure is how you could have sent me to this penny-ante town and not known she was here. That's not like you, Lefty. You're always on top of the most minute details. How could you have missed this one? And when I called, how come you didn't remember who Katharine Lafferty was?"

"How come you didn't?" Lefty countered. "I didn't sleep with her, you did."

Mac's anger spilled over. "Are you sure of that? Sounds to me like you were a little more solicitous of her than you needed to be."

"Jeez, Mac, the girl was brokenhearted. Not to mention being half my age. Besides, she was in love with you, and she'd just seen you gunned down, practically in front of her eyes. She had no one to turn to—her mother was cold, disapproving and her best friend wasn't much help."

"You're remembering an awful lot for someone who didn't even know her name a few hours ago."

"You're a fine one to talk to me about remembering. No, I didn't sleep with her. She was too busy mourning you to even realize I was male."

"It doesn't matter to me whether you slept with her or not," Mac said promptly.

"Sure it doesn't," Lefty drawled, obviously not convinced. "So how much did you tell her?"

"Nothing."

"Nothing? You just waltzed in there, said, 'Hey, I'm not really dead, how's it going?' and left it at that?"

"How long have I worked with you, Lefty? I know what I'm doing. I gave her just as much truth as she needed, and then went into my cover story. As far as she's concerned, when they revived me I turned state's evidence and then changed my name and my life. I told her I was simply a hardworking newspaperman who, through some rotten, shortsighted coincidence, happened to end up in the same small town she now lived in."

"And she swallowed that?"

"I don't know. She wasn't being completely rational by the time I took my leave. She threw a lamp at me, and then grabbed my gun."

"Your gun? You were fool enough to take your gun?" Lefty shrieked.

"Lefty, I didn't know who the hell she was," he said with a sigh. "She could have been part of the Miller gang, or connected to the Kansas City operation. Of course I took my gun."

"And what did she think about mild-mannered Clark Kent having a gun?"

"I don't know if that's dawned on her yet."

"It will," Lefty said grimly. "She was one smart cookie ten years ago, and I doubt she's gotten any dumber. You're going to have to come up with a better story."

Mac lit a cigarette, still cursing. "I think you ought to pull me. I didn't want this job, and you know it. I wanted out. You talked me into doing one last job, and like a fool I agreed to it. This isn't even my kind of thing. Roberts is better qualified, so is O'Malley."

"Don't get cold feet on me, Mac. I need you there."

"I'm not getting cold feet," he snapped. "I just think my effectiveness has been compromised. You don't know how small a town this is. I hadn't run into Katharine before, but I'd certainly heard her name mentioned any number of times. Everybody knows everybody around here."

"That's why another stranger would cause even more comment. I trust your expertise, Mac. You'll be able to explain the gun, just as you'll be able to explain everything else. Besides, it sounds as if she's so mad at you she won't even be speaking to you."

"We can only hope," he said grimly. "I still think you should pull me."

"You promised, Mac. She can't still mean something to you after all this time. Hell, you didn't even recognize her...."

"She doesn't mean anything," he said instantly.

"And you can't matter to her. She's engaged, isn't she? Isn't that why she turned up at the newspaper office? So as soon as she cools off, she'll probably put you out of her mind. Sure, she's mad about being lied to, but she's made a new life for herself, got herself a hotshot banker for a fiancé, the world's her oyster. She's not going to throw it away just to get even with you for dying. Or for not dying."

"You can almost convince me," Mac said dryly. "I'll give it a week. If I'm not getting anywhere with your little project, or if Katharine decides revenge is better than a big wedding, then we'll talk about it."

"I knew you'd be sensible. It's not like you still have any feelings for her."

"No," Mac said in a hollow voice, "it's not like I have any feelings for her. Just tell me one thing, Lefty."

"Sure thing."

"How come you knew her fiancé was a hotshot banker?"

Chapter Eleven

Katharine had every intention of rising early and throwing herself into her work. She was going to shower and head for the bank, and spend the entire weekend enmeshed in accounts, trying to pull a semblance of her normal life back together again.

She woke at a quarter past eleven. The house was flooded with light from the curtainless windows, illuminating the stark, colorless interior. She lay facedown on the bed, her bandaged right hand beside her face, and moaned. She hadn't slept past eight o'clock in the morning in more than a decade.

It was only natural, she told herself as she quickly showered, keeping her bandaged hand out of the stream of water. Her sleep had been disrupted, first by Mac's unwelcome appearance, then by nightmares. Maybe for once she deserved to sleep late. As a rare lapse it was excusable, as long as she kept it to once a decade.

Her cut hand looked better than it felt. She rewrapped it, this time with gauze she found neatly tucked under her sink, then poked through her closet in search of something to throw on while she made herself some lifesaving coffee.

For some reason she bypassed the beiges and grays. At the far end of her closet was a fuchsia silk kimono some half-blind relative of Henry's had given her for her thirtieth birthday. She'd never worn it, planning on passing it on to someone more suited to it, but that morning she pulled it on over her underwear, absently relishing the feel of it against her skin.

"Keep to your regular habits," she muttered to herself as she went downstairs. It was too late for her usual dose of morning news, so instead she went to the stereo, turning on the easy-listening FM station she favored. Barry Manilow was singing something ultimately forgettable, and Katharine was halfway to the kitchen before she turned around, went back to the stereo and spun the tuning dial.

She came up with an oldies station playing Led Zeppelin singing "Whole Lotta Love." She turned the volume up, loud, and went in search of coffee.

THERE WAS NOTHING Mac hated more than the feeling that someone was lying to him. And it was more than a feeling. In the years he'd worked with Lefty Siegal he'd learned all the nuances. Lefty was lying to him, but for the life of him Mac couldn't figure out what the lie was, and why.

Lefty's excuse had been quick enough last night. He'd admitted to running a preliminary check on Katharine Lafferty, and there was no way Mac could prove otherwise. He'd simply have to bide his time, push Lefty when he was ready to be pushed.

In the meantime, it made the current situation particularly complicated. Because in the initial stages of his investigation, it had become more than clear that whatever was going on in the small town of Dexter went directly through the Dexter National Bank. And the Dexter National Bank was the Osmands, Henrys junior and senior, and by extension, Katharine Lafferty.

Maybe that was why Lefty was holding out on him. Maybe he didn't think he could be that detached, despite his protests of no emotional involvement.

But Lefty knew him better than that. Lefty knew that, after all these years, he'd turn his own mother in if he found she was guilty of something slimy. He'd do it regretfully, painfully, but he'd do it.

The past ten years had been filled with a complete reversal in his personal life. He'd gone from a minor mob hireling to the straightest of the straight arrows, all with the prodding of Lefty Siegal. Lefty had given him a start in this business, just as he'd given Lefty the toehold he'd needed. Now that he was ready to end it, he owed Lefty this last job. Much as he hated it, with its added complications, he had to see this one through.

The current situation wasn't his usual sort of job. But he'd learned with his years in the business that you went where they sent you, did what they asked of you, and sooner or later it worked out.

He'd figured out a couple of years ago that keeping on with his current job was nothing more than a form of penance. Penance for the mean years as a teenage hoodlum on the streets of south Boston, never caring who he hurt, who he trampled on in his quest for money and power. He'd stopped short of dealing drugs, of running prostitutes like the almost forgotten Leon, of doing anything more violent than persuading the occasional deadbeat that gambling debts were affairs of honor, and that you let your kids starve before you welshed on a bet.

But if fate, in the form of a half-crazy, violent kid like Billy Ray, hadn't taken a hand, he probably would have crossed each and every one of those invisible moral lines.

So he'd leaped at Lefty Siegal's offer of work with the Internal Crime Task Force. After all, he was perfectly suited for the jobs Lefty came up with, what with his firsthand knowledge of how organized crime worked, not to mention his familiarity with criminal types. And the ICTF had been just his sort of organization—small, secretive and autonomous. He only had to answer to Lefty, who answered to God knew who. If things got too hairy he got bailed out, and someone else cleaned up the mess left behind.

He'd been fool enough to convince himself he was making the world a safer, better place. It was only recently that he had realized he was doing all the rotten things he'd always been afraid he'd end up doing. He was just doing them for the good guys this time around.

So this was his last job. Though this time it was white-collar crime, damnably neat and only faintly sleazy. The massive collapse of the savings-and-loan institutions in the country had been brought about by a combination of mismanagement, greed and stupidity. But somewhere along the way a few people managed to get very rich indeed, including a handful of upper-echelon banking executives from Sacramento, California.

Lefty and his cohorts had been on the trail of the very substantial sum of money for over a year, and gotten exactly nowhere. While Mac had been instrumental in closing up an extortion scheme in the bucolic pastures of northern Wisconsin, Lefty had been closing in. It wasn't until they decided to look out of state that they'd finally had a break in the case. They'd traced the money as far as Dexter, Washington. Namely, the Dexter National Bank, owned by the Henry Osmands, junior and senior. Now all they had to do was prove it, put the final pieces to the puzzle and they'd have the bad guys dead to rights.

Mac had argued like crazy when Lefty had asked him to take on this final job. He wanted out, he wanted a life of his own and he didn't get too excited about white-collar crime. He knew all the arguments, that it hurt the little people down the line, and so on. And he certainly had nothing but contempt for the elitist criminals who didn't even comprehend that they were no better than the neighborhood thug, despite their three-piece suits and M.B.A.'s.

But like it or not, Mac had developed an unfortunate taste for blood and pain. If he didn't see people hurting, the crime had no immediacy for him. That was another reason he had to get out of the business. Sometimes it seemed as if the only time he felt alive was when someone was trying to kill him.

Lefty knew how to pull his strings, of course. The cover as newspaper editor was something he couldn't resist. He'd had the same cover several times during the past decade, and to his amazement he'd discovered he had a real knack for it.

If he'd been born someplace other than south Boston, had a real family, a normal life, then maybe that's what he would have ended up doing. Maybe it was still in his future.

Right now he couldn't afford to think about the future. This easy, boring little job was proving a lot tougher than he'd expected. And having Katharine Lafferty smack in the middle of it made it almost impossible. She was engaged to marry one of the major suspects in the money-laundering scheme, and she was too smart not to guess what was going on. So even though the wise, sane part of him wanted to get as far away from her as quickly as he could, the responsible part told him no way. She was part of the investigation—he was going to have to keep an eye on her. Maybe a close eye on her. And the stupid, insane part of him reveled in that fact.

He woke up late, didn't bother to shave and dragged himself into the tiny kitchenette of his apartment. It took up the second floor of an old Victorian house. His landlady was a sweet, white-haired old lady who was insatiably curious, another drawback. She was also, fortunately, nearsighted and almost deaf.

He flicked on the radio, filling the room with some romantic mush. He snorted, flicked the dial and stopped on Led Zeppelin singing "Whole Lotta Love."

KATHARINE COULDN'T FIND her hairpins. She had several sets of heavy tortoiseshell ones that kept her thick hair in place, and every single one seemed to have disappeared during her early-evening rampage through her house. She didn't even have the simple option of stopping off at the local drugstore and buying more. In these days of loose-flowing hair there were very few places where one could buy heavy-duty hairpins. She'd found her current ones in a specialty store in the nearest mall. Unfortunately, the nearest mall was an hour and a half away, and she wasn't about to make a special trip for something as unimportant as her hair.

She was half tempted to take a pair of scissors and hack it all off. A wiser recourse would be to call Myrtle's Shear Perfection and have her trim Katharine's mane to a manageable length.

In the end she simply shoved the still-damp tendrils behind her ears and set out for the bank, in a vain search for a trace of normalcy in her suddenly topsy-turvy world. Besides, the *Dexter Argus,* like most of the businesses in the area, did their banking locally. She was going to be very curious to check their records for the past couple of months, particularly since Seth Price hired a new managing editor.

She should have known an empty office was too much to hope for midday on a Saturday. Hank Osmand was just locking the side door when Katharine pulled up, and she couldn't help noticing the odd furtiveness in his manner. What would Hank have to be furtive about, she wondered. After all, it was his bank. He had a board of directors to answer to, but they were all his golfing buddies and his children's godfathers, et cetera. He pretty much managed to charm them into a policy of benign indifference, and the bank had certainly prospered.

Indeed, it had always surprised her just how prosperous the Dexter National Bank was. She didn't for one minute suspect anyone of misconduct—the Osmands had the unassailable rectitude and honesty seldom seen in these sleazy days. It was one of the things that had drawn her to Dexter. That, and the surprisingly healthy salary she was offered, nearly double the salary she'd been making at her old job in California.

She slid out of the car, shoving her long hair out of her face. "Good afternoon, Hank."

Maybe she'd imagined the furtiveness of his movements. He turned to her with his huge, welcoming smile. "Katharine!" he boomed. "I should have known you'd be in sooner or later. Don't you ever take a day off?"

"Not if I can help it," she said pleasantly enough. "Is everything all right? I thought you were spending the weekend in Sacramento."

"Just a small glitch, all taken care of," he said smoothly. Suddenly his gaze narrowed. "You look different, Katharine."

She managed a smile. She knew it fell far short of the usual serenity she projected, but under the circumstances it was the best she could do. "It must be my hair. I don't usually wear it loose."

"It's very becoming," Hank said. "You don't usually wear anything so colorful, do you? That red sweater looks quite nice."

Standing around in the bank parking lot discussing her choice of clothing was not what Katharine had had in mind when she left for work. "It was the only thing I could find that was clean."

"I don't believe that for a moment." Hank's hearty laugh boomed out. "You're always neat as a pin, and I'm certain your house is just as well organized as your bank records. That's one of your most sterling qualities, Katharine, your sheer dependability."

As a compliment it fell far short of what she would have liked, but then, Hank's compliments were usually a little too fulsome. This time perhaps he was being more honest.

"I'm going in. Is there something I can do for you?" she asked politely.

"Not a thing, not a thing." He waved her away. "We'll be seeing you at the Morrises later tonight, won't we?"

"I forgot," she said. "What time is it?"

"Six to eight. I'm sure Henry is planning to pick you up. After all, the Morrises are one of our major investors. He always has the bottom line firmly in mind."

"Of course. Exactly why are the Morrises having a cocktail party tonight?"

"Do they need a reason? The Morrises love to entertain."

"But they usually have some sort of excuse."

"You're right about that," Hank agreed. "I believe this one's in honor of the new editor down at the paper. Seth wanted him to meet the right people, make some friends.

Maybe he'll soften that hard edge the paper's taken recently."

Damn, Katharine thought. It only needed this to make a miserable day turn worse. "I like the hard edge," she found herself saying, much to her surprise.

Hank was equally startled. In the year since he'd wooed her away from the Sacramento-Silver Savings and Loan he'd never heard her state a conflicting opinion.

"Well, to each his own," he murmured, heading toward his Mercedes. He paused, turning back to her. "I like your hair, Katharine. You should leave it loose more often."

Katharine watched him leave. For the first time in a long time she found herself immune to his spell. She might be planning to marry his son, but he wasn't going to be a father to her. And she suddenly had the unpleasant notion that that gleam in his eye wasn't the slightest bit paternal.

When she stepped inside the hushed, luxurious interior of the bank, she stood very still, waiting for the cocoon of warmth and security to wash over her, wash away the misery eating up her insides. She waited, and it didn't come.

All right, she told herself. She was still suffering from a delayed reaction. All she had to do was get through the day, get through the evening, seeing Mac under normal, social circumstances, and then she'd be able to get on with her life.

Funny that she thought of him as Mac, not Danny. The Danny she'd known and loved really had died ten years ago. The man who'd taken his place was colder, harder, older. Different, in ways so elemental that it didn't matter that he had the same eyes, same face, same crescent-shaped scar beside his mouth. He was no longer Danny. All she had to do was accept that fact, and then maybe life would return to normal.

Another odd thing, she thought as she mixed herself a cup of instant coffee. Her insides felt as if they had been put through a wringer. She had a pain in her chest, a rawness in her throat, a burning in her eyes and the world's worst headache.

She did not, however, have an upset stomach. Her beginning ulcer had taken the most stressful time of her life and decided to take a rest. She ought to be grateful for that small favor. Instead, she felt annoyed, as if even her body had taken Mac's side.

Her state of mind wasn't improved by her perusal of the corporate records of the *Dexter Argus*. It was a simple enough matter to bring up everything on the computer, up to and including every check written. Hank Osmand had a weakness for the newest toys and latest technology, another inducement when Katharine had moved north.

In the past three months not a single check had been written to John T. MacDaniels, either from the *Argus* account or Seth Price's personal checking account. Indeed, of all the outgoing checks, there was none that was the slightest bit suspicious, despite the fact that Katharine discovered her friend Liz made a lot more than she bitched about.

The only thing interesting about the business account was several large deposits from an organization known simply by its initials, ICTF. The amount was substantial, and Katharine spent a few moments trying to guess what those initials might stand for. International Committee for True Facts? International Corps of Technicians and Flatlanders? Whoever they were, she couldn't begin to guess why they'd be paying Seth Price such large sums of money.

"Everything okay, Ms. Lafferty?" a voice asked, and she jumped, spilling her cold black coffee all over her spotless desk.

She never spilled things, never made a mess. She cursed, grabbed a cream cotton sweater she usually left on the back of the chair and began to mop it up. "Everything's fine, Jimmy. I didn't realize you were here."

Jimmy Martin had red hair, pale skin and freckles, and the unfortunate tendency to blush. He did so now, clearly embarrassed. "I startled you," he said. "I should have made more noise."

"That's all right." She dumped the coffee-soaked sweater in the trash, not even hesitating. "Why are you here?"

Jimmy blushed a darker red. He'd been hired as a security guard a couple of months ago. He was in his early twenties, with not much education and a sweet, shy demeanor and a talent for appearing silently where someone least expected him. "I was driving by and I saw your car. I also saw someone else had been parked here—there were fresh tire marks on the pavement, so I thought I'd check and make sure everything was okay. You can't be too careful, Ms. Lafferty."

Now why didn't she believe him? Why was she suddenly suspicious of his aw-shucks demeanor, his sturdy innocence? Why did she think there was a much smarter man behind those bland brown eyes?

"You're right," she said, turning off her computer. "You can't be too careful." She must be going crazy, suspecting everyone of everything. First she'd started distrusting Hank, the man she'd most wanted to be her father, and now she was seeing ghosts where nothing but a helpful security guard existed. "Will you lock up after me?"

"Sure thing, Ms. Lafferty. You have a good weekend."

She managed a wry smile. "I don't imagine I will. But I'll give it my best shot."

She was almost out the side door when she heard the noise. When the bank was open there were enough people talking to cover the noise, but in the current silence it was loud and clear. The quiet little blips of someone dialing the phone.

Estelle Richard's desk was near the door; her space-age telephone had a red button lit up. With all the stealth she could muster she pushed the button and picked up the receiver, scarcely daring to breathe.

Jimmy's voice no longer had its country twang. It was terse, crisp and authoritative. "Mac," he said, "both Osmand and the girl have been here."

"Where are you calling from?" There was no doubting his voice, even if she'd never heard it over a telephone.

"From the bank. She just left...."

"Get the hell out of there. You should know better than to trust anyone, particularly someone like Katharine Lafferty." A second later the dial tone buzzed, and she had a moment to marvel at the speed with which Jimmy complied before she bounded for the door.

She was just pulling out of the parking lot when Jimmy appeared in the door. She gave him a gay little wave as she pulled out of the driveway, keeping her friendly smile plastered to her face. It vanished the moment she was out of sight. What the hell was going on here?

HENRY ARRIVED AT HER HOUSE promptly at six. Katharine had been extremely busy since she'd left the bank. First of all, she'd done what she usually did in moments of stress. She'd gone shopping. The town of Dexter didn't offer a great deal in the way of shops, but the local hardware store had any color paint she wanted, not to mention a junior artist's set that would have to do for the time being.

Rachel's Fine Fashions tended to go in for queenly sizes and muted colors, but the racks were so crowded that eventually Katharine emerged triumphant. Her final stop was the grocery store. Ignoring Chock full o' Nuts and Maxwell House, she went to the gourmet coffee section and bought chocolate almond roast. She bought croissants instead of oat bran cereal, sinfully expensive raspberries instead of green bananas, topping it all off with a chilled bottle of Moët champagne that should have been saved for a memorable occasion.

For some reason tonight felt like a memorable occasion. She was coming out of her cocoon, shedding her protective coloring, and she was going to say goodbye to the last vestiges of emotion she held for Mac. And then she was going to find out exactly what he was doing here, and do her best to nail him to the wall.

Hell hath no fury like a woman abandoned, she thought grimly, not bothering to glance in the mirror when she heard Henry at the door. If she couldn't find peace, at least she could find revenge.

Henry stood there, tall and perfect as always, a slightly sullen Melissa at his side. "Good evening, Katharine. I thought you wouldn't mind if we brought Melissa with us. She's fighting with her current beau...."

"I know," Katharine said. "Would you two like to come in and have something to drink?"

"I think we'd better get going. Er...Katharine?"

"Yes, Henry?"

He cleared his throat. "Where did you get that dress?"

Katharine did a mocking little pirouette. "Rachel's finest. Don't you like it?" She wasn't surprised by his reaction. The dress she'd found had been way in the back beyond some old pantsuits that hadn't sold in the seven years they'd been sitting on a rack. It was red. Not pale pink, or rose, or burgundy, or any of the more acceptable shades that Katharine had always avoided. It was a bright, fiery red, cut low in the front, lower in the back, exposing her elegant shoulders, slender waist and admittedly decent chest.

It was cut high, to the hemline flirting with her knees. And the material, some sort of synthetic, clung in a way that might almost be indecent. She hadn't done anything with her hair, simply let it hang down her back. In the humidity of Washington's rainy climate, it was thick and curly, and she'd topped the effect off with a huge pair of silver hoops that she'd bought years ago and never worn.

Melissa's eyes had narrowed. "I think she looks fabulous. Better than you deserve, Henry."

"I wouldn't have thought that was the most suitable thing for business," Henry began, a tiny frown forming between his beautiful gray eyes.

"But this isn't business, is it, Henry?" Katharine replied. "This is a party, and I intend to enjoy myself. You spend too much time thinking about work."

Henry opened his mouth to protest such heresy, then shut it again with a hard little snap.

"Come on, Henry, don't be such a stick-in-the-mud," Melissa said. "If I don't mind that Katharine is going to outshine every woman there tonight, me included, then you shouldn't object.''

"I'm not objecting," Henry said sternly. "I just think there's a time and a place for everything."

"And the time and the place is now," Katharine said, sliding her arm through Henry's and giving him her most devastating smile. He simply blinked in return, stunned by the exotic creature on his arm.

And then he pulled himself together. "Let's go, then," he said briskly. "Though I can't rid myself of the feeling that this is not going to be a peaceful night."

"Nonsense," Katharine said cheerfully. "We're going to have a wonderful time."

"Somehow I doubt that," Henry muttered morosely.

Chapter Twelve

Wilbur Morris owned Rachel's clothing emporium, the Ford dealership, Cox's Drugstore and the local dry cleaners. Less public was the fact that he owned the Dew Drop Inn out on Route 5 and took a cut of the action, both legal and illegal, without reporting it to the IRS.

Katharine had stumbled across that fact, not at all by accident. She'd never liked the bluff, overbearing lecher, and she hadn't liked the almost pristine neatness of his accounts. It hadn't taken long for her to ferret out the dirty little secrets, but she left things at that. As much as she disliked Wilbur, she was fond of his blond, fading wife Blanche. Besides, what went on between a client and the IRS was none of her business until a subpoena was issued, and so far Morris had managed to pull the wool over everyone's eyes.

She hadn't bothered to confide her discovery to Henry or his father. For one thing, if they were even remotely as professional as they should be, they'd be fully aware of Wilbur Morris's hanky-panky. And if they weren't, she didn't want to be the one to tell them.

Still and all, he and his wife did manage to throw a great party. As Katharine walked into the crowded room she was aware of the stir she was making. Henry was sticking close beside her, but she could feel him looking at her as if she were some rare, exotic bird who'd landed on his arm, one he was afraid might lean over and take a chunk out of him.

She hadn't intended to be that outrageous. When she'd stopped by Rachel's that afternoon she'd simply been interested in something with a little color. The tasteful neutrals in her closet suddenly made her feel claustrophobic—a simple rose or pale blue would have been change enough.

But something had drawn her to the red dress, something she'd been ignoring for far too long. And once she'd tried it on she'd been lost. Rachel herself had been both horrified and impressed, and had almost lost her sense of entrepreneurship and tried to talk her out of purchasing it.

But common sense had reared its ugly head, in the matronly Rachel if not in Katharine, and the dress now clung to her body like a second skin.

She could see Hank from across the room, see his eyes bug out of his head, and she gave him a cool smile, a smile that faded when she saw Jimmy Martin in the background. What in heaven's name was that spy doing here? But of course she knew the answer. He must have somehow wangled an invitation so that he could meet his confederate.

Mac wasn't there, of that one thing she was absolutely certain. She wished she didn't have reliable instincts where he was concerned, but for now, until she could manage to control them, she knew intimately whether his eyes were on her or not. And if he were in the room, he'd be watching her.

"Katharine, dear." Hank had materialized by her side. "Er... this is a new look for you, isn't it?"

She felt Henry stiffen beside her. "She looks wonderful," he announced, with just a trace of defiance. Once again there was that thread of tension running between father and son, a tension that was very recent.

"Doesn't she?" Melissa piped in. "I think..." Her voice trailed off suddenly, and Katharine knew exactly what had distracted her. "Who is that fabulous-looking man?" she demanded, looking over Katharine's shoulder.

"I imagine you're talking about Wilbur's guest of honor," she said dryly, loath to turn around. This was her night for finally breaking free. It was what she needed to do, but she was frightened. Just a moment or two more, she promised herself. Then she'd turn around and feel absolutely nothing at all.

"You've met MacDaniels?" Hank demanded, frowning.

"Of course she has," Henry answered for her. "She was over at the *Argus* choosing wedding invitations. You haven't told me what you picked yet, darling."

He was coming closer, she knew it. She could feel it through her pores, through her skin, through her heart. She could see it in Melissa's widened eyes and parted lips, she could hear it in the sudden hush around them.

"As a matter of fact," Mac said from directly behind her, "she didn't have a chance to choose."

"Why not?" Melissa asked breathlessly, fluttering her beautiful eyes at the man standing directly behind Katharine's almost nude back.

Katharine had no choice, she had to step back and allow him into the small circle of people. Indeed, feeling him so close behind the bare skin of her back was intensely disturbing—meeting his midnight-blue gaze couldn't possibly be any worse.

"Mac, how are you?" Hank boomed, his professional bonhomie firmly in place. As usual he didn't wait for an answer. "You know my son, Henry, and I gather you've already met his fiancée. I'd like you to know my younger daughter, Melissa."

His magnetic eyes swept over Melissa with practiced charm, practically ignoring the woman beside him. Which was just as well, Katharine told herself. Henry was still stuck at her side, and if she hadn't known him well enough to believe him above such petty emotions as jealousy, she would have thought he was being overprotective.

"So why didn't Katharine have a chance to choose wedding invitations?" Henry demanded. "We're already well past the time when we should have been sending them out. I hate doing things in a rush."

Mac turned to Katharine, a devilish light in his eyes. "This is a rushed wedding?" he inquired. "Are we anticipating a happy event?"

She drew in her breath with a silent, shocked hiss, but the others, even Henry, responded with amusement. "Clearly you don't know my brother or his fiancée very well," Melissa said, sidling up to him, her huge eyes shining with blatant admiration. "They don't do anything spontaneous or unplanned. When the time comes they'll have the requisite two point three children, and not a moment sooner."

"Sounds exciting," Mac murmured.

Katharine smiled thinly. "It suits us."

"Why are we discussing our future children?" Henry demanded in a faintly querulous voice. "I hardly think it appropriate cocktail conversation."

"So why are you in such a rush to get married, Henry?" Mac asked.

Henry glared back at him, and Katharine realized that not only were the two of them at least marginally acquainted, neither of them liked the other very much. "He's afraid I'll run off with some gangster."

Amidst the polite chuckle Mac's dangerous blue gaze suddenly blazed into hers, and she felt it all the way to the tips of her toes. It was a mistake, she realized belatedly, to tweak the tiger's tail. He was looking at her with more intensity than she'd seen in a man's eyes in a long time. Ten years, to be exact.

"Madcap behavior is not your sort of thing," Henry said with an indulgent smile. "That's why I'm still wondering why you didn't choose the wedding invitations."

There was no way he was going to let go of it, Katharine realized with a trace of desperation. He was like a bull terrier with a juicy little rabbit. He had the notion by the neck and was shaking it into submission.

"I didn't have time to show her the books," Mac said. "I told her she had to come back Monday. We've got a deadline to meet every Friday afternoon. If the paper doesn't get put to bed then we're in deep trouble. I figured the world wouldn't end if your wedding invitations waited another few days."

She stared at him in utter amazement. She never would have thought he'd come to her rescue. Indeed, much as a part of her wanted to accept that easy out, the stronger, angrier part of her refused to give in. She wanted nothing from him, including a convenient excuse.

"He's lying," she said flatly. "The fact of the matter is, I fainted at his feet."

"Don't be ridiculous," Henry said in an irritable voice.

"I'm not. I took one look at him and keeled over. He reminded me of someone in my scarlet past."

"Do tell?" Melissa leaned forward, her bright red lips parted eagerly. "I never realized you had a scarlet past."

"She doesn't," Henry snapped. "She's pulling your leg."

"I never realized Katharine had a sense of humor," Melissa countered. "Tell me about your past, Katharine. Who does Mac look like?"

Mac stepped on her foot, hard. It was all done with such astonishing smoothness that Katharine almost believed it was an accident. Someone in the crowded room conveniently stumbled against Mac, and Mac fell against Katharine, his foot coming down hard on her instep, his glass of whiskey drenching her dress.

For a moment all was a riot of confusion, voices and handkerchiefs offering solace, but Katharine refused them all, from Melissa's sympathy to Hank's too-busy hands as he tried to mop up the spilled whiskey from her cleavage. Over their heads her eyes met Mac's for a brief, telling moment. *Don't mess with me,* his expression seemed to say. *I can play this game far better than you ever could.*

"I think I'd better see whether this dress can be salvaged." She kept her voice light. "I'll be right back."

"I'm terribly sorry," Mac said again, his eyes dark and dangerous.

"I'm sure you are," she said, walking away.

"She doesn't seem to like you very much," Henry observed with a trace more perception than he usually had.

"That's all right." Melissa's seductive voice carried to Katharine's ears as she walked away. "I more than make up for it."

Fine and dandy, Katharine thought, fuming, as she made her way to Blanche Morris's huge powder room. Let Melissa keep Mac busy. After all, he'd always liked teenaged girls. Or at least, he'd liked her when she was a teenager.

The splotch of whiskey across the low-cut front of her clinging dress spoiled the effect. Not to mention that she smelled like a distillery instead of Anaïs Anaïs. She sank down in front of the wall-length mirror, staring at her reflection while several other women chattered around her. The woman staring back at her was a stranger, one with too much hair, too big eyes and a ruined dress that probably was better suited to Melissa than to a formerly staid banker. She'd been so determined to force her life back to its safe old ways. But somewhere between her initial determination and the passage of the day, all her resolutions had fallen by the wayside.

The first thing she had to do was go home, find her ecru linen cocktail dress, find some way to pin her thick hair back, even if she had to resort to paper clips and rubber bands, and then come back and see if she could salvage some of her reputation. Henry was already looking deeply disturbed, and Melissa seemed both shocked and envious. As for Mac, she didn't give a damn what he thought.

It was simple enough at that small-town party to get someone to give a message to Henry, telling him she'd be back shortly. It was simple enough to slip out the side entrance, through the garden, where no one would see her and ask leading questions. It should have been simple enough to cross the brick patio, the frozen lawn, and reach Henry's car. But she hadn't been counting on Mac.

"Running away again, Katharine?" The question was rhetorical, since the hand that had clamped down on her forearm wasn't allowing her to go anywhere.

She shivered in the chilly winter wind. She hadn't bothered to go in search of her coat—she didn't want to answer any more questions than she had to, and right now she was regretting it. "I'm going home to change the dress you ruined," she said, her voice as frosty as the late-November air.

"It's a shame about the dress," he murmured. "But I couldn't very well let you come out with something incriminating before I explained a few things to you."

"I'm not interested in explanations."

"Actually that word is a euphemism. I don't want to explain so much as warn you, Katharine."

She looked up, startled, into his midnight-blue eyes as a stray shiver danced across her skin. "Warn me?"

"Don't go shooting your mouth off about my past life. I'm not ready to go into lengthy explanations, and you seem to have developed a fair amount of clout in the short time you've been here. I'm afraid they'd take your word over mine any day."

"How did you know I hadn't been here long?"

"I have my sources. Listen, Katharine, I don't want to play games with you. You carry on with your life, with your dull fiancé and your wedding plans, and I'll carry on with mine. It's a small town, we're bound to run into each other, but I imagine if we use a little discretion and self-control we can carry it off."

She heard all this in a white-hot haze of anger. "Dull fiancé?" she echoed, enraged. "You've got a hell of a lot of nerve, passing judgment on Henry. Just because you've never done an honest day's work in your life doesn't mean you can insult people who have."

"What makes you think I haven't done an honest day's work in my life? What makes you think I haven't been working at newspapers since I finished school?"

She shouldn't taunt him, but she couldn't resist. His hand was still manacled to her arm, and a light, chilly mist had begun to fall, leaving a faint film across her bare skin. "Several things," she said unwisely. "I have access to the paper's financial records, among other things. I know that in the two or three months you've been here you've never been paid one cent."

His eyes narrowed. "That's between Seth Price and me, isn't it? What right do you have to poke your nose where it doesn't belong?"

"I have the right of pure rage. I don't trust you. I don't believe a word you say. Your confederate isn't as smooth as you are. I got a chance to listen in when our new security guard gave you a little call this afternoon. He's probably looking for you right now, ready to pass you information." She took a deep breath. "You're no more a newspaper editor than I am a topless dancer. You're lying, and I've already learned that where you're concerned, people get hurt. I don't want to see anyone else lying in a pool of blood, unless, by some great good fortune, it happens to be you."

"Sorry, I have no intention of obliging you. Believe it or not, I'm just here to do a job."

"Oh, I believe it all right. I just don't believe it's the job you say it is."

He stared at her for a moment in mute frustration. The light mist had grown a little more enthusiastic, and it sparkled in his dark hair, misted his glowering face, danced across the worn tweed jacket and gray striped shirt. He looked like the real thing all right, as far removed from the minor-league hoodlum she'd once known as she was from the impassioned teenager. "What am I going to do with you, Katharine?" he said wearily, the edge of anger still tight in his voice. "I can't have you saying things that I don't want spread around."

"Why not? If you're who and what you say you are, why should it matter what I tell people?" she countered between her teeth. She could feel the damp cold deep in her bones, and it was trying to shake its way outward. She tried to control it, to keep herself very still, but the chill was winning.

He released his bruising grip on her wrist, but the move was unexpected, and by the time she'd pulled herself together enough to make a dash for it he'd slid his hands up her wet, bare arms to her shoulders, clamping down, his thumbs caressing the edges of her collarbone. She stared up at him in mute surprise as the long-suppressed tremors broke forth, shivering across her lightly dressed body. "You're driving me crazy, Katharine," he said in a low voice. "If I had any sense at all I'd get rid of you. You're going to cause me nothing but trouble, and even if you were willing to listen to reason and behave yourself, you're still too damned distracting."

"Let me get this straight." Her voice was wavering from the cold, as shiver after shiver racked her body beneath his strong hands. "You want me to be a good girl, keep my mouth shut and go away, or you're going to kill me?"

"Not exactly. Where the hell is your coat? Don't you have enough sense to wear something when you go outside in November? You're going to catch pneumonia."

She shoved her damp, curling hair away from her face. "That hardly matters if you're going to kill me. Besides, I was trying to sneak out without anyone seeing me."

"I'm not going to kill you," he said in an irritable voice. "Tempting as the thought might be. I don't suppose you'd feel like giving me your word that you'll keep quiet."

She considered it. Her body was shivering, the warmth from his hands burning into her, making her tremble even more. This was the man she'd loved, the man she'd mourned for ten endless years. He was standing close enough for the heat of his body to penetrate a chill that ran so deep she thought it would never go away. His hands were touching her, and she wanted to reach up and put her own hands over his, to draw those hands down the skimpy front of her dress.

She fought it. She fought the drugging pull of him, of her own long-buried needs. She didn't want to want him. She hated him. But she wanted him all the same.

"You're driving me crazy," he said again, in a different voice. He pushed her up against the house so that the cold, rough brick was at her back and his warm, strong body was pressed along the front of her, and his mouth was cold and wet from the heavy mist. And then it was warm, she was warm, her arms had slid around his waist, under his open jacket, and she could feel his body pressed intimately against hers, fitting perfectly, with an instinctive knowledge that defied anger and the passage of time.

She didn't even bother to wonder why she was kissing him back. She knew she shouldn't, but that no longer seemed to matter. Henry kept his mouth closed when he kissed her; Mac didn't. He used his lips, his tongue, his teeth, he kissed her with a devouring thoroughness that she could only begin to respond to as she trembled in the tight circle of his arms.

He was hard against her. Feeling it, knowing it, added to her confusion. As far as she could tell, Henry had never been that excited. Maybe he was built in such a way that she couldn't tell. Or maybe she was in for a major disappointment on her wedding night.

Mac had broken the kiss, moving back a few inches, and his eyes were hooded. "What are you thinking about?" he asked, his voice husky.

She wanted him to keep on kissing her. She wanted to tumble under the bushes on the Morrises' perfectly landscaped lawn, she wanted to rip his clothes from him and feel love again.

But she wasn't going to let it happen. She wasn't going to let her heart be ripped apart again. This time she wouldn't survive. She looked up at him with a sweet smile. "I was wondering if Henry was as well endowed as you are."

His eyes darkened suddenly, and for a brief moment she was satisfied that she'd managed to startle him. He released her, stepping back, just as the rain began to fall in earnest.

"Don't you know?" he asked softly.

He didn't stop her as she ran this time, her high heels sinking into the muddy ground. She didn't glance behind her as she jumped into Henry's car and pulled out, almost directly into some late arrival's Cadillac. She was shaking so hard she could barely drive, despite the fact that her body still burned from where his had touched it, despite the fact that her chattering teeth and frozen mouth could still feel the imprint of his. He'd warned her not to play games with him, warned her with nothing more than a look. She should have known.

She was hopelessly outclassed. He knew how to cut to the bone, swift and deep, so that her puny efforts at attack were useless. He knew how to touch her and still make her melt. He knew she wasn't really going to tell anyone about him.

And he probably knew what had taken her almost thirty-six hours to figure out. She was still in love with him. And always would be. And the hot tears pouring down her face as she drove home did nothing at all to warm the deep ice that had invaded her heart and soul. She had the feeling she'd never be warm again.

"YOU WANT TO TELL ME what's going on between you and the banker lady?" Jimmy Martin materialized beside him, seemingly oblivious to the rain.

"Not particularly. I'm in charge of this operation, remember? I know what I'm doing." He reacted with a growl, furious at himself, at Katharine, at Lefty Siegal for putting him in this damnable position.

"Hey, I'm only asking," Jimmy said quickly, holding up his hands in a sign of surrender. "We've worked together before, and I know you're just about the best in the business. I figure you know what you're doing. I just wondered whether you needed me to take a hand."

"Like what?"

Jimmy grinned. He was known for being particularly effective with female suspects. His boyish grin and willingness to give his all in the line of duty made for a number of jokes among his comrades. "It seems as if her jealous fiancé isn't keeping her busy enough, and as far as I can tell you don't want her. Maybe I should see if I can provide a little healthy distraction."

Mac controlled his deep desire to plant his fist in Jimmy's white teeth. "I wouldn't try it if I were you," he said calmly. "She knows you're working with me."

"How?"

"You were dangerously sloppy, calling from the bank. She didn't trust you showing up like that, and she listened in on our conversation. Mistakes like that can cost you your life, Jimmy. You know that as well as I do."

"You think Katharine's in that deep? I didn't realize there was much danger involved in this particular operation."

"There isn't. I'm talking about things in general. You've been in the business long enough to know you can't be too careful. As for Katharine, I don't think we're going to have any trouble with her. She's not involved in the scam, though it's possible she might suspect some of what's going on. But she's not going to get in our way."

"What makes you so sure of that?" Jimmy demanded, still smarting from his reprimand.

"Instinct," he said in a silky voice. "You got any quarrel with that?" His instincts were legendary among Lefty's rangers, and Jimmy shook his head.

"No quarrel. I'd stake my life on your instincts. So tell me, what do we do next?"

"We find out exactly how dirty Katharine's straight-arrow fiancé is," Mac said smoothly, ignoring his own irrational streak of jealousy. "And then we bring him down."

Chapter Thirteen

The light mist had turned into a freezing rain by the time Katharine skidded Henry's big sedan in front of her house. For one brief moment Katharine wondered how he and Melissa would get home after the party. There was no way she was going to go back there to fetch them and run the risk of facing Mac again. She'd simply been through too much in the past forty-eight hours.

Ripping off the flame-colored dress, she tossed it into the wastebasket as she headed upstairs. On impulse she'd bought a fuchsia T-shirt when she'd been shopping, for comfort rather than anything else, she'd told herself. She slipped it on, grabbed the faded jeans that no one outside her house had ever seen and went back down to pour herself a large glass of whiskey. She had every intention of getting nobly, gloriously drunk.

She hadn't counted on the fact that she hated whiskey. The bottle of bourbon was in residence solely for guests, and the first harsh taste raised goose bumps on her bare arms. The second made her shudder down to her toes. The rest she poured down the sink, settling for Diet Coke with a resigned sigh.

The house was too quiet. She could hear the faint hum of the refrigerator, the gas furnace, the tick tick of freezing rain against her windows. She turned on the small color television, turned as usual to PBS, but they were in the middle of some earnest British masterpiece, and she quickly switched it back off.

She wasn't in need of anything purportedly good for her. She wanted something shallow and stupid and mind-numbing. Turning on the radio, she jumped a mile when some heavy metal group shrieked loudly, and she almost switched it back off. Something seemed to stop her hand. Instead, she turned the volume up a notch higher, drained her Coke and turned back to face her neat, bland living room, a determined glint in her eye.

It was after ten when she heard the sound of her doorbell. She still had the stereo up high, drowning out any sounds she didn't wish to hear, and she'd unplugged the telephone. The faint buzz of the doorbell, muffled beneath the Rolling Stones, followed by a furious pounding, made her wonder whether the neighbors had called and complained. She didn't think so. Her house was very tight, and old Mrs. Landon on the left was almost totally deaf. The Perkins family on the right had three teenagers and were hardly strangers to noise and loud rock and roll.

She stood in the middle of her empty living room, considering whether it might be Mac. Then she dismissed the notion. Mac didn't seem to need such niceties as an invitation. If he wanted to come in he'd find a way to do it, and it wouldn't involve ringing the doorbell.

Henry was standing in her doorway, tall and furious. The freezing rain sparkled in his dark hair, his eyes were disapproving, his handsome mouth set in a thin line. As he took in her appearance his eyes widened faintly, and his mouth grew even grimmer.

"What the hell is going on?" he demanded.

"Don't swear at me," Katharine said mildly enough.

"You've suddenly turned into a stranger," he said bitterly. "Just look at yourself! Your hair is a mess down your back, your face is covered with splotches of paint, your clothes are better suited to a teenager. On top of that, you race out of an important cocktail party, a business cocktail party, and leave both Melissa and me stranded. And then you act as if you don't owe anyone an explanation."

"I don't," she said.

For a moment he simply stared in outrage. "It's a lucky thing for you MacDaniels offered us a ride over here. Otherwise we would have had to hitchhike...."

"Mac's here?" she demanded in horror, getting to the heart of the matter.

"He dropped me off and is driving Melissa home. As a matter of fact, I believe they're going out for a drink first. He seemed quite taken with my little sister. And at least he's slightly more presentable than the muscle-headed jocks she's been hanging around with."

Katharine was having a hard time absorbing all this information at one time. She picked on the easiest part. "I thought you didn't like Mac."

"I don't. I don't trust him, I think the paper's taken much too hard-edged a turn. He doesn't understand small-town politics. We're all friends here." He continued to glare at her. "I didn't come over here to discuss MacDaniels, Katharine. I came over for an explanation."

"Actually, you came over for your car," she said. "If you're going to lecture me you might as well come in. I expect half the neighbors in this friendly small town of yours are watching us with great interest."

That succeeded in breaking through Henry's outrage. With an unnerved glance over his shoulder, he quickly stepped into her living room, shutting the door behind him.

"Good God, Katharine," he gasped. "What have you done?"

She shrugged, moving ahead of him, stepping carefully over the drop cloths. "I was painting."

"Where's all your furniture? And could you turn down that infernal racket?" His voice had risen to a quiet shout in an effort to compete with Steely Dan.

"The furniture's wherever I could stash it. Mostly under drop cloths," she said as she clambered over a heaped-up pile to the stereo. It was with real regret that she turned down "Aja." At least it wasn't "Hey Twenty," an age already too loaded with memories. The sudden silence was deafening, like a thick woolen blanket closing down around their ears. She looked across her shambles of a living room at the man she had thought she'd make a life with, and wondered whether she'd just woken up after a long sleep.

Henry was looking at the brightly colored mural she was in the midst of creating on the once-pale wall, and his expression was both concerned and fretful. "What's that supposed to be?" he demanded in an aggrieved tone.

Katharine glanced at the streaks of crimson, purple and gold. "A butterfly," she said. "Emerging from a cocoon. Or a phoenix. Take your pick. Would you like a drink?"

"Ten o'clock isn't cocktail hour."

"I think you need a drink, Henry. I need to talk to you, and I think you'll feel better with a drink in your hand."

The fretful expression left his eyes, replaced by something pathetically close to fear. "We can talk tomorrow," he said, turning to leave. "It's late, and you need time to think about things before you say anything rash."

"It's not that late, Henry, and what I have to say won't take long."

"Katharine..."

"I'm breaking our engagement." There, the words were out. For a moment she was swamped with relief that it hadn't been nearly as painful as she'd thought it would be to actually say it. And then she got a good look at his expression.

"You don't mean that," he said, but it was clear that he knew what she'd been about to say, and had wanted to avoid it.

"I'm afraid I do," she said, her voice gentler as guilt swamped her. Looking up at Henry's tall, handsome figure, she was overwhelmed with the sudden realization that this self-assured, somewhat pompous but basically kind man loved her. Really loved her. And she had no choice but to hand him that love back. "Come into the kitchen and have a drink and we can talk about it, Henry," she said, surprised that there was a note of pleading in her voice.

"I don't think that's necessary. I'm not going to be able to change your mind, am I?" He'd managed to wrap all his considerable dignity around him, but his gray eyes were hollow.

"No," she said. "We really wouldn't suit at all. I'm not the kind of woman you thought I was. You fell in love with an unemotional, self-contained banker. I'm torn apart by emotions I thought I'd buried years ago. I don't know who I am and what I want in this life, but I know that everything that seemed so simple and clear a few short days ago now seems totally confused."

"Then why rush into anything? Why not give yourself some time to think things through? I don't know what's happened to send you into a tailspin, and I'm not about to ask. You'll tell me if you need to. But you don't have to throw away an eminently suitable marriage because you're feeling a little restricted. We don't have to get married next month—we can postpone it until sometime in the spring. If you're having some sort of premature midlife crisis I can be very patient."

"Henry," she said. "I don't love you. I don't think I ever did."

He flinched. "I don't believe we were discussing undying passions. I thought we simply decided we'd make one hell of a couple. I still believe that, Kay. You just need a little time to think things through and you'll agree. Don't throw away something that could be so right for both of us."

"Henry..."

"I'm not taking the ring, Kay."

She'd pulled it off her hand and was holding it out to him, but he simply turned on his heel and walked back toward the door. He held himself very straight, and once again the searing guilt swept through her. She'd never realized that someone like Henry Osmand could fall in love. And not with someone as remote as she'd been.

She followed him, catching him by the door and tucking the flawless diamond in his jacket pocket. "I'm sorry, Henry."

He simply looked at her, and she suddenly remembered the expression on Melissa's face as she bewailed her broken heart. If only Katharine could trust that Henry would bounce back as quickly.

He didn't slam the door as he walked out into the freezing rain. He closed it very quietly, and moments later she heard his car take off into the night at a sedate, well-ordered pace. If it weren't for the expression in his eyes she could have convinced herself that things had gone very well indeed.

But she'd recognized that expression. And that was one more thing she could chalk up to Mac's account. She'd somehow managed to break a good man's heart, when she'd never even realized he had one in the first place.

She turned the radio up even louder than she had in the first place. She didn't recognize who was singing, and she didn't care. The music was loud and passionate and angry, matching her mood exactly. Picking up her palette, she turned back to her mural and began to paint.

MAC ONLY CONSIDERED Melissa Osmand for a second or two before deciding to get her back home as quickly as he could. For one thing, she was too damned young for him. He'd had twenty-year-olds, one in particular, when he'd been a suitable age to appreciate them. Now, to a man at the advanced age of thirty-four, someone with Melissa's youth and self-absorbed innocence seemed almost obscenely young.

It didn't matter that her bright gray eyes were more than willing. It didn't matter that she obviously had a luscious, well-trained body and a healthy enthusiasm for physical endeavors. It didn't matter that she smelled like musky flowers and her hand brushed his thigh or touched his arm whenever she spoke to him. He simply didn't want her.

He didn't want Barbara Collins, either. They'd been seeing each other on a very casual basis since he'd come to the area. She was a real estate lawyer in the next town over, a mature woman with no illusions as to their relationship, and he'd enjoyed her company, and her body, tremendously.

If he had any sense he'd give her a call and then drive twenty miles through the freezing rain to spend the night in her experienced arms.

But he wasn't going to do that, either. He had a few scruples, and one of them involved not using one woman in place of another. He wasn't interested in Melissa, he wasn't interested in Barbara, he wasn't interested in anyone. Except Katharine.

He didn't know why he couldn't keep his hands off her, he thought as he parked his treasured MGB outside his apartment. He'd been alone with her twice in the past two days, and both times he'd ended up kissing her. It wasn't as if he was a man who couldn't control his desires. In the past ten years he'd never let sex get in the way of a job he was doing. He'd been able to compartmentalize, and if things started to overlap he'd simply dropped the relationship. It had been only his body involved, not his heart and soul.

But it wasn't so simple this time around. Katharine Lafferty was engaged to marry the major suspect in a money-laundering scheme, the man he'd come to this small northwest town to catch. The only sensible thing to do would be to keep as far away as possible.

So why was it taking every ounce of his concentration to keep from driving over to that little house and making sure she got home safely?

He knew why, he thought as he let himself into his apartment, dumping his rain-wet jacket across a chair and heading for the kitchenette and a bottle of Olympia. Just as he knew he hadn't done anything as simple as forgetting Katharine Lafferty during the past ten years.

He hadn't forgotten her, he'd deliberately, ruthlessly blocked out all memory of her. She'd been lost to him forever, both by the life-style he'd chosen and his one noble gesture. And having ruthlessly torn her out of his life, for both their sakes, he'd simply refused to allow himself to think of her.

Once that block had been broken, however, he found he was thinking of nothing else. When he least expected it memories would come flooding back—Katharine in the shower, wet and hot and wanton. Katharine sitting in his car, filled with a mixture of longing and panic. Katharine lying in his arms, fitting there perfectly, her body in tune with his.

Hell, he thought, dropping down on the sofa and draining half the beer. It was probably just hormones. She'd happened to hit him at his sexual peak. It had worked out to the best sex he'd ever had, but that was all it was. If he went to bed with her now it would be nothing but a major letdown.

Damn, why was he even considering such a thing? She wouldn't let him get within ten feet of her.

Except that she had. She'd even kissed him back, outside that stupid cocktail party with the icy rain dripping down over them.

And he knew full well it wasn't a question of if he went to bed with her again. It was a question of when. And she knew it just as well as he did.

The metallic *brrr* of the phone broke the stillness. He stared at it for a moment, unmoving, even though it was directly beside him. There was no one he wanted to talk to at the moment. No one except Katharine, and she certainly wouldn't be calling him.

Still, it might be Lefty. Maybe if things started to move a little more quickly he'd be able to wrap things up and escape before he got in too deep.

"Yeah," he barked into the telephone.

"Trying to scare me off, Mac?" Lefty replied. "You should know I don't scare easily. How are things coming?"

Mac's reply was one brief word.

"Still the same Mac," Lefty said cheerfully. "I've got some good news for you, buddy boy. Looks like things are going to come to a head in a matter of days. By this time next week you should be out of there."

"Terrific," Mac growled. "Just what I wanted to hear."

"So why don't you sound more enthusiastic?" Lefty taunted him. "Maybe you aren't so eager to get away from the small-town ambience. Maybe you've found a reason to stick around."

"Maybe you've got rocks in your head," Mac snapped back. "Give me what you've got and stop being so damned playful."

"There's another chunk of money coming through. Cromwell, the banker down in Sacramento, is putting through one last chunk. He knows we're on to him, but the dumb bastard doesn't realize how close. He's too greedy to cut his losses and wait, he's going for one last killing. And we're going to nab his northwest connection when he does. How's Jimmy doing?"

"The man needs to work on his cover—he's almost blown it several times in front of the girl."

"What girl?"

"Woman," Mac corrected himself edgily. "Katharine Lafferty."

"Well, that's no big problem. I doubt she's in on any of this," Lefty said expansively. "And I wouldn't worry about you calling her a girl. You probably still remember the good old days, young love and all that."

"That sound you hear is me gagging. Spare me the young love crap. And what makes you think she doesn't have anything to do with this? You're half a continent away, and you haven't seen her in ten years."

"I did some checking the moment you said she was there. I'm thorough, even if I'm not farsighted. She's lived an exemplary life. Hardworking, serious, no social life to speak of. No fun to speak of. If I didn't know better, I'd say she's been in mourning for the last ten years."

"But you know better." Mac's voice was dangerous.

"Sure I do. So do you. No woman of any intelligence is going to pine after a worthless bum like you, and Katharine Lafferty always struck me as a woman of great intelligence. Too good for the likes of you.''

"Why do we keep talking about Katharine Lafferty?''

"I don't know. Maybe you keep bringing her up. Listen, Mac, keep your mind above your waist and we'll get through this just fine. The money's coming up on Tuesday—how or when we're not sure. That part is up to you and Jimmy. Once we nail Osmand, or whoever, you can concentrate on renewing old passions.''

"Lefty...''

"Yeah?''

"Stuff it.''

Lefty's only response was an irritating chuckle.

He figured he had two choices. One was to keep up with the Olympia, maybe switch to Scotch and numb himself into bed for at least a semblance of sleep. Or he could give it up right now, make a pot of coffee and go over what he'd learned in the three months in Dexter, Washington. What he'd learned about the money-laundering scheme, that is. Not what he'd learned about Katharine Lafferty and his blocked past.

The latter seemed the more sensible road, much as he cherished the idea of a stiff drink. He was used to making do on little or no sleep—the lack of rest only tended to make his wits sharper, at least in the beginning. If he was going to finish things up, not mess up at a crucial juncture because he was still mooning over an ancient romance, then he better apply himself, and fast.

Things fell together quickly enough, aided by a pot of French roast coffee and too many cigarettes. Jimmy showed up just after midnight, made a dent in Mac's supply of Olympia and disappeared around three, leaving Mac to fill out the rest of the night with a few fitful hours of sleep, the caffeine still jangling his nerves into intermittent wakefulness, his hormones still tormenting him with erotic memories of a twenty-year-old Katharine who was somehow even more luscious as a thirty-year-old.

Sunday went by in a haze of work and coffee, and by the time he rolled out of bed on Monday morning he was thoroughly hung over from lack of sleep, too many dreams and too much caffeine. The digital clock flashed a gloomy eight-thirty at him, slothfully late, but then, who did he have to impress? In another few days he'd turn his back on the newspaper and never have to think about it again.

It was a shame about that, though. He'd discovered he liked what he was doing, liked running the small, radical paper. He'd even discovered a latent talent for writing. Of course, Lefty always told him he wrote the most literate reports in the bureau, but he'd dismissed that. All he knew was that he never had to sweat writing them the way other agents did.

Maybe he'd get a job in the newspaper business when he decided to go back to work. In the meantime, all he wanted was heat, sunshine and no more of this damned northwestern rain.

A shower and shave brought him a small measure of alertness. Another two cups of reheated coffee opened his eyes a few more centimeters, and if his hands trembled slightly as he lit his first cigarette, no one else would notice.

The ice storm of last night had vanished in the unexpected warmth of the day. Even the sun seemed to be trying to make an effort. Maybe Washington wasn't such a miserable place after all.

He drove his precious sports car to work, parking it well out of the way of careless drivers, and managed to get through the day concentrating on newspaper business, only thinking about Katharine two or three times every half hour. It was late when he was ready to leave. The office was deserted, and he took time to check in with Jimmy, only to find that neither of the two Osmands, father or son, had shown up to work that day for more than a couple of hours. Katharine had appeared for half a day, setting the place in an uproar, and then taken off herself, and it had taken Jimmy the better part of the afternoon to find out what was causing such a ruckus.

"She broke her engagement to the boss's son," Jimmy announced.

"You think I care?" Mac shot back, squashing down his own incomprehensible reaction to the news.

"It might mean she found out what was going on," Jimmy said mildly enough.

"Or she might have gotten bored with him."

"There's always that. I'm going to work on the computers tonight after everyone leaves. I'll come by around midnight whether I've gotten any further or not."

"You'll have gotten further. Lefty says another chunk of money is coming through tomorrow. If we haven't cracked it by that time it might be our last chance."

"Yes, boss. Maybe it'll be closer to two in the morning."

"I'll be waiting."

The night air was fresh and crisp when he left the deserted newspaper office. His vintage M.G. was glistening beneath the streetlights, and he took a moment to admire it. He'd always wanted an M.G., and it had only been Lefty's ability to unearth the car of his dreams that had tipped the scales and sent him to Dexter. He had every intention of taking the perfectly maintained beauty into retirement with him.

He saw the bright glare of the headlights in the deserted street, and he had a sudden, sickening knowledge of what was about to happen. He didn't need to look beyond the lights to see Katharine Lafferty's serene face as her Toyota bore down upon his precious car. For half a moment he was tempted to throw himself into the street, into the pathway of her oncoming car before it smashed into the beautiful hunter green of his sports car.

Sanity prevailed. The screech of tearing metal echoed in his heart as she plowed into the side of the M.G.B. She hadn't been going fast enough to do any structural damage—she would have known that her car would suffer more punishment than his. It simply ripped and tore at the beautiful finish.

For good measure she put the Toyota into reverse, backed up and then slammed into the M.G.B. again. And then she drove away, waving cheerfully in his horrified direction before she disappeared into the night-shrouded streets of Dexter.

Chapter Fourteen

It was a lucky thing for Katharine Lafferty that she'd smashed the fender of his M.G. down over the wire wheels. He was able to vent the first moments of fury yanking the metal away. By the time he got the car on the road to take off after her it was making an ominous grinding noise, and the steering was a joke. He simply compensated, speeding after her with a furious determination.

Katharine's luck held. He was stopped by the police two miles from her house.

The policeman was a clean-cut man with the name Finnegan on his brass badge. The brass was still shiny, proclaiming that the policeman was new on the job. He perused Mac's Chicago driver's license and registration with a wary eye. "You want to tell me how your car got banged up, Mr. MacDaniels? We're not talking about a hit-and-run, are we? It's against the law to leave the scene of an accident."

Even later he couldn't figure out why he did it. "I sideswiped an oak tree in my driveway, officer. My fault alone, and I'm going to call my insurance company first thing in the morning."

Finnegan looked skeptical. "Was the oak tree painted dark blue?" he inquired, picking a fleck of paint off the side of the green M.G.

Mac considered his options. It would serve Katharine right if he got her hauled into court for hit-and-run. On the other hand, it might prove a needless complication.

"Mind if I get some more identification?" he asked in a resigned tone.

"As long as you do it carefully," the policeman said, clearly prepared for Mac to pull a gun.

Mac's gun was in the glove compartment, complete with license, but Officer Finnegan didn't have to know that. He simply handed him his ICTF identification.

"Damn," the policeman muttered, handing it back along with the license and registration. "I thought I had a live one for a moment."

"Boring job?" Mac asked with real sympathy.

"The worst. This town is so squeaky clean you could eat off the sidewalks. No one does anything worse than cheat on their wives and their income taxes," he said bitterly.

"I wouldn't count on it. If things were as boring as they seemed, I wouldn't be here."

Finnegan's eyes widened. "You mean . . ."

"I'll tell you what. When we need police backup I'll ask for you in particular. A deal?"

"I'd appreciate that, sir," he said with real enthusiasm. "You better get that car looked at, and fast. You were wobbling all over the road."

"I'll do that."

He was still intent on reaching Katharine and wringing her neck, but the car gave up the ghost half a mile from her house. He stashed it by the side of the road and walked the rest of the way. The night had grown colder, windier, and he pulled his jacket around him, trying to keep his rage at a simmering level.

Her house was locked and deserted. Locks were never any problem for him—he simply let himself in the back door without bothering with the lights and promptly fell over a piece of furniture.

He got back to his feet, trying to focus on the various shrouded shapes in the dark house. He flicked on the lights for one brief moment, just to orient himself, and let out a long, surprised whistle.

The beige blandness of her house had vanished into a welter of colorful chaos. The walls were splashes of brilliant color—huge tropical flowers, butterflies and giant birds and dark forests and bright oceans. He stared, open-mouthed in astonishment at the sheer vitality and passion of her paintings. This wasn't the house of a banker. This wasn't the house of the mild, colorless creature who'd fainted at his feet in the newspaper office.

This was the house of Katharine, the one woman he'd once thought he loved. And that knowledge, that sharp memory was painfully inescapable.

KATHARINE'S ELATION lasted approximately five minutes after smashing Mac's car. And then reaction began to set in. Not regret exactly, or fear. More a simple matter of second thoughts. Maybe she would have been much better off pretending Mac didn't exist. Certainly she was better off thinking Danny didn't.

She didn't want to go home. She'd run out of paint, not to mention wall space, and she wasn't ready to start on the upstairs. Besides, the place was so crowded she could barely move. She'd made arrangements for someone to come and haul most of her unwanted furniture away. Maybe when that happened she might feel less restless.

She made herself drive to the next town and have dinner at a small restaurant where no one knew her. She only picked at her food, her stomach tied in knots, and by the time she was driving back home she realized that she'd picked up an ominous thump in her front end. Her poor little Toyota shouldn't have had to pay the price for her revenge, but then, she hadn't actually planned to smash his car. She'd simply found herself driving by just as he was leaving, and for the first time in ten years she gave in to an emotional impulse.

No, it wasn't the first time. Ever since she'd walked into his office she'd been giving in to impulses. She could only hope they didn't start backfiring on her as her car had suddenly begun to do.

Her house was dark and unwelcoming when she got home. Her Toyota was wheezing audibly by the time she pulled into her driveway, and it rattled and trembled into silence when she turned it off. Just out of curiosity she tried to restart it, but she was rewarded with nothing but a sullen ticking. She'd have to finagle a ride in to work tomorrow, and Henry was the last person she could ask. He hadn't taken her breaking the engagement well, and he'd been even more distressed when she'd given her notice at the bank today. If she asked him for a ride he'd provide it, but he'd also provide a nonstop argument as to how she was ruining her life.

She was so tired. All she wanted was a hot shower and her bed. Tomorrow she'd have to become at least partially responsible again, phone her insurance company and make up some plausible tale about bumping into Mac's M.G.B. He might deny it, of course. He might already have the police out looking for her, ready to haul her in on hit-and-run charges. Or even, if he cared to get fanciful, attempted murder.

Not that the notion hadn't entered her brain on several occasions during the past few days. Her hurt and rage and sense of betrayal were so overwhelming she felt positively murderous whenever she wasn't crying. At least smashing into his car had vented some of that rage. Leaving her feeling guilty, uneasy and waiting for his retribution.

She flicked the light switch when she entered her house, then muttered a demure little curse under her breath. Since she'd torn her living room apart there was no longer a lamp attached to that switch. Double locking her front door behind her, she stumbled into her inky-dark living room, hands outstretched in front of her, reaching for the small lamp she'd left perched on top of the stereo.

Instead her hands encountered something solid, something warm, something alive. She let out a panicked scream, one that was quickly smothered by the hard hand covering her mouth, and her frightened struggle was just as quickly subdued by his larger, stronger body.

"I guess I'm going to have to get rid of you after all, Katharine," Mac murmured in her ear, and his deep, painfully familiar voice should have sent her further into fear.

But the room was dark and warm. The man who held her trapped against him felt and smelled like the one man she'd ever loved, and his voice in her ear was the voice she'd given up ever hearing again. Even the taste of his hand against her mouth was familiar, and arousing. She sagged against him, telling herself it was fright and weariness, knowing that for one brief moment she wanted to allow herself the final luxury of his body heat.

He didn't seem to know what to do with her sudden capitulation. His hand loosened on her mouth, and his grip no longer seemed so harsh. "Are you going to scream?"

"No," she whispered against his hand, wishing for one crazy instant that she could kiss his palm.

He moved his hand away before she could do more than fantasize. Still keeping a firm grip on her, he reached over and turned on the dimly watted light bulb, then gazed down at her out of his wary, midnight-blue eyes.

She wet her lips nervously, wishing he'd let her go even as she still reveled in the heat of his body pressed up against her. "Where's your car?"

He laughed, an odd, bitter sound that wasn't without amusement. "It crapped out about half a mile from here. You're pretty good when it comes to revenge, aren't you?"

"I learned from a master. What are you going to do to me?" She sounded no more than casually interested.

"Well, now, that presents a problem." He released her, dropping down on the littered sofa and lighting a cigarette. "I can't very well kill you, tempted though I might be. Someone would be bound to ask questions. Same goes if I simply make you disappear. I need there to be less attention, not more."

Without the demoralizing feel of his hands on her body she was feeling a tiny bit braver. "You wouldn't kill me," she said calmly, allowing herself a furtive glance toward the front door. It would take her precious moments to unfasten the double lock, moments he probably wouldn't allow her.

"No? I've killed before."

"That was when you were a second-rate gangster fighting for your life. I can't see a small-town newspaper editor murdering an old girlfriend because he doesn't want too many embarrassing questions asked."

"I was never second-rate," he corrected her. "Is that what you are? An old girlfriend?"

"It's as good a term as any." She managed a careless little shrug.

"I thought you were my one true love."

If this gentle mockery was going to be his revenge for smashing his car she might almost have preferred murder. "Not when you couldn't remember my face or name."

"You'd changed both," he pointed out carelessly. "You turned yourself into some bland creature that few men would look at twice."

"Sorry I didn't appeal to you," she shot back, her hands curling into fists. Why hadn't she rammed into the M.G. at least one more time?

"The question is, who are you now? You aren't the meek, virginal little rabbit you were ten years ago. And you aren't the faceless nonentity who fainted at my feet." His seemingly emotionless gaze flitted over her face, the thick tangle of blond hair that cascaded over her shoulders, the deep purple cotton sweater and black pants.

"No one of your concern."

"You are when you ram into my car in a fit of insanity."

"It wasn't a fit of insanity. That was one of the calmest, most rational acts I've ever performed. That's about all you care about, isn't it? Your stupid classic car? You felt the same way about your old Aston Martin. It was the only way I could think of to break what passes for your heart."

He didn't say a word, just slid lower on the sofa, watching her as she stood over him holding herself very still.

"I will admit that it was ill-advised, no matter how good it felt," she said, recognizing her banker's voice with its clipped, unemotional tones. "I'll be in touch with my insurance company tomorrow. I'm sure they'll be able to make her as good as new."

"Don't bother," he said airily. "I've already called my own company."

"Along with the police?"

"No."

"You still need my insurance...."

"No," he said again. "I told them I skidded on a slippery road and plowed into you. My fault."

She simply stared at him for a moment. "Why?" she asked bluntly.

"Let's just say that maybe I owe you."

She couldn't help it—she laughed. "So in return for my living ten years with a shattered heart you're willing to pay a higher insurance premium next time around. Very noble."

Once again he honed in on what she'd hoped he hadn't noticed. "Did you live ten years with a broken heart?" His voice was infuriatingly gentle.

She ignored the question. "Before you leave," she said pointedly, "I wanted to give you a friendly warning."

He raised an eyebrow. "Oh, really? Well, take your time. I'm not about to leave."

"Yes, you are. But before you go I wanted to tell you to keep away from Melissa Osmand. She's just gone through a hard time, and she doesn't need to be another sacrificial victim."

"Melissa Osmand isn't anybody's victim. Besides, what the hell does it matter to you?"

"I don't want to see another twenty-year-old with her heart broken."

"All twenty-year-olds get their hearts broken. It goes with the territory. Are you sure you're not feeling jealous?"

"Jealous?" The sound wasn't much more than a strangled shriek of fury. "Jealous?" she demanded again. "Of you? Of all the egotistical, overweening, monstrous..."

"You've already made it more than clear that I've blighted your life. If you loved me so much that you carried a torch for me for ten years then it stands to reason that you still have some feeling for me."

"I do. Utter loathing."

He contemplated her for a moment, staring up at her lazily. "I don't think it's that simple."

"Maybe not. But it's enough. Get out, Mac. I have painting to do." It didn't matter that she was out of paint, out of energy, out of inspiration. All she wanted to do was get rid of him. In the dark cocoon of her dimly lit house she was far too vulnerable to emotions she thought had shattered in the face of his duplicity. She had thought she'd gotten over him, completely, the moment she knew the depths of his lie. Now she knew she'd only been kidding herself. Part of her hated him with a white-hot fury. Part of her, the wild, dangerous part of her that was surfacing after years of being buried, wanted him, with a longing as intense as it was sexual. And part of her, the part she despised, still loved him, and always would. All the lies, all the games he was playing, couldn't change that. If death couldn't change it, nothing could.

But she didn't want him around. She was too afraid she was going to succumb to one of those conflicting emotions. That she was going to kill him. That she was going to fling herself at his feet and admit she still loved him. That she was going to go to bed with him.

Because he wanted her. She knew that, though how she did she wasn't quite sure. But he wanted her as much as she wanted him. And therein lay the danger.

He glanced around him. "This is part of the new you?"

"Yes, indeed," she said breezily, edging toward the door. Maybe her only hope was to run, not from him, but from her own damnable weakness. "I'm changing my image. No longer the bland little creature you were just mocking. I'm going to indulge my insatiable appetites. After all, I have to catch up on ten years of mummified behavior."

"I'll reach the door before you get the first lock unlocked," he said blandly. "Don't even try it."

She held herself very still. "And what would you do if you caught me?"

"Try it and see," he suggested affably, but she wasn't fooled. If she ran for the door he'd touch her, and this time if he touched her he wouldn't let her go. And she wouldn't want him to.

She moved back into the room, skirting the enshrouded chair but keeping well out of the way of his long, stretched-out legs. She saw the brief flash of disappointment in his dark eyes before he shuttered them, and she knew an answering regret.

"Have a seat," he said, patting the sofa beside him and dumping off the pile of mail she'd put there Saturday and still not bothered to look at.

"Why?"

"Because we've got ten years to catch up on. And I'm not leaving until I'm convinced you're going to be reasonable."

"I'll be reasonable," she said, ignoring the place beside him. The sofa was one of the few comfortable pieces of furniture in her functional little house. It was oversize, soft, the sort of thing you sank into and then had trouble climbing out of. Its beige upholstery was now flecked with lavender, vermilion and China white, but it still looked just as inviting. Particularly with Mac sitting in the middle of it.

"Prove it," he said, his voice a gentle taunt.

She leaned up against a wall, then pulled herself back, checking her purple sweater for fresh paint. The tropical mural had dried, which was her main concern. She couldn't care less if her clothes, her hair, her skin were paint bedecked. "I don't have to prove anything to you, Mac. And I don't want to talk over old times. I'm... I'm sorry I gave in to temptation this afternoon and rammed into your car, but I promise that that will be my last moment of emotional weakness as far as you're concerned."

"Like hell."

"I beg your pardon?"

"You said you were coming out of your cocoon. Ready to taste the pleasures of the flesh. I think you should start on me."

For a moment she was speechless at his audacity. And at her own desire. "You have got to be out of your mind."

"You and I both know that ten years ago we had the best sex of our lives. You've confused it with some romantic passion, thinking it was wonderful because you were in love with me. I happen to know that's just a bunch of crap. It was great because we were young, healthy animals who enjoyed each other. In light of our intervening experience I think you'll find there's nothing magical about it. You'll discover I wasn't your one true love, and you'll therefore cease to hate me."

"Very logical. But I don't need to go to bed with you to know that you aren't my one true love. Besides," she added, with what she felt was just the right amount of insouciance, "you don't happen to turn me on."

His lazy pose on the couch was deceptive. He was off it so fast she didn't realize what was happening, didn't have enough time to marshal her defenses. One moment she was lounging against her freshly painted wall, in the next she was wrapped in his unyielding embrace, his body tight against her, his mouth hovering just above her breathlessly parted lips. "Oh, yeah?" he murmured. "Prove it." And he dropped his mouth down on hers.

It was a devastating kiss, slow and thorough. She was a witless participant, holding herself very still as he gently rubbed his lips over hers, dampening them. He nibbled on her full lower lip, tugging at it, and when her mouth parted he used his tongue, deftly, slyly, teasing her into a helpless response she'd been determined not to give. He took her arms, which had been lying limply at her sides, and pulled them around his waist. He took her mouth, this time with building passion, and there wasn't a moment's hesitation in her response. For the first time in her life she didn't think about the ramifications of what she was doing. Suddenly all that mattered was that fate had given her another chance, a stolen chance, and all the common sense in the world couldn't stop her.

His hands were moving up under her loose-fitting sweater, hard hands, warm hands, pulling the cotton knit up and over her head and tossing it into the shambles of the living room. He started to pull her back against him, and then he let out a muffled groan. "I'd forgotten your taste in exotic underwear. What do you call that color—peach?"

"You'd forgotten everything," she said, her voice low and strained. "Don't talk to me, Mac. Just make love to me."

He caught her face between his hands, holding her still as his dark eyes blazed down into hers. "Why? So you can close your eyes and pretend I'm Danny?"

"Why not? Aren't you?"

"Not anymore. And it's not going to be like ten years ago. This isn't time travel, Katharine. This is here and now." There was anger in his voice, anger in his mouth as he kissed her, anger in his hands as he picked her up and dropped her down on the sofa, following her down. She didn't know where that anger came from, and she didn't bother to question it. His body was hard and heavy as he covered hers, almost as if he wanted to frighten her into calling it off.

And indeed, she knew a moment's panic, alone in the darkness with a stranger who'd once meant her entire life. She pushed at him, and he levered himself away from her, his hips still pressed against hers, legs still intertwined. "Change your mind, Katharine?" he taunted. "Say the word, and I'll walk out of here."

She could feel him against the cradle of her thighs, the solid evidence of his arousal. In the few, short-lived relationships she'd experimented with in her early twenties, she'd never felt anything stronger than mild attraction. The feel of him, the knowledge of how much he wanted her, was a fire in her veins.

She didn't waste time with words. "Don't talk," she said again. And reaching up, she tore his shirt open, scattering buttons across the living room, exposing his smoothly muscled chest, sliding her hands along his ribs, holding him tightly.

Her peach lace bra had a complicated front hook, but it simply melted beneath Mac's deft hands. Her breasts felt achingly tender beneath his touch, and when his mouth fastened on one she let out a muffled cry of reaction, part pleasure, part pain.

He must have sensed the pain, for he tried to move away, but she simply caught his head and held him there, reveling in the luxury of simply feeling anything at all. When he angled himself away from her, stripping the rest of the clothes from her body, she made no protest, determined to want this, determined to have this. When he dumped his jeans on the floor beside the couch and lay back down with her she tried to pull him back on top of her, her hands feverish, desperate.

"Katharine," he said, his voice troubled.

"Don't talk," she said again. "I want you. Now." And vainly she tried to wrap her legs around him.

But he held her squirming body still, immobilizing her by putting one leg across hers, trapping her there. She flinched at the first touch of his hand on her belly, then willed herself to relax as it moved lower, to drift gently through the tight curls, then down between her legs. The sensation was uncomfortable, but she was determined to ignore it, telling herself this was what she wanted, this was what she needed.

She could sense the curious stillness in Mac's body, his sudden hesitation. She could feel him against her leg, hot and hard and ready for her, and she wanted to scream in frustration. "Now, Mac," she said again in a tight, angry voice. "I want you now."

Suddenly he pulled away, sitting up, leaving her lying alone on the couch. "No," he said briefly, "you don't."

She didn't move. Shame and embarrassment washed over her like a tidal wave. Her only attempts at making love in the past had ended in just this sort of failure. She'd thought that once she went to bed with Mac it would somehow break his hold over her. Instead he'd found her wanting.

She turned away from him, curling up on the couch in utter shame. "Go away," she said in a muffled voice.

"I'm not going to do that, either. Who are you trying to fool, Katharine? Yourself or me? You weren't the slightest bit turned on. Did you think I wouldn't notice?"

"Go away," she said again.

"Nope." He slid his arms around her, lifting her high against his chest, and stood. She was so surprised she had to look up, despite the misery in her eyes and the red staining her cheeks. "Clearly we went about this the wrong way. We simply need to go upstairs, find that nice big bed of yours and do it right."

"What makes you think we can?" she found herself asking.

A small, endearingly arrogant smile lit his dark face. "I have the utmost confidence in my abilities. I was simply making several assumptions about you that just aren't true. We'll approach it from a different angle." And he started toward the stairway, moving deftly through the obstacle course that was her living room.

It was a strange sensation, her skin against his, as he carried her upstairs with seemingly no effort. "Why would you want to bother?" she muttered when he reached the top of the stairs and headed for her bedroom.

"Because," he said, "you're worth it. And because, just maybe, I have my own demons to exorcise."

Chapter Fifteen

She was as frail and light as a bird in his arms, trembling slightly, and he knew perfectly well it wasn't from the cold. How he could have been so intent on his rampant lust that he hadn't noticed her response, or lack of it, should have been enough to dampen his ardor. Except that nothing could. The fact that she'd been faking it, pretending to be overcome with arousal, made him more determined than ever. He didn't know what he hoped to prove, or why, but he was going to make Katharine Lafferty feel as if she were twenty again. And tomorrow he'd worry about the consequences.

Her formerly spotless bedroom was a shambles of discarded clothing. The bed hadn't been made, so it was no problem to simply lay her down on the brightly hued sheet that had replaced her serviceable white one. She was looking up at him out of those huge eyes of hers, and there was no longer any semblance of passion. She looked plain scared, and not afraid to show it.

He was amazed at his own self-control. His hand was steady as it pushed her thick mane of hair away from her pale, moonlit face. He considered turning on the bedside light, but it no longer existed, having been hurled at his head a few short days ago. Moonlight had its advantages. She was already scared enough. The full view of his aroused, battle-scarred body might scare her off for good.

Leaning over her, he rested his forearms on the sheet beside her head, and he spoke very softly, just against her lips. "Are you afraid of me?"

She shook her head, a slight movement, but enough to gently brush her lips against his. Her eyes widened slightly in reaction, and then she held herself very still again.

"Then what are you afraid of?" he persisted. He could feel the soft tips of her breasts against his chest, and it took all his self-control not to reach over and cup them. He wanted to touch them, to touch her, but he'd gone too fast. For once in his life he was going to have to be patient.

"I'm afraid of me," she said finally. "I'm afraid I'll fall in love with you all over again, and this time when my heart breaks I'll just...die."

He didn't laugh. He didn't reassure her—she wouldn't have believed him. He didn't offer to leave. She wouldn't have let him. Instead he finally did the one thing she asked. He stopped talking.

Her mouth was so damned sweet beneath his. He stretched out on the wide bed beside her, taking his time, coaxing a response from her with gentle patience that he didn't know he had. She shivered when he touched her breast, but this time he was able to coax a pebbled arousal that her body couldn't hide, an arousal that begged for his mouth. She stirred on the bed, but this time she made no demands. He allowed her her passivity—for now she needed it, she needed to be made love to, to be cherished and aroused and eventually satiated. Her skin was like silk beneath his hands, smooth and supple, and when he finally slid his hand between her legs he was rewarded with the telltale dampness that was missing before.

He kissed her again, before she could start making demands, as his fingers began a slow, languorous caress. He could feel her reactions intimately, in the flush of her skin, the pounding of her heart, the racing of her pulses. He knew when to exert pressure, when to be gentle, when to delve deep into her mysteries, when to back off, and this time when she began to tremble it wasn't with fear.

He could have taken her then—he was more than ready for her, but something made him hold back. He wanted the first time to be just for her, some small thing he could give her. Ignoring her frantic hands on his shoulders, tugging at him, he continued the inexorable play of his hand on her, until suddenly she arched off the bed, her entire body convulsing in reaction, and his mouth drank in her cries.

He didn't allow her time to come down. Indeed, his own patience was at an end. He tore his mouth away from hers and moved between her legs, pulling them up around his hips. She was panting slightly, her eyes glazed from a lingering reaction, and then he pushed forward, against her, into her clinging dampness, forcing his way past the lingering contractions until he rested deep inside her.

He was the one who was trembling now, trembling in his need for her, trembling with the last vestiges of control. And then she reached her arms up around his neck, put her mouth on his and lifted her hips, pulling him in deeper still.

He groaned then, unable to think, to prolong, to gentle her. He pounded into her, shaking the bed, shaking the universe, unable to stop, as the darkness threatened to swallow him. He could feel her fingernails digging into his shoulders, hear her convulsive little cries in the back of her throat, but he was on the edge of madness. And then her body tightened around his, clenching in unmistakable climax, and he was gone, pouring himself into her, body and heart and soul.

It was a while before he realized he had to be crushing her. For some reason he was kissing the side of her neck, and she was arching against him like a contented kitten. He didn't usually indulge in kissing women once he'd finished making love to them. Usually they were content enough so that there was no need. There was a need this time. His need. He wanted to feel her sweat-damp skin beneath his mouth, he wanted to lick the tears from her face. He never wanted to move from the sweet, tight haven of her body.

Some ounce of sanity finally penetrated his foggy brain. "I must be crushing you," he muttered, lifting his head to look down at her. Mistake number one. Her huge eyes were shining with tears and love. She was looking at him as she'd looked at him ten years ago. And the worst part of it was, he wanted that look.

Reluctantly he moved away from her, stretching out beside her in the bed, pulling her tightly against him. She came willingly, threading her arms around him, resting her head against his shoulder. He could feel the dampness of her tears, he could hear the faint trace of a sigh that had to come from the very center of her heart. And he told himself he was a rotten, soulless bastard to have done this to her. And tightening his grip, he fell asleep.

HE MADE LOVE TO HER AGAIN at some point during the long, dark night. The moon had already set, and if she had a clock in her bedroom it was probably under a pile of discarded clothes, but that didn't matter. This time she was the one who woke him up, her mouth sweet and hot and demanding as it covered his body. This time she was on top, controlling their actions, taking her pleasure with an exuberant delight that simply compounded his own. She fell asleep on top of him, her slight weight no discomfort at all, and before he drifted off he wondered at his own cockiness. He'd been so certain the only reason she'd lingered in his brain was the fact that she'd been the first woman he'd ever thought he was in love with. That what, in the ensuing years, had loomed as the best sex of his life was in fact nothing more than youthful hormones and nostalgia.

Wrong. It still was the best sex he'd ever had in his life. He'd hardly been a monk in the ensuing years, and every single woman he'd bedded had been more experienced than Katharine. But none of them moved him even fractionally as much as Katharine did, up to and including the woman he'd made the mistake of being married to for two years.

He wished he knew what the hell he was doing. On top of everything else, he'd carried her upstairs like some romantic hero, stark naked. His pants, his wallet and the protection he was never without were still resting on the cluttered living-room floor. He could only hope Katharine was protected. But despite the fact that up until yesterday she had a fiancé, he doubted it. And he cursed himself for being careless enough to take such a risk for both of them.

The sun was just coming up when she slid off his body and curled up beside him, boneless and comfortable, and her heavy fall of hair tickled him. Catching a strand between his fingers, he forgot that he never slept with women. He closed his eyes, thinking he ought to find some way to get home. Jimmy was probably there, waiting, wondering where the hell he was at such an important time. And then he slept, better than he'd slept in ten long years.

KATHARINE DIDN'T WANT to wake up. She felt warm, heavy and incredibly happy, with a happiness that reached deep inside her and couldn't be defined. It was as if all the pain and sorrow had been wiped clean, that life had started as new and as fresh as the bright, early-morning sunlight pouring in her window and battering against her eyelids.

She couldn't fight anymore. She opened her eyes, slowly at first, and found she was looking directly into Mac's enigmatic blue gaze. Her mouth curved in a helpless smile, and to her vast relief he smiled back, clearly as wary as she was with the aftermath of last night.

"What time is it?" Her voice came out in a trembly sort of croak.

"I don't know. It must be pretty early but I can't see a clock anywhere around."

"That's right. I threw it against a wall." She didn't want to move away from him. His skin was smooth and warm and wonderful, pressed against hers, and she wanted to stay forever in the shelter of his arms.

Except that they weren't necessarily a shelter. And daylight had arrived, bringing reality back home, and a world to be faced, and questions to be answered.

She pulled away, reluctantly, and he let her go, reluctantly. She sat up in the bed, turned away from him, and her thick hair hung down her back, hiding her. She could feel his hand touch one strand, lightly, and then release it.

"You should probably go home," she said, staring at the floor in front of her.

"Not before we discuss something."

"I don't know if I'm in the mood for that right now. I'd really rather..."

"Are you protected?" The question was cool, blunt, embarrassing after the heedless passion of the darker hours. She was glad her face was turned away from him. She wouldn't have wanted him to see the flush that was climbing her cheeks, the woeful expression in her eyes.

"I wasn't exactly planning this," she said. "But I wouldn't think we'd need to worry. I didn't get pregnant ten years ago, and teenagers are notoriously fertile."

"I wondered about that."

"Did you? I thought I was wiped clean out of your mind in the hospital. What did you think I did, have an abortion?"

"There would have been nothing wrong with that."

She turned then, her face creased in fury. "You still don't get it, do you? I loved you! You were the only thing that mattered to me. When you died, my life was over. The only thing that would have given me any hope at all would have been if I were carrying your baby. When I found I wasn't, I almost killed myself. So don't tell me there'd be nothing wrong with having an abortion, you son of a..." As quickly as her rage erupted it vanished, as she stared at him.

He was lying stretched out on her bed, the bed that no man had ever shared, and the brightly colored sheet was draped loosely around his waist. His face was shadowed, remote, his eyes watching her with an increasing wariness.

But it wasn't his eyes that caught and held her. It was his body.

He'd filled out from the lean young man of ten years ago. His shoulders were broader, his chest more muscular, harder, more polished. He had a tan, though where it could have come from in the middle of a rainy Washington winter she couldn't begin to guess. He also had the most horrifying group of scars she'd ever seen in her life.

One went from his left shoulder, angling down to his right hip. Another small one ran parallel, plus several smaller jagged scars were scattered across his smooth, tanned torso, with a particularly nasty one on his left shoulder.

"Yeah, I know," he said with a wry note in his voice. "It's not a pretty sight. Billy Ray had a semiautomatic, and the surgeons were into speed more than delicacy."

She met his rueful expression then, and she was scarcely aware of the tears pouring down her face. For some reason, despite her rage, her despair, her passion, not until this moment did the full reality of what had happened to him hit her. Leaning forward, she pressed her lips against one cruel scar, and then another, her hair fanning out over both of them, her tears bathing each rip in his flesh.

She felt his hand reach out and catch her head, pulling her up toward him with gentle but inexorable pressure. "Don't," he said, his voice raw with pain. "For God's sake, Katharine, please don't cry." He kissed her mouth, drinking in the tears, he kissed her wet cheeks, her nose, her eyelids, and each touch of his lips began to heal her own invisible scars.

When she awoke again it was full daylight, and she was alone in the bed. She didn't need her smashed alarm clock to tell her it was midmorning and she was late for work. She lay there, facedown on the cotton sheets, and contemplated how utterly weary she was. And how alone.

And then she heard him moving around downstairs, and she smelled the seductive scent of coffee drifting up the stairs mingling with the lingering smell of turpentine and oil paints. The relief that washed through her was completely out of proportion with the circumstances. It wouldn't have been the end of the world if he'd simply gone home this morning without saying goodbye. It just would have felt like it.

She grabbed her fuchsia silk kimono from the place on the floor where she'd left it and headed for the bathroom.

Her face looked absurd. The endless tears she'd been crying, no matter what their cause, had bleached her eyelashes and left salty runnels down her skin. Her hair was a witch's tangle that defeated even her hairbrush. She washed as quickly as she could, terrified he'd disappear as magically as he'd arrived.

He was sitting in her beige kitchen, drinking coffee from a plain white mug, when she practically tumbled into the room. "I thought you'd left," she said breathlessly, accepting a cup of coffee automatically.

"I wanted to talk to you first."

She took a scalding sip, then realized with sudden surprise that he made it the way she liked it. Milk, no sugar. If he hadn't even remembered her face or her name after ten years, how could he remember the way she took her coffee? "Okay," she said warily, expecting something unpleasant. "Talk."

"Why don't you sit down?" He gestured to the tall white stool, a twin to the one he was perched on. He looked distant and formal again, not the man who'd carried her upstairs and stormed away her inhibitions, not the scarred, tender man who'd lain naked in her bed. His red cotton sweater added a touch of color to the plain room, and Katharine had the sudden, abstract notion of painting poppies on the ceiling.

She sat down, keeping her vivid silk robe pulled around her. "I'm not sure if I'm going to like this conversation," she said, taking another sip of her coffee.

"Why not?"

"Well, I figure you're going to say something unpleasant. Like, now we both know that sex between us is merely ordinary, or—"

That wiped the distant look from his face. "Ordinary?" he echoed in a voice loud enough to make her wince. "Ordinary?" he repeated in a calmer tone. "You call last night ordinary?"

"No. But then, I suspect my experience in these matters lags quite a way behind yours."

"Last night had nothing to do with ordinary, and we both know it."

She took another sip. "So that blows your theory that one quick roll in the hay would end whatever ties we have."

"Don't push."

"I'm not pushing," she protested. "You're the one who said you wanted to talk."

"Not about us."

"Why not?"

"Because I'm not ready to. There are other things that I have to deal with first, before we can sort out what's between us."

"Of course," she said affably, plastering an icy smile on her face. "You take care of the important things first."

"I didn't say that...." He slammed his coffee cup down on the white counter, and coffee sloshed over his hand. "You're enough to drive a saint mad."

"And you, Danny or Mac or whoever you are, are no saint." She was quite pleased with herself for that one. Until she met the leashed fury in his eyes, and decided she'd better back off. She didn't know quite what he'd do if she pushed him too far, and she wasn't about to find out. Not for one moment did she think he might hurt her. But he might walk out on her, and even if he was only gone a day the very thought was too painful to bear.

"Are you going to stop baiting me?" His voice was low and dangerous.

"Yes, sir. So what do you want to talk to me about? Car insurance?"

"Forget the car. I don't want you to go in to work today."

That was entirely unexpected. "Not go in to work? Why not? Unless you can think of a better way to spend the day...?" She let the delicate suggestion trail. Her body was sore in places she'd forgotten existed, and while a day spent in bed was appealing, she didn't know whether she'd survive.

"I want you to keep away from Henry Osmand."

She simply blinked. "Are you jealous?" It was unbelievable, but utterly wonderful to consider. He quickly destroyed such a notion.

"You've already broken your engagement, haven't you? And you never even went to bed with him? No, I'm not jealous. I don't trust him."

"Mac, I promise you, Henry's a perfect gentleman. He's not going to try anything with me...."

"It's not you that I don't trust him with. He's up to some hanky-panky at the bank. I've been following leads for weeks now, and something's about to break. I don't want you caught in the cross fire."

While that added concern kept her from hurling her coffee mug at his head, her mood had definitely altered. "What do you mean you've been following leads? Henry wouldn't think of doing anything dishonest. For one thing, he hasn't the imagination for it. For another, I would have noticed."

"I wondered why you didn't," Mac said, staring into his coffee cup.

She was speechless for a moment. When she finally found her voice it was low and dangerous. "Are you accusing me of financial misdealings, Mac?"

"Of course not."

"But you're accusing Henry. You'd better have some proof."

"I have every intention of getting exactly that. I certainly can't go to press on suppositions. But I don't want you in danger while I go about getting that proof."

"So I'm supposed to step out of the way while someone I once cared about gets railroaded by the so-called free press?" she said.

"Nobody's being railroaded," Mac said wearily. "Will you listen to reason, Katharine?"

"I'm being eminently reasonable. You're just not saying anything I want to hear."

He reached across the table and caught her wrist in his strong hand. It wasn't a painful grip, indeed, his thumb was absently caressing her throbbing pulse, but she knew she couldn't escape from him unless he was willing to let her go. "Katharine, it's dangerous for you to go to the bank today. I want you to stay home, go for a drive, do something. But don't go in to work today."

"I can't go for a drive. I did something to my car when I smashed it into yours. And why is today dangerous? What's going on here, Mac? Since when has the *Dexter Argus* become a haven for investigative reporting? The Osmands are decent, boring people, they aren't criminals. Why don't you go back to reporting on Grange bake sales and leave innocent people alone?"

His jaw hardened, and she wanted to reach out and smooth the rigid muscle. "I'm trying to leave innocent people out of it. For heaven's sake, Katharine, can't you trust me?"

She looked into his beautiful midnight-blue eyes, and she knew a moment's searing regret. "No."

He dropped her wrist, pushing back from the table. "Damn it, you're just like my ex-wife. Why won't women ever listen to reason?"

For a moment she couldn't believe her ears. It shouldn't have come as such a shock. She'd already ascertained that he hadn't been mourning for her as she'd mourned him. Most people married by the time they reached thirty-four, and at least half of that number divorced. She had absolutely no reason to feel betrayed all over again.

"Ex-wife?" she managed to say in a deceptively calm tone.

This time he wasn't as obtuse. "I don't have time to explain about her now. I want your promise that you'll stay put today. When I get back I'll tell you everything you want to know."

"Don't come back."

He stared at her blankly. "I beg your pardon?"

"I said don't come back." She hurled her half-empty coffee cup at his head, splattering the room with coffee, but he'd already grown used to ducking. "Get out of here, you lying, sneaking, rotten, miserable..." She'd expected him to walk out on her mid-tirade.

Instead he walked up to her, yanked her into his arms and silenced her furious mouth with his. She fought him for a moment, punching at him, but he seemed oblivious to her struggles. Particularly since her mouth was busy kissing him back.

When the fight finally left her he released her, setting her back down on the stool while she stared at him dazedly. "Stay put," he said. And he left without another word.

She heard the front door slam behind him. And suddenly she remembered another time, ten years ago, when he'd told her to stay put. She'd done as he'd told her, and almost lost him forever.

She'd be damned if she was going to make that mistake again. Picking her way carefully over the broken shards of her coffee mug, she headed for the stairs at a breakneck pace. By the time the taxi she'd called arrived, she was outside and waiting in the Washington drizzle.

Chapter Sixteen

Tuesday was usually a busy day at the Dexter National Bank. Several of the local businesses chose Tuesday as payday, and there was always a steady stream of customers.

But when Katharine had the taxi drop her off at the back entrance she noted with surprise that there were only a few cars there. Hank's Lincoln, Henry's more sedate Chrysler and a couple of others. At this time of day the back lot should have been packed.

Her watch was somewhere beneath the drop cloths that littered her house, but the taxi driver had informed her, to her horror, that it was after two o'clock. Banking transactions closed at that hour—maybe people had simply left early. Maybe a typhoon was due, a volcano eruption, a blizzard. Absurd as such fantasies were, Katharine couldn't escape the sense of impending doom. Something terrible, inescapable, was hanging over their heads, and she couldn't for the life of her imagine what it was.

The very idea of Henry's being involved in financial misconduct was absurd. She'd be far more likely to believe it of an old phony like Hank than...

Maybe that was it. She had to accept the fact that something must be going on at the Dexter bank. For one thing, Mac was too smart, too savvy a man to imagine something like that. He must have some very substantial leads. For another, she'd run across a number of inexplicable things, starting with her own hiring, and each time she'd asked a pointed question she'd been fobbed off with vague assurances.

The Sacramento-Silver Savings and Loan had been about to go belly-up when she'd gotten her offer from Dexter, an offer she'd jumped at like a hungry fish going after a juicy worm. While she wasn't to blame for the massive mismanagement and shady dealings that had made the S.S.S. and L. an industry nightmare, she'd been afraid that merely her association with the bank and sleazes like its president, J. Wallingford Cromwell, better known as Wally the Crumb to his irreverent junior officers, would put a shadow on her résumé.

The Dexter offer was manna from heaven, something she'd accepted without wondering why an out-of-state bank would make her such a generous offer when she hadn't even been sending out résumés. As the savings-and-loan scandal widened, besmirching everyone, she'd simply been grateful to have escaped in time.

Grateful enough not to have pushed on the troubling questions that had arisen during the past year. She'd been a foolish coward, in more ways than one, looking for a safe, painless life, but the past few days had taught her that safety was an illusion. Somewhere after the time she first set eyes on John T. MacDaniels she'd come back to life. And there was no retreating into her mindless utopia.

Whatever was going on at the Dexter bank was connected with Sacramento-Silver, or she'd eat Mac's crumpled MGB. But she didn't think Henry had anything to do with it. For one thing, he'd had nothing to do with hiring her—Hank had made the offer. For another, Hank was an old golfing buddy of Wally the Crumb. The old-boy network was still going strong—somewhere between Hank and Wally lay the answer.

The back door of the bank was locked, an unheard-of situation during daylight hours. Katharine simply used her key, stepping into the unnatural silence of the building with only the faintest prickling of fear at the back of her neck.

There was no one in sight. She looked out past the old-fashioned iron teller cages to the lobby. Completely deserted. There was a large sign across the front, facing out into the street, but the green shades had been pulled, foiling passersby. The bank was officially closed down. Maybe Mac had already had his scoop. Or maybe he'd missed it entirely when he was in bed with her.

"What are you doing here?" Estelle Richard, the plump, comfortable loan manager was heading for the door, her arms loaded with papers.

"Coming in to work. A little late, I'll grant you. What in heaven's name is going on here?"

Estelle shook her head. "You missed all the excitement. Would you believe someone called in a bomb threat next door at Calderwood's Insurance Agency? Now why would anyone want to bomb an insurance salesman? No, don't answer that question. You and I both know that Scott is one of the sweetest guys in the world. The police figured it was just some bored teenager, but they still had to follow through and evacuate half the block. By the time they found there was nothing there Hank decided it wasn't worth reopening. I imagine it'll be a madhouse around here tomorrow."

"But it's perfectly safe now? The bomb was definitely a hoax?" Katharine persisted.

"Supposedly. Hank still thought it would be better if everyone cleared out. Besides, the computer system's down, and you know no one can accomplish a blessed thing when the computers go out."

Katharine's sense of distrust was increasing by leaps and bounds. "This computer system never goes down, at least not completely. It has too many safety overrides."

"Well, the impossible happened. We're lucky the security system still works. That new boy, Jimmy Martin, disappeared a few hours ago and no one's seen any trace of him."

Uneasiness quickly shifted into outright fear. "Isn't anyone looking for him?"

"Things have been pretty busy the last few hours. The police department's had more than they can handle. I'm sure he'll show up sooner or later. I'm heading out now, and I'm the last one to leave. Why don't you come along, too? Hank doesn't want anyone hanging around."

"Is he still here? His car's outside."

"No one's here, I told you. He and Henry went off for some private discussion and they haven't been back since." Estelle reached for the door handle. "You coming?" she asked again.

"Not right now. I want to catch up on a little work, seeing as how I've only got two weeks left."

"I told you, the computers are down."

"Believe it or not, I do have paperwork. I'm not as firm a believer in electronics as Hank is. See you tomorrow, Estelle."

Estelle shrugged her plump shoulders. "Suit yourself."

Katharine waited until she heard Estelle's car drive away. And then she headed down the empty hallways to her office.

It was odd—she used to feel so at home, at peace in the empty bank. But not today. There was a cold malice in the air, the sense of something lingering, and if she had any sense at all she'd turn around, head home and wait for Mac to return like the great white hunter and inform his meek little woman what had happened.

Well, she wasn't meek, and she wasn't the type to sit and wait. Whether or not she was his woman still remained to be seen. But she wasn't leaving the supposedly deserted environs of the Dexter National Bank until she made a thorough search and found out everything she could possibly find out. Including what had happened to the duplicitous Jimmy Martin.

She stopped at her office more out of habit than curiosity, but the moment she poked her head in she had the very strong sense that something was different. Up until several days ago she'd been a woman of compulsive neatness, and her metamorphosis hadn't had a chance to hit her office.

Her loan applications should have been in a neat stack on the lower right-hand corner of her desk, her business accounts on the upper left. Three number-two pencils, freshly sharpened, should have rested at the edge of her spotless blotter, and her computer terminal should have been at a precise forty-five-degree angle.

To the untrained eye there would have been no difference. But to Katharine the evidence screamed at her. Someone had been rifling her desk. But why?

She heard their voices coming from a distance, and even in her abstracted state she knew them well. Hank, Sr., and Henry, Jr., father and son involved in a bitter, low-voiced quarrel.

She considered diving under her desk, then thought better of it. Whoever had searched her office might not have finished, and if she was found hiding she'd have a hard time explaining it away. She couldn't leave—the two men were coming from the back hallway. She could either head to the right, ending up in the spacious lobby of the deserted bank, or to the left and the kitchen area that was one of the perks for the pampered employees.

She decided on the kitchen, simply because there'd be more places to hide, either there or in the adjacent dining room or rest rooms. There was even a possibility of climbing out a window, though that was unlikely. The bank was wired to prevent intruders—each window was securely locked and fastened with an alarm that could raise the dead.

She barely made it to the kitchen before she heard their voices, and she cursed to herself. Just her luck—instead of heading to Hank's elegant office where they could argue in comfort they were also heading for the kitchen. She considered opening the refrigerator and making herself a sandwich in an attempt to pass off her presence in the deserted bank as natural, then decided her hands were shaking too much to carry it off. Their voices were getting louder, angrier, and she didn't dare hesitate a moment longer.

She ducked into the first door she came to, then stopped dead still as she surveyed the one room in the Dexter bank building she'd never seen.

The men's rest room was clean, blue tiled and chilly. It was also occupied, in a manner of speaking. Jimmy Martin was lying stretched out on those cold blue tiles, bound and gagged and obviously unconscious.

She was about to rush over to him, to make sure he was still breathing, when the swinging door banged open, slamming her into the narrow space against the wall. Whoever stood there didn't move, didn't let the door swing shut, thank heavens, to see her standing there, caught like a rat in a trap.

"He's still out cold." Hank's booming voice sounded cheerful, ominously so. "I told you there was nothing to worry about. By the time he comes to there won't be a trace of evidence. I've been spreading the word that he had a drug problem—Monty down at the police station isn't about to take an outsider's word over mine."

"You've got to stop this," Henry said fiercely, and Katharine allowed herself a brief flare of triumph. At least she hadn't misjudged him.

The door swung shut again, and she let out a sigh of relief. She didn't dare move. She could only hope that whatever they'd done to Jimmy, he had a tough enough constitution to survive it.

"Don't be such a wimp, Henry," Hank said irritably. "I've gotten this down to an art. Once the delivery's made it'll take me a couple of hours to launder it through the computer and transfer it across the border. There'll be no trace at all, and we'll have done a favor for a friend. Your godfather, as a matter of fact. Not to mention having made a tidy profit both for ourselves and our stockholders."

"Stockholders," Henry said faintly. "You mean you pass the money along?"

"I told you, I've got it down to an art. If you'd just lend me a hand I could handle it in even less time, minimizing the danger. This is the last time, I promise you, boy. Once we

get this handled Wallingford's getting out of the country
and we're back on the straight and narrow."

"No."

"You wouldn't turn your own father in," Hank said, the
faint pleading note in his voice nothing but a sham. He knew
perfectly well Henry wouldn't do such a thing.

"I haven't yet. I've suspected something for over a year,
and I've been cowardly enough to turn my back on it. But
no more, Father. This is the last time."

"The absolute last. I promise." Hank's voice moved away
from the closed door, but Katharine knew he hadn't gone
far. She was so intent on listening to the conversation that
she didn't notice that someone was opening the door to a
stall she'd assumed was empty.

"You've got to understand, Henry," Hank was saying.
"This savings-and-loan mess has affected everybody. Wally's been a victim just as much as his investors. There's
nothing wrong with trying to help him salvage something...."

"If he's a victim why is he leaving the country?" Henry
said coldly. "And he's salvaging something in the neighborhood of six million dollars, which is hell of a lot better
than his investors."

"Six million minus our cut, which is substantial," Hank
reminded him, not without some misplaced pride. "Obviously we're not going to agree on this. I need you to promise you'll continue to keep your mouth shut, even if you
won't help me."

There was a dead silence. A silence pervasive enough that
Katharine heard the faint creak of the hinges. Looking up,
she saw Mac moving across the blue-tiled floor, quiet as a
ghost. He knelt by Jimmy's supine body, pausing long
enough to send a glare in her direction that would have par-
alyzed her if she hadn't already been stiff with fear. She
watched as he checked Jimmy's pulse, then nodded with
satisfaction. She breathed her own sigh of relief, too loudly,
and then realized the two men were no longer saying a word.

Suddenly Hank's voice broke through, louder again, closer to the door, and once more she flattened herself against the wall, hoping to God the man didn't have to use the facilities. The urinals were in direct sight of the door—once he turned to leave he'd see her.

"I told you, there's no proof, and that snoopy newspaper editor isn't going to get any," he said loudly. "As for that nosy ex-fiancée of yours, I couldn't find anything on her desk that suggests she's figured out what's been going on, but she's too damned smart for her own good. That's why Wally got her out of Sacramento. I've managed to keep her so busy she hasn't had much time to wonder about certain things, and I'd been counting on you to fill up her social time. Why you let her break the engagement is beyond me. If you won't do anything else to help me, at least get her to agree to marry you again. Romance the woman, boy. Haven't you got a manly bone in your body?"

The bathroom door slammed open with sudden force. Before she had time to cower, Hank had reached in and yanked her from behind the door, dragging her into the kitchen. In her panic she fought him, looking over her shoulder for her white knight. Mac had disappeared once again, leaving her to fend for herself.

"Look what I found in the men's room, Henry," Hank boomed, shoving her into the kitchen. "The little lady herself. You never told me she was into kinky tricks. I wouldn't have thought that would have been your thing at all."

Henry barely gave her a worried glance. Clearly he was too caught up in his father's situation to spare much attention to a snoopy ex-fiancée. "Let her go, Father. You're just making this worse."

"I don't think it can get much worse. I've got a son who's going to turn his back on his own father, I've got a nosy security man tied up in the men's room, I've got a young lady who's too smart for her own good. This is beginning to annoy me." He shoved Katharine down in a chair with a little too much force.

She should be terrified, she told herself. Hank, if he wasn't deranged, was so egocentric that he thought he was invincible. "You're not going to get away with this, Hank." She tried for a firm voice, but it came out lamentably wavery.

"Why not? There's no proof. I can cover my tracks—having you pussyfoot through my computers taught me to do just that. If anyone wants to go searching for evidence they're going to have a damned hard time finding it."

A sudden, shrill buzzing sliced through the kitchen, making them all jump. "Who the hell is that?" Hank said furiously, reaching into his pocket and pulling out a very serviceable-looking gun. Both Katharine and Henry stared at it in numb horror. "The delivery isn't due for another hour. Let's just hope it isn't some dumb cop."

The buzzing sounded again, and at the same time Katharine saw the men's room door begin to open. Hoping to distract Hank, she tried to stand. "I think I should go see..."

"Sit down!" Hank roared, but she kept moving, determined to distract him.

"Father, the bathroom..." that wimp Henry said nervously.

Hank spun around, the gun drawn.

"Mac, watch out!" Katharine shrieked. "He's got a gun."

Her mistake. Hank didn't start blasting away at the bathroom door like someone out of a cheap TV show. He simply grabbed her, clamping her against his slightly paunchy body, and held the gun to her neck.

"Come on out, MacDaniels. I've got the little lady right here, and if you don't want to see her hurt you'll come out very slowly."

"Father..." Henry pleaded, his hands hanging limply at his sides as he made no effort to help her.

"Shut up. I know what I'm doing. Are you coming out, MacDaniels?"

The door opened, slowly enough, revealing Mac. His hands were empty, held over his head, and his face was distant and unreadable. "Don't you think things have gone far enough?" he asked in a deceptively calm voice. "Let her go before you make any more stupid mistakes."

"I haven't made any mistakes at all. I found Ms. Lafferty trying to make off with bearer bonds. My son was trying to talk me into not pressing charges, but I haven't made up my mind."

"Fast thinking," Mac said. "So why are you holding a gun at her throat? And why is a man tied up on the bathroom floor?"

"That's her accomplice. She does seem to be a regular Mata Hari, doesn't she? She's got my son wrapped around her little finger, and now it appears like she's got you, too. Pretty slick work for someone who seemed so harmless."

"Let her go and we can work out a deal," Mac said, and Katharine heard the edge of desperation in his voice.

"I'm not interested in deals. No one has anything on me yet."

"Maybe not. But it shouldn't take long."

Whoever had been ringing the doorbell somehow managed to get in. They could hear a strange creaking noise as they stood poised in the kitchen, a tableau of fear and danger, waiting for fate.

The reality was momentarily prosaic. A tall man in an ill-fitting jumpsuit proclaiming Bossie's Milk's the Best wheeled milk cartons into the kitchen. "Door was unlocked," he announced, seemingly oblivious to the tensions in the little room.

And then Katharine recognized Wally the Crumb beneath the ill-fitting uniform.

Everything happened in a blur. The bathroom door slammed open again, revealing Jimmy and half a dozen uniformed policemen, guns pointed directly at Hank. And therefore at Katharine.

"Freeze!" several of them shouted in a ragged chorus, but Hank only tightened his grip.

"I don't think so," he said. "I'm getting out of here, and the little lady's going with me. You can't shoot me without endangering her, and I don't think Dexter's finest is going to risk that. Out of my way, Henry."

"No, Father."

Katharine was too frightened to feel even a momentary surprise, but Hank simply ignored him, dragging her past his motionless son. Henry's bravery was only verbal, and he made no move to stop the old man. And then something broke through, and he shoved at his father with all his force, so that his grip on Katharine broke and for a moment she was dazed and free, still too shocked to run.

Mac moved, so quickly it was almost a blur, diving toward them. He tackled Katharine, bringing her down out of Hank's reach and then rolling away as the gun spat in his direction. And then it was over, the policemen clambering over them to grab the suddenly defeated Hank.

Katharine didn't move, huddled on the floor as waves of reaction washed over her. A second later a pair of strong arms were around her, and Mac was drawing her to her feet, holding her shivering body against his, while in the background someone was droning on about "you have the right to remain silent."

She glanced up, about to tell Mac she loved him, when she saw the delivery man trying to sneak out the back. "Don't let him get away," she shrieked. "He's part of it."

Jimmy moved fast, collaring him. "Who the hell is he?"

"Wally the Crumb," she said, glaring at the fallen bank executive.

"J. Wallingford Cromwell," Henry said in a low voice. "President of the Sacramento-Silver Savings and Loan."

Suddenly everything got very businesslike as the motley crew got herded toward the door. Henry moved along with them, but at least he wasn't handcuffed. "I trust we can count on your cooperation, Mr. Osmand," Jimmy was saying, sounding years older than his boyish cover as a security guard.

"Yes," he said wearily. "It's the least I can do." He paused to look back at Katharine, and his heart was in his eyes. "Kay, I'm sorry...."

Mac's arms tightened around her, just slightly. "I know, Henry," she said. "I know."

Mac didn't say a word as he bundled her into the rental sedan he had parked outside the bank. She was hardly aware of the looks passing between him and the policemen left on guard, hardly aware of anything at all until they were back in her untidy house with the early winter evening closing down around them.

"We didn't have to go with the police," she said, belatedly realizing that blessing as she wandered into her living room.

"Don't worry, they'll get to us sooner or later," Mac said in an abstracted voice as he turned lights on against the gathering gloom.

"I suppose so," she said, getting on to more important things. "You're jealous of Henry."

"Why should I be?"

"You shouldn't. I feel sorry for him, but I don't love him. I love you. And you still love me."

"Don't be ridiculous," he said irritably. "Who said I ever loved you?"

"You did. Many times, as a matter of fact," she announced triumphantly. "And you still do. You risked your life to save mine. You must love me."

"Hank wasn't going to shoot you."

"He almost shot you," she pointed out.

"Listen, Katharine," he began, sounding harassed.

"No," she said firmly, suddenly very sure of herself. "You listen to me." She came to him and began unbuttoning his shirt. "You love me. You always have, you always will and you're too damned stubborn to realize it. I know perfectly well you couldn't have shown up here by accident. Fate doesn't work that way. You came to find me. You don't have to lie anymore, Mac. Or Danny. Or whoever the hell you are. I love you. We were made for each other, and

I don't want to hear any more arguments." Leaning up, she kissed him full on the mouth. His response was instantaneous, his arms coming around her and holding her tight against him.

When they finally paused for breath she looked up at him, love shining in her eyes. "Now are you going to keep arguing," she demanded, "or are we going to go to bed?"

"We're going to bed," he said flatly. "We'll argue in the morning."

Chapter Seventeen

This time Katharine woke up before Mac did. She was simply too happy to stay in bed, sleeping peacefully in his arms. Besides, after the past two nights she needed a long, soaking bath to soothe her aches and pains, she needed coffee, she needed time to just sit and grin like a happy idiot.

The bath did such wonders that she was almost tempted to crawl back into bed with him, then thought better of it. He needed his sleep. They'd kept each other awake most of the long, glorious night, and she had a vested interest in taking care of him. They'd lost too much time already—she wanted to make the most of the next sixty or seventy years.

She grabbed the phone on the first ring just as she was sitting down to coffee, hoping it wouldn't wake him up. The familiar-unfamiliar voice on the other end sent the first prickles of uneasiness through her buoyant optimism.

"MacDaniels there?" the voice asked.

Her first instinct was to deny it. Who would possibly know he was there? Unless it was the police, ready to ask the questions they'd been able to avoid so far.

It would be a waste of time to deny it. "He's asleep right now," she said carefully. "Who's calling?"

"Asleep, is he?" The man on the other end chuckled. "I knew it was going to work out."

Suddenly she recognized that voice from another, terrible time. And she had the sense that this time wasn't going to be much of an improvement. "Lefty?" she said. "Is that you?"

"Imagine you remembering, Katharine," Lefty Siegal said. "You were feeling so rotten I didn't think you even knew I was around. I'm sorry I couldn't tell you the truth about Mac, but it had to be that way."

She had a sudden, painful vision of Lefty holding her hand, holding her while she sobbed against his burly shoulder. "You knew all the time?" she asked, her voice low and steady.

"Of course I did. I wasn't sure that he was going to come and work for us at the crime task force then, but I thought the chances were good. And look at how well it's worked out. You two are back together again. Maybe you can even talk him into staying on another year or two. Burnout level is high on a job like his, but you ought to be giving him a new lease on life."

"A job like his?"

"Sure. We have an even higher turnover rate than the FBI and CIA combined. Working undercover takes a toll on a man, even when it's something that he likes. He'd done newspapers before, so I knew this last job would be a piece of cake. He usually specializes in something a little more dangerous than white-collar crime, but I wanted to give you two a chance. I felt I owed you."

Mac had entered the kitchen, dressed, his shirt still unbuttoned, a wary expression in his eyes. "You sent him here?" she asked, wanting to be very clear on this.

"Of course. He had no idea you were there. Came as a hell of a surprise to him, I can tell you that. But I knew it would work out, given time. I'm glad as hell Osmand senior had sticky fingers, or I don't know how I would have gotten the two of you together. But all's well that ends well, isn't it?"

"Sure," Katharine said, her voice numb. She set the phone down on the white counter very carefully. "It's for you," she said. And she walked past him, out of the room.

MAC'S PHONE CONVERSATION with Lefty was brief, furious and to the point. By the time he went in search of Katharine he was shaking with what he told himself was rage. And knew, deep down inside, was fear.

She was sitting upstairs in her white bedroom, the welter of brightly colored clothes strewn around her. She wasn't moving, wasn't looking at anything in particular. She simply sat there.

"Are you going to let me explain?" he asked in a rough voice.

She looked up at him, surprised. "I hadn't realized you were still here," she said in a pleasant, detached tone.

"Where the hell would I have gone?"

"Back to where you came from. To your crime task force with Lefty Siegal, wherever that is. After all, you've accomplished what you came for. Hank Osmand is in jail, along with Wally the Crumb. Everything worked out very neatly."

"I never told you I came here for you. I always said I didn't know you were here."

"Of course," she said. "I don't know why I didn't believe you. Maybe it was your history of dishonesty that made me assume everything you said was a lie, particularly the things I didn't want to believe." She smiled up at him brightly, but her eyes were hollow and dead. "You've earned your early retirement. You've even taken care of unfinished business with me. Now you won't have to worry about some fool woman mourning her life away. But then, you'd forgotten I'd existed, hadn't you? So you wouldn't have been worried anyway."

"Katharine..."

"So there was no need for Lefty Siegal's ham-handed matchmaking after all, was there? I hope you tell him so when you see him next." She kept this all up in a cheerful, pleasant little voice, never meeting his eye.

"Look at me, Katharine."

She stared down at her hands. They were lying loosely in her lap. She still had a light bandage around one, and there were flecks of paint on her long, unvarnished nails. He wanted to go down on his knees to her, to take her hands in his and say...

He couldn't say it. Part of him was still fighting it, still not ready to trust it. And he wasn't going to be forced into any kind of statement that he might spend the rest of his life regretting. He was never going to tell Katharine Lafferty that he loved her until he was absolutely certain it was for eternity. He owed her nothing less.

"Katharine," he said roughly, "what do you want from me?"

She did look at him then, and he saw the answer in her huge, tear-filled brown eyes. But she gave him a calm smile, ignoring the pain. "I want you to go away," she said simply.

And without another word, that was exactly what he did.

"YOU'RE A BEAUTIFUL BRIDE, Kay," Melissa said, fluffing the lacy white veil around her face. "A little pale, but then, all brides are pale, aren't they? Maybe you could use a little rouge."

"It doesn't matter," Katharine said. "The veil will be covering my face, anyway."

"Don't you want your wedding day to be perfect?" Melissa demanded with a certain amount of asperity.

Katharine looked at her bridesmaid. Melissa had more emotion invested in this ceremony than she did, she thought with her usual absence of emotion. But then, the entire Osmand clan needed something to cheer them up, and she and Henry were the perfect sacrifices. While the front page of the *Dexter Argus*, under new management, was filled with Hank Osmand's upcoming trial, the society pages were filled with the Osmand wedding. It was no wonder the entire family was feeling schizophrenic.

"I just want my wedding day to be over with," Katharine said calmly. "I wish we hadn't had to go through all this fuss. I would have been happy enough with a civil ceremony." Indeed, the two months needed to plan this elaborate affair had only been two months of doubts that she'd continued to squash down. Two months of waiting to see whether Mac would call, would write, would make any move in her direction. He hadn't.

"You know why we're going through this big to-do. Henry wants to show the world that the Osmands aren't beaten."

Katharine bit back her instinctive retort. It had been hard climbing back into her cocoon after Mac had left that morning two months ago. It had taken three coats of white paint to cover her mural, and even now she could still see traces of the tropical birds.

She'd gone back to beige clothes and her hair tied back. She'd agreed to Henry's renewed proposal out of apathy more than anything else, and Henry was willing to accept her on those terms, even though her interest in her upcoming nuptials was just about nil. She'd let Melissa and Henry choose her wedding dress, saying she had no taste in such matters. Looking down at it, she swallowed her dismay. The damned thing had hoop skirts like something out of *Gone With the Wind*. It had lace dripping from every possible spot, it had white ribbons and seed pearls and embroidered cupids, and it came equipped with a train that needed fourteen flower girls to manage. Since there were no flower girls available it was up to Melissa and Katharine to manage on their own, and the very thought made Katharine's ulcer flare up.

The veil was the worst of all. Fully as long as the train, it consisted of six layers of tulle, attached to something that resembled a white satin bird's nest. When she'd first seen it she'd thought Melissa was kidding. She wasn't.

"Aren't you going to look at yourself?" Melissa demanded. They were in the upstairs lounge of the Dexter Country Club. It was an unseasonably warm and sunny day in mid-February, a beautiful day for a wedding. Katharine had counted on clouds and rain to match her mood when they'd reset the date, but fate had, as usual, dealt her a losing hand.

Katharine glanced at herself in the mirror. "Lovely," she said briefly. "Are you ready?"

Melissa shook her head in patent disgust. She was currently madly in love with one of the bank examiners who'd taken up residence in Dexter and in Henry's back pocket, and she thought the world should be equally enraptured. "We have to wait until someone comes to get us. Just relax, Kay."

"I'm relaxed," Katharine said, sinking down on a stool and watching with dismay as her skirt billowed up around her.

"That's part of the problem," Melissa complained as she moved to the window that overlooked the parking area. "A bride shouldn't be relaxed. A bride should be fussing with her appearance, nervous as a cat. You just sit there looking like an ice cream sundae."

"You chose the dress," Katharine pointed out mildly.

Melissa stared out the window. "Don't you love Henry, Kay?"

It didn't used to be a lie. Two and a half months ago she would have said yes and never doubted it. Now she knew it simply wasn't true.

But so did Henry. And he was still willing to risk it. Because he loved her. Because he wanted to prove to the world that everything was normal, even as his boisterous, egocentric father awaited trial. Because he thought he could make her love him, and she was determined to do so.

Fortunately Melissa wasn't expecting an answer, too caught up in the sight outside. "There's father, the old reprobate. I'm surprised you invited him to the wedding."

"We could hardly exclude the father of the groom, could we?"

"At least you wouldn't let him give you away," Melissa said. "Maybe that'll teach him a lesson."

For the first time that day, and probably the only time, Katharine laughed. "There's no limit to the ends I'll go to," she murmured.

"Look at that car," Melissa murmured. "I've always wanted one like that."

"Like what?" Katharine asked, not really caring.

"I'm not sure. Maybe it's a Jaguar. Or a Lotus. I'm not that familiar with British cars, but it sure is a beauty."

She was unprepared for the pain that sliced through her. She hadn't expected to think of Mac, had fought off all memory of him. And now someone's stupid British sports car had snuck in behind her defenses and brought the pain soaring back.

"Are you ready, Katharine?" Henry stood in the door, handsome and elegant. He'd taken to calling her Katharine since they'd reinstated their engagement, and she hadn't bothered to stop him. She tried very hard to keep no secrets from him, but as usual the guilt came back every time she looked at him.

"You shouldn't be here!" Melissa shrieked. "It's bad luck."

"We're not worried about luck, Melissa," Henry said. "Besides, there's been a slight change in plans. Seth Price was feeling a little faint, so he won't be able to escort Katharine up the aisle. So I brought in someone else."

Standing behind him was a burly little man, not more than five feet four, with a bald head, tiny little raisin eyes, a shaggy gray mustache and impressive jowls. Katharine simply stared at him for a moment, and then recognition dawned.

"Lefty," she said, not moving, when she wanted to throw her arms around him and cry again, cry as she hadn't since Mac had walked away from her.

"Hi, there, Katharine. Got any objections to me giving you away?"

She had a thousand, but she shook her head, rising, and gave Lefty her arm. In the distance she could hear the wedding march. Henry's choice—safe, traditional, easy to move to. Melissa rushed forward and pulled the veil over her face, shoved the bouquet into her hand and started ahead of her, moving at a decorous, measured pace.

"You look beautiful, Katharine," Lefty said in a hushed voice. "You must be pretty nervous, huh?"

"I'm not nervous." They were moving past the hordes of guests, nearly the entire town of Dexter, and every eye was trained on her.

"Could have fooled me. Why is your hand trembling?"

"It's cold."

"It's hotter'n hell in here," Lefty said frankly, glancing nervously around him. "Listen, Katharine, you can't do this to him."

"Can't do what to whom?"

"Geez, I love it when you say whom. You're the only person I know who can do it."

They were halfway to the front of the room. The justice of the peace was waiting, Henry was waiting, his gray eyes watching her with a curious resignation.

"Shut up, Lefty," Katharine said sweetly.

"He loves you. The poor sap's been eaten up alive, trying to figure out what's best. When he heard you were going to get married he went on a bender that'll go down in the history books. You marry Osmand and Mac'll never get over it."

"He'll survive. He's tough."

"He'll survive like you did when you thought he was dead. Survival is all it'll be. He's already told me he won't retire, but the man's burned out. If I send him out again he'll come back dead. Then how will you feel?"

Melissa had reached the front and taken a decorous left-hand turn, waiting for Katharine to reach them.

"Did he send you here to plead his case for him, Lefty?"

"Hell, no. He'd kill me if he knew I was anywhere near you. He agreed to drive me to the wedding because he wants to look at you one last time. But he wouldn't even come in. He's sitting in his car, waiting for this to be over, waiting for one last glimpse of you."

"You're breaking my heart," she said as they reached Henry.

"You don't have a heart to break," Lefty shot back.

"Not for ten years," she agreed.

The next few minutes passed in a daze. Lefty handed her over to Henry, putting her icy-cold hand in his, and the justice of the peace, one of Henry's less felonious godfathers, began a traditional ceremony.

She could feel Henry watching her, his gray eyes troubled, as the words sailed right over her head. She heard the words about "let him speak now or forever hold his peace" and she held her breath, her hand clenching Henry's tightly, as she waited for Lefty to speak up, waited for Melissa to protest.

In the sudden, endless silence, Henry cleared his throat, and Katharine glanced up at him, startled. For the first time her eyes looked into his, and a wealth of reluctant understanding passed between them. Without a word he let her go, just a tiny nod, a wry smile, and his hand released hers.

She turned as the justice of the peace was about to go on. Standing in the sunny doorway, not moving, was a tall, motionless figure.

He was wearing jeans, a leather jacket and boots. He looked the antithesis of Henry's proper attire, and his expression was guarded. It didn't matter. Suddenly Katharine was alive again, gloriously, painfully, joyously alive.

"Well," she said, her voice carrying through the hushed, packed room. "Are you just going to stand there, or are you going to say something?"

That moved him. He straightened up, and there was a devilish light of pure happiness in his eyes. "Get your tail out of here, woman," he said. "You belong with me."

The shock wave that rippled through the middle-class assemblage was even greater than the one felt by the small town when Hank Osmand was arrested. White-collar crime they could understand. Social solecism was a little harder to accept.

Katharine raced down the center aisle, her train and veil flying after her, her absurd hoop skirts knocking against the chairs as she went. Flinging herself into his arms, she was totally oblivious to the shocked guests she was leaving behind. All she was aware of was Mac, dragging her toward an old Jaguar XKE.

He paused long enough to kiss her, with a hard, fierce passion that left her breathless. "I love you," he announced, kissing her eyelids. "I love you, I love you, I love..."

She reached up and caught his face between her hands. "I know," she said gently. "I know."

"We're driving to Nevada. We'll be there by three in the morning, and we can get married then."

"Fine," she said with a breathless laugh.

"We'll live anywhere you want. I can get a real job on a newspaper. I've got money, you can paint, you can be a banker, you can do anything you please."

"Fine."

"But if you ever do a fool thing like think you can marry someone else I'll sic Lefty on you."

"He does a good job. I have only one problem."

"What's that?"

"How is this ridiculous dress going to fit in your teensy little car?"

IN THE END IT WAS very simple. Henry walked through the crowd of sympathetic well-wishers, his sister by his side, his back straight and proud, disdaining any sympathy. He decided that despite the fact that he'd been stood up at the altar and his heart was broken he was feeling not bad at all. Damn good as a matter of fact. Sort of noble and long-suffering. A lot of mileage could be made out of that when Hank went to court. Maybe old Judge Miller, sitting in the second row with his tear-bedewed wife, might be willing to give the old man a suspended sentence.

By the time he reached the front door Katharine had gone. Tearing down the highway was a hunter-green Jaguar with a mound of white lace trailing along behind it. A moment later the veil went sailing, left behind on the road.

"Are you okay, Henry?" Melissa asked.

Katharine was going to live a colorful, exciting life. The very thought of it was enough to tire a man out, Henry thought. When it came right down to it, he'd had a lucky escape. ''Just fine, Melissa. Let's go get drunk.''

Which is exactly what he did.

HARLEQUIN®

Don't miss these Harlequin favorites by some of our most distinguished authors!
And now, you can receive a discount by ordering two or more titles!

HT #25645	THREE GROOMS AND A WIFE by JoAnn Ross	$3.25 U.S./$3.75 CAN.	☐
HT #25648	JESSIE'S LAWMAN by Kristine Rolofson	$3.25 U.S.//$3.75 CAN.	☐
HP #11725	THE WRONG KIND OF WIFE by Roberta Leigh	$3.25 U.S./$3.75 CAN.	☐
HP #11755	TIGER EYES by Robyn Donald	$3.25 U.S./$3.75 CAN.	☐
HR #03362	THE BABY BUSINESS by Rebecca Winters	$2.99 U.S./$3.50 CAN.	☐
HR #03375	THE BABY CAPER by Emma Goldrick	$2.99 U.S./$3.50 CAN.	☐
HS #70638	THE SECRET YEARS by Margot Dalton	$3.75 U.S./$4.25 CAN.	☐
HS #70655	PEACEKEEPER by Marisa Carroll	$3.75 U.S./$4.25 CAN.	☐
HI #22280	MIDNIGHT RIDER by Laura Pender	$2.99 U.S./$3.50 CAN.	☐
HI #22235	BEAUTY VS THE BEAST by M.J. Rogers	$3.50 U.S./$3.99 CAN.	☐
HAR #16531	TEDDY BEAR HEIR by Elda Minger	$3.50 U.S./$3.99 CAN.	☐
HAR #16596	COUNTERFEIT HUSBAND by Linda Randall Wisdom	$3.50 U.S./$3.99 CAN.	☐
HH #28795	PIECES OF SKY by Marianne Willman	$3.99 U.S./$4.50 CAN.	☐
HH #28855	SWEET SURRENDER by Julie Tetel	$4.50 U.S./$4.99 CAN.	☐

(limited quantities available on certain titles)

	AMOUNT	$
DEDUCT:	10% DISCOUNT FOR 2+ BOOKS	$
ADD:	POSTAGE & HANDLING	$
	($1.00 for one book, 50¢ for each additional)	
	APPLICABLE TAXES**	$_____
	TOTAL PAYABLE	$_____
	(check or money order—please do not send cash)	

To order, complete this form and send it, along with a check or money order for the total above, payable to Harlequin Books, to: **In the U.S.:** 3010 Walden Avenue, P.O. Box 9047, Buffalo, NY 14269-9047; **In Canada:** P.O. Box 613, Fort Erie, Ontario, L2A 5X3.

Name: _____

Address: _____ City: _____

State/Prov.: _____ Zip/Postal Code: _____

**New York residents remit applicable sales taxes.
  Canadian residents remit applicable GST and provincial taxes.

HBACK-AJ3

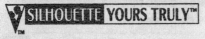

Silhouette ROMANCE™

What's a single dad to do when he needs a wife by next Thursday?

Who's a confirmed bachelor to call when he finds a baby on his doorstep?

How does a plain Jane in love with her gorgeous boss get him to notice her?

From classic love stories to romantic comedies to emotional heart tuggers, **Silhouette Romance** offers six irresistible novels every month by some of your favorite authors!
Such as...beloved bestsellers **Diana Palmer,**
Annette Broadrick, Suzanne Carey, Elizabeth August
and **Marie Ferrarella,** to name just a few—and some sure to become favorites!

Fabulous Fathers...Bundles of Joy...Miniseries...
Months of blushing brides and convenient weddings...
Holiday celebrations... You'll find all this and much more in
Silhouette Romance—always emotional, always enjoyable,
always about love!

SR-GEN

Harlequin Romance ®

Delightful

Affectionate

Romantic

Emotional

Tender

Original

Daring

Riveting

Enchanting

Adventurous

Moving

Harlequin Romance—the
series that has it all!

HROM-G

Harlequin® Historical

If you're a serious fan of historical romance,
then you're in luck!

Harlequin Historicals brings you
stories by bestselling authors, rising new stars
and talented first-timers.

Ruth Langan & Theresa Michaels
Mary McBride & Cheryl St. John
Margaret Moore & Merline Lovelace
Julie Tetel & Nina Beaumont
Susan Amarillas & Ana Seymour
Deborah Simmons & Linda Castle
Cassandra Austin & Emily French
Miranda Jarrett & Suzanne Barclay
DeLoras Scott & Laurie Grant…

You'll never run out of favorites.

Harlequin Historicals…they're too good to miss!

HH-GEN

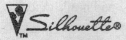

Tom Cruise
and
Nicole Kidman

Tom Cruise and Nicole Kidman were married on Christmas Eve in Telluride, Colorado. Openly affectionate with one another, they seem to have one of the few successful Hollywood marriages. They often make extra scheduling efforts to dedicate time to their adopted children, and both are very protective of them in regard to publicity and media exposure.

A close family friend states that one of the secrets to the success of the Cruise marriage is the ambition of both partners. "They both want to be not just superstars," he asserts, "but the number-one box-office stars in the world."

B-CRUISE